"Sarah Aldridge's effectiveness in recreating the emotions, experiences and connections between women of all ages and circumstances in various periods of time from the 1890s to the present is evidence of her growing ability as a writer. Her contribution to lesbian literature over the past ten years has been substantial. Her novels are educational and entertaining and obviously written with a love for the women in them and a love for the women who read them."

—Stephanie L. Gotlob

TOTTIE

A TALE OF THE
SIXTIES

TOTTIE
A TALE OF THE SIXTIES
BY
SARAH ALDRIDGE

the Naiad Press inc.
1985

ISBN: 0-930044-01-0

To
TW

Lesbian Novels by Sarah Aldridge:

Latecomer	*1974*
Tottie	*1975*
Cytherea's Breath	*1976*
All True Lovers	*1978*
The Nesting Place	*1982*
Madame Aurora	*1983*

and in Summer, 1985
watch for

Misfortune's Friend

TOTTIE
A Tale of the 'Sixties

Chapter One

In the spring of 1968 Constantia Elizabeth Norton was twenty-seven years old and an associate in the law firm of Bryanston and Clay, one of the largest on the East Coast and credited with being a forcing bed for promising young lawyers. She had been there two years and there were moments when the boundless enthusiasm and pristine self-congratulation that had been hers in her first days with the firm sometimes wore thin under the influence of a growing sophistication. At such times she had to remind herself that she had done well in the time and under the circumstances allotted to her.

She was in such a mood now. She stood in the window of her tiny office—well, at least she had it all to herself, even if it was the smallest on the floor—gazing out. The long spring evening was still light. Obeying an impulse, she snatched up the papers strewn on the desk before her and shuffled them into a hasty sort of order. The girl who did her typing and took her dictation had gone some time since. This evening her patience seemed suddenly exhausted. She was not in the mood to struggle with reversions and estates in trust, nor to spend half an hour in the rituals of tidying up.

No, she was not in the mood, she thought, as she reached for the suede jacket that hung on the coat rack. Half of the windows in the surrounding office buildings still showed signs of occupancy. She might spend another hour working, waiting for Roger. Roger never left his office before seven and he would expect her to be there till then. But she was not going to stay and work. If Roger did not find her in her office, he would come directly to her apartment and then she could give some excuse for her early departure.

He would probably be a little put out. Roger was Bryanston and Clay's most promising young man, brainy, ambitious, committed to achieving an outstanding place in the legal profession. Also, he had, after they had gone together for six months and without putting it into words, let her know that she met his specifications for a wife—goodlooking, amiable, intelligent, ready to subordinate herself to his ambitions, the sort of wife who would fit well into the career he was energetically building. But he did not like impulsive actions. She would not try to explain to him really what had prompted her, her sudden sense of frustration, her momentary mood of impatience with her lot in life. He would not believe her, would not take her explanations seriously. He would say, You are acting just like a woman. You don't know your own mind. His saying this would goad her into recalling a thousand instances of his own inconsistency. Then he would be offended and she would spend hours soothing his hurt feelings.

She took her hand off the doorknob. The sound of another door opening and closing caused her to turn around. A tall, well-built man, carrying a briefcase, was walking down the long corridor towards her. He said at once, "I was coming to look for you. I've had a call from Stuart. He says I had better go out to Chicago this evening. We have got to have depositions from three of the witnesses in the Wiseberger case and two of them will be unavailable if we don't act fast. I'll drop you at your place and go on out to the airport."

Connie sighed in relief. Roger gave no sign that he noticed it. In the cab he talked with singleminded earnestness of the problems confronting him. She accepted his perfunctory kiss under the eye of the cabdriver as he left her on the sidewalk in front of her apartment building.

There was no doorman—The Park Towers was not quite that pretentious—but the switchboard operator sat behind a counter at the far side of the lobby, discreetly observing their parting through the glass doors. Roger was well-known to the woman, since he came so often to fetch Connie for the evening or to bring her back on the nights when they did not stay till morning at his place. Roger had certain fixed ideas of propriety, of the proper outward appearance of things. For a year now they had gone to bed together, as matter-of-factly as a married couple, but always in his bed, not hers. His declared reason was that the people at his own apartment house were less curious and observant of their comings and goings, since he was a bachelor and therefore more or less expected to have a girl with him frequently. That it was always the same girl did not matter. Whereas the people at her place would take more notice if he stayed with her through the night. She did not argue the point with him.

The switchboard operator said now, "There is a phone message for you, Miss Norton."

Walking to the elevator Connie read the message on the slip of paper: "If you remember me, would you like to see me again? Phil." A telephone number followed.

Phil Quinn. Riding up in the elevator Connie was aware not only of surprise but of a certain lifting of spirits. Years ago—it seemed years ago—she and Phil had been the best of friends, in their junior year in college. Then in their senior year he had gradually faded from the group of which they had been a part. His politics had become radical, he had disappeared for days at a time, and when he turned up again she learned he had taken part in demonstrations of one sort or another. Early in his senior year he had dropped out of college, saying he was no longer interested in finishing. She had protested against this sudden capriciousness, right at the end of his college course, wasting, she pointed out, four years of effort. But he had brushed aside her protest and disappeared for good.

Of course she would like to see him again. She wondered how changed he would be.

Letting herself into her apartment, she paused only long enough to take off her jacket before reaching for the telephone. The phone at the other end rang for a number of times but when it was answered there was unmistakeably Phil's voice, a cheerful, light baritone, familiar and calm, bringing back another age in her life, another atmosphere. Within a few minutes they were back to the old, comfortable banter. No, she was not married. No, she did not live in the bosom of her family. Had he forgotten that she was a poor, lorn orphan, with only aunts who lived elsewhere in the country? In any case, yes, she was free for that evening and would love to see him. He would be there at once, he said, and rang off.

Her mind running on the past, she changed her clothes, absent-mindedly choosing an ultramarine blue dress that favored her eyes, brushing her chestnut-colored hair, which she wore in a long bob, fastening a blue bandeau to keep it out of her eyes, clasping around her neck the pearl necklace that had been her mother's. Only after some time was she aware that she had not given a thought to Roger, somewhere on his way to Chicago. The hint, in the back of her mind, of the possible awkwardness with Phil at the end of the evening was brushed aside. She had never been one to cross a bridge before she got to it.

Her current of thought was interrupted by the signal on the telephone from the switchboard operator. Mr. Quinn was there and should he come up?

When she opened her apartment door to him she stood for a moment nonplussed. It was undoubtedly Phil who stood there smiling at her. Her remembrance of him after all was very vivid. But the slender man standing there wore his bright brown hair long, to his shoulders, held back from his face by a broad band of many-colored strands across his forehead. His beard was full and neatly trimmed. He wore an orange silk shirt and a pair of tight-fitting trousers. But his dark coat was well-cut and the bare feet in the open sandals were pinkly clean.

"Surprised?" He smiled broadly and eyed her miniskirt and the long, shapely legs it revealed.

"You know I am. I couldn't have been more astounded when I got your message."

"I'm a little astounded myself," he said, gazing around the room. "Do you live here by yourself?"

"Yes."

He glanced around again. "Then I'd say you are in a higher income bracket than you used to be. You used to be poor but honest. Are you still honest?"

"It depends on what you mean by honest," she shot back.

"But, seriously, how do you pay for all this?" They were still standing in the middle of the room.

She laughed. "I get a salary now."

"A salary. Then you are a member of the Establishment."

"Right. In fact, I'm a lawyer, an upholder of the in-group."

He continued to look at her blandly. "Let's go and have dinner and catch up with ourselves."

They sat for a long while in a dark corner of a dimly-lit restaurant. Phil refused a drink but ordered one for her when she said she wanted it. Seeing him drinking water she cast back to the days of their earlier friendship, when scotch and bourbon had been staples of an evening out.

She told him about law school and being lucky enough to be taken on as an associate in Bryanston and Clay. Her narrative began in detail and with warmth, but she found it quickly becoming more sketchy and perfunctory. Phil did not interrupt her and he seemed to listen attentively, but she had the feeling that a great gap had after all opened up between them, that their viewpoints were now so different that she could not take his understanding and sympathy for granted as she would once have done. He made no comment of any sort when she detailed the moments of triumph and uncertainty in her affairs. Hurriedly she brought her story to an end and she noted that he did not seem to regret the sketchiness of her account. She had the feeling that he found what she told him remote and unimportant.

She broke off and asked, "What have you been doing, Phil? Somebody told me you had been drafted."

He nodded. He was prompt in telling his own story. He had been drafted. He had served in southeast Asia as a medical corpsman, since he decided he could not bring himself to learn how to kill people. Besides, she interjected, it would be useful experience for somebody who intended to make medicine his career.

"Oh, but I don't. I gave that idea up a long time ago."

"Why?"

He looked down at his empty plate. "It's just not my scene."

She found difficulty in following his explanation. But she gathered in general that he objected to the fixed patterns into which the lives of professional men perforce fitted. No, he was not a Marxist, nor the adherent of any political ideology. He had investigated the religions and philosophies of the Far East. He had experimented with the hallucigenic drugs in a cautious way. He was sorry for the younger kids he had seen who had not realized where their heedlessness might take them. A lack of historical perspective, he went on, kept a lot of them from learning from the experience of others. It was as if civilization had to begin afresh with every new generation—

Connie cut him short when he was well-launched on what seemed to be a favorite theme of his. "But what do you intend to do, then?"

"My own thing." A slightly mocking smile emphasized his use of the phrase.

"And what is that?"

He answered in undogmatic tones, replying to her prodding with sometimes vague, sometimes evasive explanations. Disease, poverty, social injustice, racial prejudice—all these things had to be confronted. But he had to do this in his own way. There was too much about the ways of organized society—public welfare, school systems, government management—that struck him as wrong, criminally wrong, and he could not lend his energies to perpetuating such modes of action.

Connie, watching his faintly smiling, serenely handsome face, found herself falling further and further away from her old intimacy with him. He had the air of an ascetic, with a goal she could not identify.

Chapter Two

In the week that followed Connie learned a great deal more in detail about Phil. He came every evening. The first time or two she came home at her usual late hour, adhering to the work pattern she had built up in unconscious accommodation to Roger, she found Phil sitting in the lobby, carrying on a gravely polite conversation with the switchboard operator. After that she impulsively threw conscientiousness to the winds and came home at six o'clock, awaiting him in the apartment. Phil always brought her home at midnight, in time for her to receive the phone call that Roger always placed at that time.

The first night Roger had told her that he would be delayed in Chicago for several days. Unforeseen complications had arisen. In the middle of the week he said he would have to stay into the next weekend. He spoke in a tone of magnanimous concern, as if he regretted disappointing her but that obviously his professional duties came first. Connie was relieved at the reprieve, relieved that for the moment she need not tell him about Phil.

Phil himself continued to puzzle her. When he brought her back to the apartment at the end of the evening he sat for a while in amiable conversation, with no suggestion that he was interested in going to bed with her. After perhaps half an hour he got up and said goodnight, at the same time asking her if she was free the next evening. His cool companionability slowly dissipated the slight tension that had unconsciously mounted in her as the evening wore on. She liked Phil, she told herself, quite as much as she ever did, but she did not want to go to bed with him. In fact, she did not want to go to bed with anybody, even Roger. With Roger it had become a dutiful ritual, like that of any long-married couple. Seldom, lately, did sheer desire make her welcome the process of preparing herself and waiting for Roger to join her in bed. She was greatly relieved that Phil showed no interest in the matter.

On Friday evening, when they left her apartment, he stood on the sidewalk beside her and said, "This evening, if it's all right with you, I'd like us to have a bite to eat somewhere and then go and visit some friends of mine."

At her look of surprise he explained that he was about to leave town again and there were people he wanted to see, people who were likely to be at his friends' place. As he and Connie walked to a small restaurant in the neighborhood, he made a few more disconnected comments about the friends to whom he was taking her. They were artists, he said. The man earned money as a commercial illustrator, enough to support him and his wife. But aside from that they lived as free as they could of the demands of a money-making culture. You could find almost anybody at their apartment—Zen Buddhists, rock artists, people dedicated to all sorts of causes, just plain kids trying to identify themselves. Connie listened to him in silence.

Phil's friends lived on the second floor of a big old house in what was once a fashionably residential neighborhood, so their rooms were large and lofty, furnished with a haphazard assortment of inflated chairs, outsized sofas and hassocks of various shapes. When they arrived, there was a din of clashing cymbals and electric guitars that drowned out all attempts to communicate names, so Connie had to be content to make her hostess's acquaintance in pantomime. She was a thin young woman who wore a robe that had an asiatic quality about it in fabric and design. When the guitarists, seated on a huddle of cushions in one corner of the room, fell silent, Connie learned that she invented designs for dress and curtain materials. Their conversation was brief and since Phil had immediately wandered from her side, Connie had leisure to watch the people who sat about the two big rooms. Some of them, she saw, were very young, dropouts, she supposed, from college. Remembering her own college days, she wondered whether at twenty-seven she was already too old to fit easily into their world. The idea amused her and she was further amused at the thought of what Roger's response to all this would be. Roger's energies were always controlled, motivated, directed towards a well-defined goal. He had no use for the vacillating, the confused or even those who questioned to no purpose, or what appeared to him to be no purpose.

She found herself shortly sitting in a corner of a sofa next to a long-haired boy who made no response to her remarks but looked at her out of glazed eyes. Phil had said that his friends drew the line at only two things. They allowed neither minors nor drugs on their premises. This, said Phil, was the result of a brush with the police, which they did not wish to have repeated. Well, she supposed the boy had taken his drugs elsewhere but he certainly seemed still under their influence. His head gradually fell

back against the sofa cushions and Connie got up and walked
slowly over to a counter that stood at the end of the room. Beer
and soft drinks and a loaf of bread and some sliced ham and cheese
had been placed there. Connie poured herself a beer and eyed a
bowl of pretzels and saltines. Phil had disappeared into the far
room where she could hear a loud argument in progress about the
efficacy of violent protest. Someone said that the indiscriminate
placing of bombs aroused people, made them conscious of the
things that should be changed. Nobody could ignore the effects,
the threat of an exploding bomb. She heard Phil's voice, quieter
but more emphatic, saying that this was hardly a new or revolu-
tionary concept. Protest-bombing had a long history. Connie ceased
to listen to the argument in the babble of voices surrounding her.

She had not heard the girl approach who was now standing beside her. Connie's first reaction was that, this evening at least,
Phil's friends' prohibitions were being honored only in the breach
and that a minor as well as a boy on drugs was part of the scene.
The girl was no taller than an average ten-year-old, skinny, with
bare feet thrust into sandals consisting only of a sole and one
thong. Her face was at first hidden by her long, pale blonde hair
that hung down well below her shoulders. She was dressed in a
pair of faded jeans, ragged around the cuffs, a white shirt and a
dark woolen poncho that hung down below her knees. A small,
bony white hand reached up from under it toward the bowl of
saltines. Then, as if in response to Connie's fascinated stare, she
drew her hand back to push her hair aside and look up at Connie
with a cold, fixed blue eye.

"Hello," said Connie involuntarily.

The girl nodded and turned back to the table. Taking a bottle
of orange soda and a handful of saltines, she immediately put one
of the crackers in her mouth. She stood there, looking at the cap
on the soda bottle, as if defeated by it. The long hair had fallen
over her eyes again. Connie leaned down to see her face. "The
bottle opener is over there," she said, pointing to it.

She caught a glimpse of the girl's blue eye through a hanging
lock of hair. Suddenly the girl thrust the bottle into her hands and
said, "Please open it for me."

She spoke in a soft, childish voice and Connie without hesitation took the cap off the bottle and gave it back into the narrow,
bony little hand. With an odd feeling that she would have liked to
have said something or made some gesture of reassurance, to
offer the girl protection against some undefined menace, she

watched her walk away into the next room. Thereafter she saw
the girl only at a distance, sitting by herself as if absorbed in her
own thoughts, unaware of the people who pressed around her.

A couple of hours later Connie and Phil took a bus back to her
apartment and it was only when they had got out and were walking up the block that she had the chance to say, "I thought you
said your friends didn't allow minors to come to their place."

Phil glanced around at her with surprise. "They don't. Sometimes a kid running away from home will have the police out looking for him—or her, more likely. A nasty situation can develop
out of that. Neither Jim nor Nadia want to get mixed up in a charge
of contributing to the delinquency of a minor."

"It certainly looked as if they had an underage kid there tonight. Who was the little girl in a poncho?"

Phil stared at her. "A little girl in a poncho?"

"Yes. She came just to about here." Connie pointed to a spot
on her own arm between elbow and shoulder.

"Oh! That must have been the girl that came in with those two
boys who were arguing with me about bombs. Oh, no, she is not
a minor. She is over twenty-one."

"She had better carry her birth certificate around with her.
They'd never let her into an X-rated movie or give her a drink in
a bar otherwise."

They had reached the lighted entrance of the Park Towers
and she could see that Phil was grinning. "She's about the smallest
woman I ever saw. Her name is Mary Gilray and she earns a little money writing items of student news for the local papers. I
think she is supposed to be a poet."

"It can't be a very lucrative job," said Connie, remembering
vividly the thin hand that reached for the saltines. "Doesn't she
have a home and parents?"

Phil gave a little shrug. "She has probably run away from them.
Probably doesn't like their life style."

Once inside the door of her apartment he stood in the middle
of the livingroom rug and took Connie's hands in his own.

"Well, it's goodbye again, kid. I don't have much time left now
to pack up and be off." He stood looking into her eyes, a friendly
smile in his own as he added as if on sudden impulse, "Don't rush
into anything you will regret. There is plenty of time to take second thoughts."

Connie was aware that her surprise must have shown in her
face. It had not occurred to her that her own uncertainties and

inner debate had been apparent to him. She looked away from his smiling scrutiny.

"There is not much left to decide in my future, Phil. It seems pretty well ordained. If we meet again, I expect I'll be married and concerned with children."

Phil continued to smile but a certain tightness appeared at the corners of his mouth. "Oh," he said cheerfully, "we'll meet again some time. I don't believe in final farewells. But don't let anybody bully you, Connie. You're too easy-going. And think some more about alternatives before you take any irrevocable steps. I know you well enough to know that you don't find it easy to back down from a bad bargain. You're a bitter-ender."

Irritated Connie freed her hands from his. Yet she regretted his going away. She would miss his undemanding, cheerful companionship. As if he was aware of her irritation he went on to talk cheerfully of the pleasure he had had in the last week with her. In a few minutes he was gone, jauntily walking down the corridor to the elevator and turning to give her a last wave before the door closed after him.

Alone in the apartment she walked restlessly about, mechanically tidying up the few signs of disarray. Phil's remarks had left her face to face with the problem of her relationship with Roger. Lately Roger had made remarks that indicated that he considered the time had come for them to marry. Perhaps it was this awareness that had roused in her a sense of not being ready to take that step. But what would she do otherwise?

In a mood of self-disgust she went to bed.

The next morning, which was Saturday and not a regular working day in the office, she did not wake until the sun was full in the room. She turned over to reach the turn-on button of the small radio beside her bed. The announcer had already begun his newscast: It was several moments before she could understand what he was talking about. Then she gathered that he was giving spot news of something that had happened within the preceding two hours. An explosion had ripped through a downtown post office, destroying part of the building and seriously injuring one clerk who had been in the mail sorting room. It had happened before the place was open to the public and that had prevented further injuries. But the police and firemen were searching the debris for other possible victims. Two suspects had been arrested, who were being held for questioning. It was believed that this latest incident was another in a series of such bomb attacks, which the police believed was the work of a radical group of students who had instigated riots and sit-ins at several college campuses since the first of the year.

The newscaster then went on to his next item, the usual daily tabulation of the number of deaths in the Vietnamese fighting. Connie reached over and switched off the radio. This daily, casual ticking off of the number of lives snuffed out while she slept—not entirely an accurate thought, she said to herself, given the difference in time zones, but nevertheless a sickening idea. When she had mentioned this once to Roger he had said that he thought she was being morbid. He had done his service in Germany and took a rather Olympian view of the military operations in southeast Asia.

Since it was Saturday she dressed and breakfasted at a more leisurely pace than usual. She could, if need be, work on into the afternoon. She even toyed for a while with the idea of not going to the office at all. A mood of rebellion and restlessness had settled in her. Roger expected to be back next day, Sunday. When he had called her, shortly after Phil's departure, he had said that he was tired from a week of long hours and exasperating witnesses and that he proposed to take his time in winding up the case. He would have an uninterrupted night's rest before he returned to take up the work he had dropped in order to go to Chicago.

On the way to the office she picked up a late edition of the morning paper and when she reached her desk she spent half an hour reading the various stories concerning the bombing attack. She scrutinized carefully the photographs of the two suspects under arrest. For some reason, the recollection of the two boys who had argued about bombs with Phil kept coming back into her mind. Except that the photographs showed young men with long hair and beards, she could not say that she saw any particular resemblance to them. The biographies of several other young men and two girls said to be members of the radical group were given, with photographs. She recognized none of them.

The paper said that the two suspects had been caught by mail guards as they had tried to escape through the alley where the mail trucks were parked. Whether others had escaped by some other route was not known. But one eyewitness had reported that she had seen a girl—dressed in jeans and a slouch hat—in the immediate vicinity of the post office a short while before the bomb went off. No one admitted seeing her after the explosion and speculation was that she had entered the building. The police and firemen were sifting debris looking for the remains of victims, one of whom she might have been. It might be days, they said, before they would know definitely whether there were anyone's remains in the ruins.

At last Connie threw the paper into the waste paper basket and tried to bring her attention to her work. Fairly early in the evening she left the office and after walking about somewhat aimlessly she went to an expensive restaurant and had a meal alone. Back in her apartment she stepped out onto the narrow balcony that over-looked the park. The sun had long since gone. The light lingered indistinctly amongst the big trees and flowering shrubs of the park. It was still the dinner hour. Ordinarily, she and Roger would just be setting out for an evening's entertainment. Leaning on the par-apet of the balcony and looking down into the streets where she could see other people setting out for the evening, she thought ruefully that at twenty-seven she was no longer a fresh young thing, new to most of the common experiences of womankind. In fact, her age almost put her beyond the pale for the kids with whom she still instinctively identified herself, the kids struggling through college and facing the first challenges of adult life, kids like those who dropped out of college to protest against the things they did not want to accept in the world they were encountering— kids, in fact, some of them, like those two boys who had thrown the bombs into the post office.

Or like that strange girl in the poncho. What was she making an issue of?

Chapter Three

The thread of sound reached her ear and brought her back to an awareness of her surroundings. The evening had darkened into early night. The street lights were lit and cars moved with headlights on. The sound had reached her from inside the apartment, through the door open behind her. The sounds from the street had almost overwhelmed it. She turned around, warily, listening. She disliked to dwell on the idea of breakings and enterings, rapes and assaults, though her friends were constantly calling her attention to the dangers of living alone even in a well-guarded apartment building. Roger had insisted on her having an extra lock put on her front door. She did not tell him that half the time she forgot to use it.

She listened for the sound to be repeated. If someone had managed to get into the apartment, he was between her and the front door and also between her and the telephone.

She had almost given up the idea that there had in fact been a sound when she heard it again, this time more distinctly. It must be a knock on the front door, a very timid, gentle knock. She stepped into the dark room and switched on the nearest lamp. The sudden flood of light showed her an empty room. The soft knock sounded again. What in the world, thought Connie. Surely whoever was out there must be acquainted with doorbells and the fact that the small button on one side of the doorjamb rang the two-toned chime that served as such. Then the further thought occurred to her that no one who was not a tenant of the building was supposed to be allowed up in the elevator without stopping at the desk in the lobby, to be announced. She then remembered that she often noticed that the student who took the place of the daytime switchboard operator during the evening had the habit of studying with such concentration that he sometimes did not glance up when she passed through the lobby. Obviously someone had walked by him this evening.

She went to the door and called through it, "Who is it?"

A small voice responded promptly, nervously breathless. "Just me. I'm not dangerous."

Connie opened the door. She was unprepared for what she saw.

A small figure stood in front of her, wrapped in a dark woolen poncho and wearing a very large, limp black felt hat, the brim of which drooped almost to her shoulders. A thin, white hand reached up and turned back the front portion of the hat brim so that the girl's face was visible. Connie was chiefly conscious of the pair of cold blue eyes looking up into her own with a strange sort of challenge.

"I want to come in," the girl said.

"Of course," said Connie, stepping back to let her enter.

The girl stepped across the threshold and halted. She looked around and asked, "Is there anybody else here?"

Connie hesitated in surprise. "No. I'm alone."

The girl persisted. "Does anybody live here with you?"

"No. I live by myself."

The girl gave a small sigh of relief. "Then can I stay here for a while?"

Connie, even more astonished, said quickly, "Why, yes, of course." Then gazing at the girl in curiosity she said, "What is the matter? Are you running away from home?"

The girl gave her a glance of startled suspicion. "Why would you think I'm running away from anything?"

The suddenly flashing blue eyes disconcerted Connie. "Oh never mind, never mind. I just don't like the idea of getting into trouble for helping a minor run away from her parents."

"Oh, that!" said the girl contemptuously. "I'm not a minor so you needn't be afraid of that. Just because I'm small doesn't mean that I'm a child. But I have to stay here for a while."

"Well, if that's the case, why don't you take off that hat?"

The girl hesitated for a moment before lifting the big black hat off her head and putting it gently down on the nearest chair. She made no move to take off the poncho. Her pale blonde hair straggled over her shoulders. She shook it back off her face and stared up at Connie. Her face was indeed not that of a child. It was narrow, with prominent cheekbones, high-bridged nose and deep eyesockets. Her skin was astonishingly white and transparent, with no color to relieve it except the faint blue of veins and the suggestion of a violet shadow in the inner corners of her eyelids. Her mouth was small, with thin lips tightly closed. It was the sort of face, Connie thought, that one might suppose would belong to an aristocratic woman of another age—an age before sunbathing and hatlessness. It had none of the marks of beauty accepted by current standards and it bore no trace of cosmetics. And yet she found it beautiful.

It also looked a hungry face. Remembering the thin hand reaching for the saltines, she said impulsively, "Wouldn't you like something to eat? I haven't had my supper yet. We could go down the street to a place I often go to. Or—

The girl cut her short. "Don't you have something to eat here?"

"There're some eggs in the icebox and I've plenty of cans of things. Come in the kitchen with me."

The girl followed her docilely across the room to the kitchen. Then, while Connie broke eggs and put a package of frozen peas in a pot to boil, she sat at the counter like an obedient child, one hand resting on its edge, the other tucked under the poncho.

"You might tell me who you are," said Connie over her shoulder as she used the electric can opener. "What am I to call you? It is obvious you know who I am. How did you find out my name and where I live?"

"I asked that man you came to the party with last night."

"Why did you do that?" Connie asked, pausing to look at her with curiosity.

"I wanted to know who you were. I thought you would probably help me sometime."

Connie showed her surprise. She remembered her impulse to protect the girl from some unrealized menace. As she turned back to the can opener she said, "That was Phil Quinn. He said your name is Mary Gilray."

"There! See!" said the girl, triumphantly. "You knew who I was all along."

Their conversation then was very desultory. The girl did not speak unless Connie made a remark and then her replies were brief. She spoke with a sort of peremptory terseness that both annoyed and intrigued Connie. Suddenly, as Connie was taking plates from a shelf and carrying them into the livingroom to place on a small table she used when she ate at home, the girl got up and, following her, demanded, "Where is your bathroom?"

"In there, through the bedroom."

While the girl was gone, Connie pondered, I've never met anyone that young who seemed so old-fashioned. She has the manners of someone's maiden aunt. But no maiden aunt would have such a piercingly direct gaze. As soon as she comes back in here, I'm going to ask her a few straight questions.

But the minutes passed and there was no sign of the girl. Finally, half in alarm, Connie went to the bathroom. The door was ajar and she heard the sound of water running in the wash basin.

"Mary, are you all right?"

She could see the girl's back, and the reflection of her face in
the glass of the medicine cabinet. The girl turned her head. She
was holding her right hand under the faucet. Connie stepped into
the bathroom behind her and looked into the basin. The water
swirling down the drain was faintly pink. The small white hand
held under the stream from the faucet was badly gashed.

"Good lord!" Connie exclaimed. "Why didn't you tell me you
had hurt yourself. Here, wait a minute. I'll get something to bandage it with."

She rummaged hurriedly in the medicine cabinet and then snatching up a towel, wound it around the girl's hand. The girl made no
outcry when Connie applied first-aid to the gash and bandaged
her hand with cotton and gauze.

"What did you do to yourself?" Connie demanded.

"I had to get over an iron fence and the ground on the other
side was steeper. I cut myself hanging onto it before I fell."

"Did you hurt yourself anywhere else?"

"I think I have some bruises, but they don't hurt me now. I could
have broken a leg." She said this with an air of plaintive disgust,
as if frightened of the idea.

Connie gazed at her in concern. "It must have shaken you up a
good deal. Would you like a drink before you eat?"

She was nonplussed at the sudden angry glare the girl gave her.
"No thank you. I do not want anything of that kind."

Connie, disconcerted, said weakly, "Well, perhaps some food
will help," and walked back to the kitchen, pausing on her way to
point to the chair she had placed at the table in the livingroom.
When she brought the dishes from the kitchen she found the girl
seated, her head propped on her good hand, dejection showing in
the droop of her body. "Here, Mary, I'll cut things up for you."

The girl ate quickly at first, awkwardly managing her fork with
her unbandaged left hand, waiting patiently while Connie buttered her bread. Halfway through the meal her appetite seemed to
flag and she began to eat with a finickiness that Connie judged to
be her more usual manner.

When they reached the coffee, Connie suggested that they move
to more comfortable chairs across the room. The girl waved aside
her suggestion of a liqueur. Connie, with a strange feeling of embarrassment, served herself a glass of the brandy Roger had given
her at Christmas.

"Don't you think " she said, sinking down into the soft cushions
of the big sofa, where she faced the girl in the armchair opposite,

"you might give me a clue to your problem?"

"What makes you think I have a problem."

"Come now. There must be some reason why you've invited yourself here as my dinner guest. Or is it house guest?"

The girl did not hesitate. "House guest."

Connie gazed at her for a while, conscious of irritation, indignation. Then she said, "You know, I've no objection to putting you up for a few days, if that's what you want. But I do think I am entitled to know who you really are and why you feel the need to take refuge here."

"You know who I am. I've told you. I want to stay here because I haven't anywhere else to go and I haven't any money."

Connie surveyed her ragged jeans and soiled white shirt. "Don't you have any belongings? Are those the only clothes you've got?"

"No, I don't own anything."

"Well, where have you been living up till now?"

"In a boarding house. At least, I had a room in a house. But I can't go back there because I owe the woman money."

"She has your things, I suppose."

"I tell you I haven't any things."

Connie took a deep breath and set down her glass. "And I tell you that I don't believe a word you say. It is not true that I know who you are. All I know about you is that I've seen you once before, in some rather funny company. It was Phil Quinn who told me your name is Mary Gilray and that you do freelance writing for the newspapers. He also said he supposed you had run away from your family. If it is true that you are not a minor, I suppose they can't pursue you and force you to go home."

The girl did not respond. She sat passive, looking down at the rug at her feet. Connie went on, seeking the advantage of momentum. "I really believe that you are a fugitive, that you are involved with the police and that you have chosen to come to my apartment because you think no one will look for you here. But, you know, if that is the case, you're laying me open to a charge of harboring a fugitive from justice. If you're involved with people who have committed a felony, I can be charged with being an accessory after the fact."

There was silence in the room for a long moment. Then the girl said in a quiet voice, "You're a lawyer, aren't you?"

"Yes, but I'm not in criminal practice. If you need a lawyer to defend you, I can find someone for you."

The girl shook her head. "I don't need a lawyer. I'm not a criminal. I haven't done anything wrong. I just meant that you talk like a lawyer."

"But you are running away from something or somebody. Sometimes a person can find himself in an incriminating situation. Then he needs a lawyer to defend him just as much as if he were guilty."

The girl did not answer.

"Besides, how do I know that you are not really involved with the law?"

"Because I tell you so," said the girl calmly.

Connie, speechless with indignation, looked at her. The girl was gazing across the room, preoccupied.

"Will you be so good as to tell me, then," said Connie, her voice loaded with sarcasm, "how long you intend to be my house guest?"

The girl responded only with a glance. She got up from her chair and walked across the room and peered into the bedroom.

"You have just this bedroom?" she asked.

"Yes. You've seen all there is of the apartment. But I can make a bed out of that settee."

The girl glanced briefly at the piece of furniture she indicated. Then she asked abruptly, "Do you have a man who comes here to sleep with you?"

Connie, startled, said lamely, "No. That is, there is someone who comes most evenings. But we spend the night at his place." Inwardly she was amazed at herself for docilely offering explanations for her actions. She was after all accountable to no one, not even Roger, yet here she was defending herself to this strange little girl, who was looking at her with an expression that was half anxiety and half displeasure.

"Does he come into your bedroom?" the girl persisted, watching her with most concentrated attention.

Connie, even more dumbfounded, said slowly, "Well, I suppose sometimes he does—if he needs to go to the bathroom. But he usually likes to go out for the evening. He just fetches me and brings me home." She found it difficult to explain that Roger did not feel at ease in her apartment.

"It isn't that man you were with at the party?"

"Phil? Oh, no. Phil has gone away. He was only here for a few days."

The silence between them lengthened. Connie said finally, "To get back to you. What are you doing here and why do you want to stay with me?"

The girl answered only after a pause and in a quiet little voice.

"I've told you, I'm here because I've nowhere else to go. I knew you would let me stay with you."

Connie, disarmed, said gently, "You must be exhausted. Would you like to go to bed? You can have the bedroom. I can sleep out here." Then she thought, Good Lord! What next is the girl going to make me do? Why shouldn't she sleep out here?

The girl's quiet voice broke into her thoughts. "I'd like to have a bath, but I can't manage it with my hand bandaged up."

Connie glanced up to see her standing in the middle of the room, gazing at her bandaged hand. "You could, if I helped you. Shall I?"

The girl said, "Yes," and walked to the bedroom. Connie got up and followed her. The girl sat down on the seat in front of the dressing table and took off her sandals. She then stood up and took off the poncho. Her other garments consisted of the pair of jeans and a white, long-sleeved cotton shirt, too big for her. This she was beginning to unbutton as Connie went into the bathroom and turned the water on in the tub. When Connie came back into the bedroom to get a towel out of the cupboard, she saw that the girl had unbuttoned the shirt and that she wore nothing under it.

"The tub will be full in a minute. It fills very fast. Shall I help you take off your jeans?"

In answer the girl stood up and waited for her to undo the fastener at the belt and pull down the zipper. She stepped out of the jeans as they fell to the floor. She wore nothing under them, either. In the shirt, which hung down her thighs, she walked to the bathroom. Connie, giving her time to get ready to get into the tub, heard her flush the toilet. When Connie entered the bathroom the girl was in the tub, her bandaged hand held up out of the water.

Connie knelt down on one knee by the side of the tub and helped the girl wash herself. When they had finished she helped her out of the water and, wrapping the towel around her, rubbed her vigorously. The girl said nothing until suddenly she flinched and a half-suppressed "Oh!" escaped her. Connie, holding the towel away, saw a large black bruise on one thigh and buttock. The girl, noticing her stare, said quickly, "That's where I landed. My leg is pretty sore."

"You had better let me rub it with some liniment."

The girl made no protest. When she was dry, Connie paused for a moment before fetching the liniment and looked at her. Naked, she was undoubtedly a woman, the smallest mature woman Connie had ever seen, with soft full breasts, big in proportion to her small waist and narrow hips. The line of her flat stomach hollowed slightly before it disappeared in the downy blonde hair between her thighs. All over her body her skin was the same transparent white as on her face and hands. The big bruise and several smaller ones stood out in vivid blotches against the whiteness of her skin.

Aware that she had been surprised into staring for several moments, Connie hastily wrapped the towel around the girl again and went to fetch the liniment. The girl stood patiently, with no apparent selfconsciousness. At last, with the towel around her she walked back into the bedroom and went straight to the bed, which Connie had turned down—thinking, as she did so, "She can jolly well use my sheets." The girl cast aside the towel and rolled into the bed, pulling the covers up over her.

"I was going to offer you my shortie nightgown," said Connie. "I expect it would come down below your knees. Shall I turn out the light?"

The girl settled herself further down on the pillow and shook her head, her eyes closed. "Not till you come to bed," she said drowsily.

Connie, thunderstruck, stood looking down at the girl. Her face was sunk deeply into the pillow, the long lashes showing darkly against her white cheeks. The idea that she had expected to share her bed had not occurred to Connie, but at once she decided to accept it. It was a big bed. It could easily hold the two of them.

Slowly Connie undressed and prepared for bed. As she did so, her mind searched through what she remembered of the evening's conversation for explanations, which seemed to be just beyond her grasp. By the time she got into bed the girl was fast asleep. Connie propped on her elbow, watched her for several minutes before she put out the light. As she settled herself for sleep, the girl rolled unconsciously against her and sighed. How long has it been, Connie wondered compassionately, since she has had a real rest? The girl murmured something unintelligible in her sleep and frowned, as if in her dreams some fear still troubled her. Connie stroked her forehead gently and the frown vanished as, with another little sigh she seemed to sink more deeply into sleep. Connie put out the light.

Chapter Four

Once or twice in the night Connie roused, surprised at the warm presence close to her in the bed, until she remembered the evening's events. Finally she awoke to daylight. The sun was not yet up. She lay watching the sky grow brighter and remembered that this was Sunday. The girl beside her still slept deeply, undisturbed by the growing light. At seven o'clock Connie slipped stealthily out of bed, dressed quietly, and let herself out of the apartment. Just before closing the front door she paused and listened. There was no sound from the bedroom. She went out and walked briskly along the deserted streets to St. Thomas's for communion, as she always did on Sunday mornings. When she came out of the church there were more people about and she stopped at the nearby hotel where the Sunday papers were available. She glanced at the headlines and saw that there was a further account of the bombing of the post office. Not waiting to read it, she walked back to her apartment house.

She inserted the key in the lock slowly so as to make the least possible noise and closed the door carefully behind her. She crossed the livingroom quickly and pushed the bedroom door further open to look in. The girl was sitting up in bed, her eyes wide with apprehension.

"Where have you been?" she demanded, in a frightened voice. She sat propped up on her unbandaged hand, the bedclothes turned back so that her naked body was uncovered. Connie, disconcerted by the fierce stare of the cold blue eyes, said hastily, "I went to eight o'clock communion. I usually do on Sundays."

The girl lay back on the pillows, drawing up the covers around her shoulders. Connie went over to the bed and looked down at her. The girl's bandaged hand lay outside the blanket. Connie touched it gently. "Does it hurt you?"

"It throbs," said the girl, unhappily.

"I had better look at that dressing. Wait a minute while I change my clothes."

In a few minutes, having changed into the slacks and shirt she wore around the house, she brought a basin of warm water and proceeded to unwrap the bandage. The gashes looked worse in the morning light, though the girl bore the handling without a cry.

Connie, alarmed, said urgently, "I think you should have this attended to by a doctor. It may be infected. Let me take you to the emergency room at the hospital."

The girl closed her mouth tightly and shook her head. "It will be all right. Just bandage it up again."

But Connie said stubbornly, "I don't know what you are afraid of, but you had better be more afraid of tetanus. Lockjaw, I understand, isn't a nice thing to die of."

"I've had tetanus shots."

"How long ago?"

The girl shrugged. "It doesn't matter. I can have a booster if anything goes wrong. Please just bandage it up again the way you did before."

This time Connie did as she asked. The girl accepted the inevitable pain passively. When the bandaging was finished she lay back again in the bed and said in a small voice, "I ache and I'm terribly stiff. I went to the bathroom while you were gone and I could hardly walk."

"Do you want me to rub you again?"

The girl nodded and Connie went to fetch the liniment. Then she returned and pulled back the covers. The girl lay stretched on her back and did not move except to turn over when Connie directed her to. At last when Connie finished and pulled the bedclothes over her, she looked up at her and said, "You mustn't let anybody know I'm here."

Connie said sharply, "I shall do just what I think I should."

The girl continued to look up at her, her eyes all at once pleading. "But you mustn't!"

Connie turned her eyes away. "Oh, all right. We'll let it go at that for the time being. I'm going to fix some coffee and rolls."

The girl nodded and Connie went to the small kitchen. When she came into the livingroom with the rolls and butter and marmalade, the girl was sitting at the table where she had eaten the evening before. She had evidently rummaged in the bedroom closet and found a short terry-cloth bathrobe, which she had put on. The skirt reached halfway down her legs and she had rolled up the sleeve to free her bandaged hand. The other sleeve still hung down over her hand and she held it out to Connie to roll up. Her feet were bare. The pale blonde hair hung loose over her shoulders. At a quick glance she looked more than ever like a little girl but when Connie looked into her face, she realized that this was no child. The extreme fineness of her skin and her thinness gave her an appearance of fragility. Her blue eyes answered Connie's scrutiny with a sort of imperious calm.

"How old are you, Mary?" *Why does she have this effect on me?* Connie wondered. *The very first time I saw her she seemed to claim my protection. I can't look at her, I can't be in the same room with her without feeling that I must comfort and encourage her as if she has some special and undeniable right to me and everything I have.*

"Twenty-five," Mary answered.

"Then you're through college."

"No. I dropped out at the midterm." Noticing the surprise on Connie's face, she added, "I was late getting started in college here. I went to school abroad before that. I decided to go to college when I was twenty-one."

Connie poured the boiling water into the coffee cups. The girl accepted the roll she offered her. "Please butter it," she said.

"Well, if it was your own idea," said Connie, buttering the roll, "why did you drop out?"

The girl did not reply at once. Then she said, holding a piece of buttered roll in the air, "I lost interest. That was last year."

"Well, what have you been doing since then?"

The girl answered with a shrug and a shake of her head. Instead she asked, "Your name is Connie Norton, isn't it?"

"Of course. You must have known it to find me here."

"Yes. I am glad I found out who you were. I knew you would take care of me. That is why I came to find you."

"After you were hurt? It would have been better if you had gone to the emergency room of the hospital."

The girl shook her head. "I couldn't. The police would have found me."

"Oh, I see! So it's true after all that the police are looking for you!"

The girl remained unruffled. "Not for me, exactly. Just for somebody who was dressed like me, after the—"

She stopped and Connie finished for her, "After the post office was bombed. So you are the girl they are looking for there?"

"I tell you, they are just looking for somebody like me."

Connie said indignantly, "A very small girl dressed in jeans and a black poncho and wearing a big black hat. How many girls like that do you think were at the post office when it was bombed?"

The girl said stubbornly, "I did not have anything to do with that."

"Then what are you afraid of? Weren't you mixed up with the

two boys who were arrested?"

The girl shot her a glance of real alarm. "Did they catch them?"

"They were arrested trying to escape from the premises after the blast. Were they the two boys who were arguing with Phil at the party?"

The girl nodded. "But that doesn't mean anything. Lots of people talk like that."

"Are you telling me that you don't think they planted the bomb?"

"No. They did that." She spoke so casually that Connie stared at her in consternation.

"But you say you had nothing to do with it? Why were you there, then?"

The girl did not answer. Connie, upset, got up and began to clear away the breakfast. When she returned from the kitchen the girl suddenly asked, "What is the rest of your name?"

Connie, startled by her sudden switch of subject, said, "My full name is Constantia Elizabeth Norton."

"And everybody calls you Connie?"

"Yes. I've always been called Connie."

"Well, I think I'll call you Stantia."

Connie gazed at her in wonderment. There was something in the manner in which she spoke that gave what she said the quality of a pronouncement, a declaration that had the power to change the course of events. It was an absurd idea, and yet Connie could not avoid being held by the feeling. It is as if, she thought, I was being christened over again. She made no rejoinder aloud and the girl was busy finishing her last cup of coffee.

Connie said, "I brought a Sunday paper in with me. Would you like to see some of it?"

Once more the girl shook her head. "Is that what you do on Sunday mornings when you come back from church?"

"What, look at the paper? Yes, I look at the paper and listen to some music. I have a very good hi-fi set."

"By yourself?"

"Do you mean, do I do this by myself? Yes, I'm getting set in my ways. I'm almost thirty."

So I am, she thought. And, come to think of it, that's one of the habits I'll probably have to change when Roger and I get married and live together. I certainly don't expect Roger to make changes in what he is used to doing. I wonder if I shall see any more of him on Sundays than I do now. I'll probably sit here amusing myself till he is ready to come home.

Her thoughts ran along these lines for some minutes. Presently she glanced up to find that the girl had left the table and had gone to the window, where she was kneeling on a chair, gazing out at the street and the park below.

Connie called to her. "Mary, is there something you especially want to hear? I don't like rock music. But I have plenty of Mozart and Beethoven and that sort of thing."

She was answered by silence and in irritation she looked again towards the girl at the window. "Mary," she asked sharply, "don't you answer to your name?"

This time the girl half-turned around, and said politely, "I beg your pardon. I was not paying attention."

It was on the tip of Connie's tongue to say, "That's obvious," but she did not and instead repeated her question.

"Oh, anything you like," said Mary. "I listen to rock music sometimes. But it's too noisy. I don't like noise."

Connie placed several records on the turn-table and then sat down in her usual large armchair with the newspapers. On the front page were photographs of the damaged post office building and detailed statements by the chief of police and other officials, giving their views of the probable perpetrators of the bombing. They don't know a thing about it, thought Connie. The FBI might be better informed, but if so, no spokesman for them had consented to be quoted on the incident.

"Mary," Connie called across the room, when she had finished reading the stories, "just what do you have to do with this bombing business?"

Again she was answered by silence. She looked across at the girl, still in the window and repeated, "Mary." The girl did not respond and she put down the paper and got up and walked across the room to stand behind her.

"Do you know?" she said distinctly to the back of the girl's head, "I don't think your name is Mary Gilray after all. You certainly don't answer to it."

The girl started, as if aware for the first time that she was being spoken to.

"I'm sorry," she said, looking around. "I didn't realize you were talking to me."

"There's nobody else in the room," said Connie sternly. "And I've not reached the stage of talking to myself."

For the first time the suggestion of a smile appeared on the girl's face. "You're right. I'm not used to being called Mary. But my name is Mary."

"What are you called, then?"

But the girl said quietly, "No, I can't tell you yet." She turned back to look out of the window again.

In angry preoccupation Connie also looked out of the window. Several benches in the park below now held people sitting in the spring sunshine reading newspapers. There was a desultory movement of cars and pedestrians in the street. But the girl did not seem to be really engaged in watching their activity. Her preoccupation was with something within herself.

"I think you had better come here and read the newspaper accounts of the bombing," said Connie peremptorily. "You'd see how serious the situation is."

The girl glanced at her over her shoulder and then obediently came away from the window to follow her across the room. Connie handed her the section of the paper that contained the photographs and the news stories. The girl sat down on the big sofa and began to scan them. A perplexed and unhappy expression came over her face and she soon laid the papers aside.

"Those are the boys you were with?"

"The girl looked back at the photographs and said, "Yes."

"Well, you should report what you know about them to the police."

The look the girl gave her was one of distress. "I couldn't go to the police. Besides, I don't know anything about them."

"But you were with them."

"I wasn't with them. I was just following them."

Connie studied her for a moment. "I believe you are really afraid of them."

The girl leaned against the back of the sofa and drew her legs up under her. There was an air of silent dejection about her.

"If you really are afraid of them, that is all the more reason you should go to the police. Are they blackmailing you? Are they threatening to accuse you of something—of being involved in some plot of theirs? Have they been involved in bombings before?"

Mary shook her head. "I don't know anything about them. I'm not afraid of them. It's the others I am afraid of."

"And who are they?"

"Oh, I couldn't tell you!" Mary exclaimed and there was a look of real fright on her face.

Connie gave her a long look. "Are you hiding from them?"

"Yes," said Mary, in her small voice.

"What are you afraid they will do—turn you in to the police?"
The girl shook her head wordlessly.
"Assault you?"
"Yes-s," the girl answered uncertainly and then added in a
mere breath of a voice, "Kill me."
"Kill you! Why?"
Again the girl failed to answer.
Connie said cautiously, "That is pretty extraordinary. There
must be some reason why you should fear that." Is she out of her
mind, she wondered. There was no sign that the girl took drugs.
There were no needle marks on her and she did not otherwise give
the appearance of someone confused and jittery from drugtaking.
But there are other forms of aberration, thought Connie, of alien-
ation of mind, that are not drug-induced. The girl could simply be
a pathological liar, someone with an imagination that carried her
beyond the bounds of reality. Or she might be suffering from a per-
secution mania.
Connie examined her more closely, covertly. The girl sat now
with her head resting on her arm stretched across the back of the
sofa. She seemed desperately unhappy, on the verge of tears.
"Don't you think you had better tell me what your predicament
is?"
The girl lifted her head and looked at her. Her eyes were filled
with tears which she seemed to have difficulty keeping back.
"You are very kind," she said, with a curious formality. "But I
can't tell you— yet."
"Yet! If I am to help you, you should tell me now, at once. Pro-
crastinating won't help."
But the girl shook her head and in a few minutes she seemed to
have recovered her self-possession. She got up from the sofa and
announced that she wanted to get dressed.
"I washed out your jeans and shirt last night," said Connie. "I
expect they are dry. They are hanging in the bathroom under the
heat lamp."
"Thank you," said the girl, and she looked at her bandaged hand.
"Yes, I'll help you," said Connie, answering the unspoken request.
They went into the bedroom and the girl dropped the bathrobe
off her shoulders and stood naked,waiting for Connie to bring the
jeans and the shirt. Connie, returning with the clothes in her hand,
stopped and looked at her. She is a little beauty, she thought, eye-
ingthe gentle line of the small back and shapely legs. Connie could

not resist passing her hand over the girl's back. The girl did not
seem surprised. Instead she reached up with her sound hand and
stroked Connie's cheek. Connie, aware of an almost irresistible
wish to take her in her arms, like a precious, fragile doll, held out
the jeans for her to step into. Neither of them said anything.

They spent the rest of the day in an amicable semi-silence, with
very little to say but without any sense of a compulsion to speak.
Or so Connie felt and in glancing occasionally at Mary came to the
conclusion that the other girl felt the same. Connie, used to Sunday as a day she spent alone until the evening, caught herself from
time to time experiencing a new sensation, of not being alone and
yet not being under the constraint that usually came with someone
else's presence, even Roger's. She corrected herself—especially
Roger's. Roger liked to spend Sunday unhampered. Occasionally
he worked through the weekend. Otherwise, he played tennis with
some of his male friends. He had been a champion in his college
days and he still played, as he did everything, with a fanatical drive
to excel that made no allowance for the shortcomings of others.
Connie played a good enough game of tennis for her own enjoyment but she early realized that this was nothing but an irritation
to Roger. He had soon indicated that tennis was one of the things
he must do with his peers—and his peers in tennis did not include
women. He belonged to a club where he could play indoors in bad
weather, so she saw little of him until Sunday evenings, when, satisfied that he had worked off the frustrations of the week's professional problems with violent physical exercise, he came to take
her out to dinner and to spend the night with him. The fact that he
sometimes exercised to the point of somnolent taciturnity did not
strike him as important. It's my own fault, thought Connie. I don't
tell him when I'm bored to tears. And he doesn't like sudden changes
of plan. Life to Roger was a well-ordered routine, thoroughly under his control.

Chapter Five

In the middle of the morning Roger had called from the airport, the ring of the telephone shattering the peace of a long silence. It startled Connie, although she had been expecting it, almost as much as it did Mary. He would come by at seven o'clock, Roger said. They could go to his club for cocktails and then to dinner. Connie was careful to answer him as casually as he spoke. When she hung up she was aware of Mary's stare.

"Is that somebody coming here?" Mary demanded.

"Yes. My fiance. He is coming at seven o'clock to take me out to dinner."

Mary looked away, biting her lip. Connie, feeling unaccountably guilty, said hastily, "There is food in the refrigerator. You can operate the electric can opener with one hand. Or if you prefer I'll go to the delicatessen and get you anything you like."

The girl made an impatient gesture but said nothing. Connie, annoyed at herself, said brusquely, "What you really ought to do is go down to that little restaurant at the corner. The food there is pretty good."

A sudden look of fright crossed the girl's face. "I can't do that!" she exclaimed, breathless. "I can't let them find out where I am."

Disconcerted, Connie stepped over to her and impulsively put her arm around her. "Mary, if you're really afraid of somebody, why don't you tell me more about it? Maybe I could think of something that would help the situation."

"No, you couldn't."

Connie tightened her hold on the girl's shoulder. "Besides, how do you know you weren't followed here—that these people you are afraid of don't know you are here?"

The girl turned to look up into her face. "No, they don't know. They didn't know I ran away until afterwards. They thought I had taken drugs—that I was sleeping off a trip."

"And were you?"

"No. I don't take drugs."

"Well, that's one less worry," said Connie, ironically. "Why are you afraid of these people?"

"Because of what they want to do to me."

"Assault and kill you, you say."

Mary did not answer. They were both silent for a moment. Then Connie said, "You admit that you were on the scene when the post office was bombed. Why were you there?"

"Because I wanted to see what was going to happen."

Connie said sharply, "Curiosity can be dangerous. Were these other people there also?"

"Yes. They were following me. I didn't know it then."

"Following you! How did you find this out?"

Again the girl returned a complete silence. The moments passed and Connie let go of her. After a while she asked, "The bomb explosion took place at seven o'clock yesterday morning. You arrived here in my apartment about eight o'clock yesterday evening. What were you doing in the meantime?"

"When I got away from the post office, I ran down a side street and these two men stopped me. I didn't know then that they had followed me there. They told me that the police would make a dragnet of the neighborhood and that I'd better go with them. So I did and we walked a long way — I don't know where, because I didn't recognize any of that part of town. Finally, we came to a house in a row. It was pretty slummy, but I'm used to the sort of pads some of these boys stay in. We went to the top floor. I didn't see anybody in the house. It seemed to be empty. I was pretty tired by then. The two men sat around for a while and then one of them said why didn't I stay there and have a fix. They would go out and get something to eat. I said I didn't take injections. First I was going to say I didn't take any drugs and then I told them I smoked it. That made them suspicious and they wanted to know where I got that habit. I said I went with a boy who had been in Vietnam and he had learned how to smoke it like a cigarette and he had taught me. So they gave me a little powder and I went into a back room, which was just bare, and I lay down on the floor and pretended to go to sleep."

The girl stopped speaking for a few minutes and sat with her head hanging down so that Connie could not see her face. After a while she went on, "They didn't talk for a while. I suppose they thought they'd wait till I went to sleep. And then one of them left, saying he'd bring back some food for both of them. When he came back they began to talk and that is how I found out that they intended to keep me there — and — "

Her voice trailed off and she was silent for so long that Connie said, "And what?"

The girl did not respond at once and when she did she ignored Connie's question. "After a while I got up and let them know I was awake. I said I had to go downstairs to the john. They didn't stop me. I pretended to go into the bathroom, but instead I went on down the other flight of stairs and went out through the kitchen. I guessed they would wait a few minutes before coming after me, thinking I was still under the influence of the drug. I acted as if I was dopey. There was a backyard to the house, with a high railing fence around it, all twisted and bent and rusty. I managed to get over it. That's how I hurt my hand. I fell down on the other side and I had an awful moment, wondering if I had broken my leg and they'd come and catch me. But I was able to get up and run down the alley. I had to stop and rest several times, because my hand hurt so and the fall had shaken me up. But the men didn't come after me right away and then I started walking as fast as I could. I got out on the street and finally I got back downtown and then I sat down in a park for a while, thinking what I would do. I didn't have any money. I was afraid somebody would notice me. Then I remembered your name, so I went into a drugstore and looked in a phone book for your address. That park wasn't very far away from here."

When she stopped Connie considered for a while. "You know, Mary, this is a pretty wild story. Are you sure you didn't imagine some of it?"

Mary said softly, "You don't have to believe me."

"That's not the point, really. If you're going to tell me something, you should tell me everything—and tell me the truth."

"That's all I can tell you now," said Mary firmly, and turned away from her.

Some time later, aware that the afternoon was fading quickly, Connie said, "I'm going to have to get dressed soon. Roger is always punctual."

"Does he have to be anywhere but in this room?" Mary demanded, anxiously.

"Why, no. I don't think so. But listen to me, Mary. Why don't you let me introduce him to you and you tell him what you are afraid of? He could probably help—especially if it is true that you need protection from somebody." She stopped, astonished at the blaze of angry vexation that suddenly leapt into Mary's eyes.

"He must not know I'm here! I've told you, nobody must know I am here! If you tell him about me, I'll have to go away right at once. And you know I haven't anywhere else to go!" She added the last sentence in a voice that dropped suddenly to pleading.

"Oh, all right! All right! I won't tell him you are here. Don't be so upset, Mary! You can stay in the bedroom. He need not know you are here."

She sighed with relief as the panic in Mary's eyes faded. She is so mixed up, she thought. I'll just have to keep her here until I can make some sense out of what she says. Aloud she said, "You'd better let me dress your hand again before I get ready for Roger."

Mary held out her hand obediently and Connie undid the bandages. The gashes did not seem so angry and Mary said the wounds did not hurt her as much as they had.

"I'm afraid you're going to have a scar," said Connie, looking at the deepest gash in her palm.

Mary gave a little shrug and sat patiently while Connie renewed the bandage. Then Connie went to dress and afterwards surveyed the livingroom for signs that more than one person had had coffee or had sat in the chairs to read the papers. She warned Mary that she rarely closed her bedroom door entirely, so that she could not do so now without causing surprise in Roger. It usually stood ajar, and therefore Mary would have to keep away from that portion of the bedroom that was visible from the livingroom or would be reflected in the dressing-table looking-glass.

"I don't know when I shall be back, Mary. We may go to Roger's apartment and I may not get back till morning. Or perhaps I shall be back a little after midnight, since tomorrow is Monday and he'll want to be on the ball first thing in the morning. In any case, I shall stop by here before I go to the office." She avoided Mary's fixed stare as she spoke. "You'll be perfectly safe here. You can manage by yourself, can't you?"

Mary turned away from her without speaking.

Roger's ring was prompt. He looked fresh and rested, dressed with his usual conservative elegance. He kissed her as he stepped into the room and said, "Hello, pigeon. Have you missed me?"

"You haven't been out of my mind," said Connie, and was appalled at her own easy dissimulation.

Her wrap lay in readiness on the back of a chair and within minutes they were on their way down in the elevator. As they had their cocktails and ate their dinner, he talked with singleminded earnestness of the days he had spent in Chicago and the recalcitrance of one particular witness, whose belligerence had threatened to destroy the whole case. Connie made the responses he expected, so that he was not aware that her attention tended to wander. She was herself surprised to find that a good deal of what he said escaped her. She saved herself by snatching at a few familiar words and answering on assumptions of what she supposed he had said.

Involuntarily her mind kept going back to the apartment. Could Mary really manage the electric can opener? Would she think to look in the lower part of the kitchen cabinet for the skillet? Were the gashes in her hand really beginning to heal, or would infection suddenly flare up and get beyond the control of the simple remedies she had available? At last, with impatience Connie reminded herself that Mary had managed to live to the age of twenty-five without her help. She was undoubtedly perfectly capable of judging her own needs. Yet anxiety lingered in the back of Connie's mind. Or was it really something else—a wish to protect the communion that was blossoming between them, which Roger's return threatened to disrupt? You really couldn't get so used to someone in twenty-four hours, thought Connie, that you missed her as if you had lived with her for years.

Roger's voice interrupted her. "I didn't have much time to pay attention to the news while I was in Chicago. What's all this about a bombing here?"

"A downtown post office was blown up. The FBI says it was done by a radical group connected with those bombings out on the West Coast last month. They've caught two suspects, running away from the scene."

"A pity they didn't blow themselves to bits."

"They think one of them may have. They're sifting through the debris looking for fragments of human remains."

"They all ought to be shot," said Roger, spearing a piece of rare steak. "This country is really in danger from these young psychopaths. If they want to destroy themselves, it's fine with me, but something ought to be done about preventing them from damaging property and killing more reasonable people."

"I suppose some of them think the state of the world is so desperate that there's nothing to be done except knock it all to bits and start over again from scratch."

"That's a nice bit of nihilist philosophy. I hope you don't expect me to sympathize with it."

"No, I don't."

Towards the end of the evening, after a silence that went on for longer than Connie realized, Roger said, with a certain emphasis, "Shall we go to my place for a little while, Connie? I've really missed you. But I've got to be up pretty early in the morning. Shall we go along there now?"

In other words, thought Connie, in a sudden flash of half-contemptuous illumination, you want a quick one to get it out of your system.

All through the next two hours, while they sat and fondled one another for a brief space, while he took her with the promptness of old habit and urgent need, while they lay together drowsily talking until he reached for the bedside clock to see how late it had become, she tried to keep her attention on the matter at hand. At several moments she had the uncanny feeling that she was experiencing someone else's casual emotions, someone else's low-keyed feelings of accomplishing a well-learned task. Finally, slightly alarmed at her own sense of remoteness, she covertly looked at Roger. He was up and dressing. He gave no sign that he had found her in any way different from what he expected. His preoccupation with his own professional affairs, which underlay all his thoughts this evening, undoubtedly blunted his awareness of her. He took her back to her apartment. It seemed natural, under the pressure of the fleeting hours, for him to give her a quick goodnight kiss just within the front door before he left her to return to his own bed.

Connie closed the door quietly behind him and turned the second lock. The lamp was on by the big armchair. She crossed the room, walking softly, and pushed the bedroom door open.

"Mary," she said quietly.

"Yes," said Mary from the bed and the room was at once flooded by the light she switched on. She was propped up on her elbow and looked at Connie steadily.

Connie, uncomfortable under her stare, turned away and began to undress. "I won't be very long," she said, in a placating voice.

There was no answer and she glanced over at the bed again. Mary had turned her back. Connie finished undressing quickly. When she came back into the bedroom from the bathroom, Mary's back was still turned and she gave no sign that she was of aware of Connie getting into bed.

With her hand poised on the lamp switch, Connie said, "Shall I turn out the light?"

Mary's voice, slightly muffled by the bedclothes, said with distinct coldness, "Do just as you like."

Connie turned off the light and settled into bed. The day seemed suddenly to have been very long and the dark was alive with all sorts of half-visualized images and remembered phrases. It was long before she could sleep. The girl beside her lay very still, too still, as if she were consciously holding herself motionless. Her awareness of this artificial quietness, which implied a rejection of her nearness, a withdrawal of intimacy, depressed Connie's already flagging spirits. At last drowsiness overtook her and she slept a sleep full of uneasy dreams. When she woke, with a start, still under the effect of a dream she could not remember, she raised herself in bed to see that it was daylight and that Mary lay with her back towards her, as she had spent the night. The clock said half-past seven. Connie cast back the covers and got up. Mary stirred and rolled over on her back. Connie smiled at her coaxingly.

"Did you manage all right getting something to eat last night? I was wondering about you all evening."

Mary did not smile but her expression was calm and she nodded.

"I'm going to fix some coffee. Shall I bring it to you here?"

The girl shook her head and sat up in bed. Connie handed her the short bathrobe she had worn the morning before. The girl let it lie on the bed and sat rubbing her face with her unbandaged hand, her knees drawn up. In a few minutes she followed Connie into the kitchen, the robe around her shoulders, making a tent over the small white body.

"Here," said Connie, putting down the butter dish she had taken from the refrigerator. "Let me help you get it on."

The girl stood passive while Connie held the sleeves of the robe for her to thrust her arms into. She was taciturn while they sat at the table in the living room and ate. Then Connie said, finishing her second cup of coffee, "Shall I help you bathe and get dressed before I start getting ready for the office? How does your hand feel?"

"It doesn't hurt me now unless I try to use it. I'd like to take a shower."

"I'll turn it on for you." She went into the bathroom and adjusted the water for the shower. When she turned around Mary was standing near her, naked.

"Let's wrap a shower cap around your hand to keep the bandage dry. I can change it after you've bathed."

She wrapped the bandaged hand in one shower cap and put another on Mary's head, tucking the long, blonde hair under it. She found herself then washing the girl as if she were a small child and drying her off afterwards with gentle thoroughness. She suddenly felt guilty as she did so, disturbingly aware of the sensual pleasure she received from handling the soft full breasts, the rounded thighs.

The girl accepted her ministrations without demur, and when she had finished, waited for her to bring the jeans and shirt and put them on her.

"There. You'll do till I get home this evening."

"Are you going to be home this evening?" The question was asked as a challenge and Connie hesitated before answering. She had given no thought to the evening, beyond assuming that at the end of the working day she would return to the apartment and Mary. The recollection that Roger was now back in town and that he might demand her company that evening suddenly assailed her.

She said finally, a note of uncertainty in her voice, "I expect to be."

"You're not going out with that man again?"

"I—I don't know. Roger may want me to spend the evening with him. We're together most evenings."

Mary's lips set into a firm line. "Tell him that you can't go out with him tonight," she ordered her.

"That's not very easy to do," Connie protested.

Mary was eyeing her keenly. "You don't really want to go out with him," she said bluntly.

Connie looked away to escape her gaze. "I'll have to do something about getting us some food to eat tonight. There is some cheese and things for your lunch."

The girl made no reply and walked away from her into the livingroom. Connie bathed and dressed and made the bed before joining her. When she went into the livingroom the girl was sitting on the sofa with her legs drawn up under her.

"Don't you have a maid?" Mary demanded.

Connie, struck by her own failure to remember that the black girl Sadie came every Tuesday to clean her apartment, stammered, "Why—yes—, of course—Sadie comes every Tuesday morning. That's tomorrow."

Mary made no reply but looked up at her with wide eyes filled with sudden fright. She glanced around as if seeking vainly for somewhere to hide and then raised her hands to her face in a gesture of distress. Connie impulsively caught her in her arms.

"Please, Mary, don't look so scared! We'll figure something out. Nobody will come here today. You'll be quite safe till I get home. Here, look. This is my office phone number, if you should want to call me."

She let go of the girl and, snatching up the telephone pad, hastily scribbled the number down. "There," she said, turning back to the girl, "you haven't anything to worry about."

Mary said stubbornly, in a faint voice, "You mustn't tell anybody I'm here."

"No, of course not. I won't tell anybody," Connie assured her. She went on talking quickly, reassuringly, as she gathered up her handbag and keys and prepared to leave, glancing at the girl every few seconds. Mary followed her to the door. As she went to close it, she paused and looked down at the girl standing close to her as if loathe to see her go. On a sudden impulse she leaned down and kissed her. Mary put her arms around her neck and rested her forehead against her for a moment. The interchange, so sudden and unexpected, was over at once and Connie went out of the door and down the hall to the elevator. Yet Mary's presence, her awareness of Mary, went with her out into the street.

"She's got to tell me more about this business this evening," she said to herself, as she headed for the bus, "She's got to. That's all there is to it."

Chapter Six

All morning, while she diligently applied herself to the books
and papers on her desk, her thoughts kept drifting back to the a-
partment and Mary and the problem that beset her. Mary had established herself in the very middle of her consciousness, so that
her attention inevitably returned to that one constant, like the
needle of a compass seeking the north pole.

At lunchtime she sought a nearby shop which carried children's
clothes. Mary, she supposed, must wear the size that would fit a
small twelve-year-old girl. The saleswoman showed her pantsuits
in sizes that seemed ample for Mary and Connie selected one in a
pale yellow wool and a neck scarf to match. She pondered over
shoes for some time and finally bought a pair of lightweight summer slippers. She completed her purchases with some panties and
socks. As she did all this she thought, nothing will disguise her
small size but in different clothes she won't be so easily recognized. She might even be taken for a child, if one didn't look too
closely. Returning with the clothes in a big paper bag, Connie was
assailed by the normal curiosity of the girls in the office. The
things were for her niece, she said, improvising quickly to account
for the small sizes. A birthday present. She escaped into her own
office before she had to answer questions of why she had never
mentioned the niece before.

When five-thirty came she closed up her work as eagerly as any
of the younger people in the office. She had seen nothing of Roger
all day. Walking absentmindedly to the elevator she did not notice that he came out of one of the partners' offices and was almost at her elbow when he said, "Why, hello! Are you leaving?"
Astonishment rang in his voice.

Connie gave a little start. "Yes." She thought quickly. "I have a
headache. I think I must be getting a cold."

"I haven't had a chance to call you all day." He was in shirt sleeves
and carrying a file in his hand. "I'm not going to be free this evening, Connie. I'll be lucky if I get through this stuff before morning."

"Oh, that's all right, Roger! I don't feel like doing anything anyway."

"Well, take care of yourself," he responded automatically, his attention already back on the file in his hand. "I'll see you tomorrow. Good night."

"Good night," said Connie, hurrying to join the three or four other people getting into the elevator.

She got off the bus at the corner before her usual one so that she could stop by the delicatessen and finally arrived at the apartment laden with the purchases she had made at noon and a sack of groceries. She set these down on the floor to unlock her door. When she got the first lock unfastened she found the second lock on. A slight sound reached her from inside the apartment. A small voice said breathlessly through the panel of the door, "Who is it?"

"Me. Connie. I have my arms full."

The second lock turned and the door opened alowly. Mary watched as she walked in with her open handbag dangling from her arm and the bag full of groceries. She set these down and went back for the clothes. Mary gave a sigh of relief as she once more closed and latched the door.

"Did anyone come to the door during the day?" Connie asked. "Did the phone ring? I didn't call because I thought it might frighten you."

The girl shook her head and followed her as she carried the sack of groceries into the kitchen.

"I got us some filet mignon. I thought you might like a good meal."

The girl made no reply but simply watched her place the meat and the carton of milk and the eggs in the refrigerator. Then she followed her back into the livingroom.

"I've got you something else," said Connie, smiling at her as she opened the bag of clothes. "How'd you like something else to wear besides those jeans?"

She drew the pantsuit out of the bag and held it up. "The question is whether it will fit you. The woman said this is the equivalent of a size five. She didn't think any grown woman would be smaller. Let's see if she's right."

She stepped towards the girl as she spoke, to hold the garments up to her to gauge the fit. Mary retreated from her and she stopped in consternation.

"Don't you like it, Mary?" she asked in disappointment.

Mary continued to eye the suit silently.

"It's almost the same color as your hair. And I think the little bit of green on the buttons is pretty." Connie spoke coaxingly.

Mary said slowly, "It's a very nice suit. I'm—I'm just not used to wearing anything like that now."

"Well, will you try it on?"

Mary only nodded and began to unbutton her shirt with her left hand. She stood patiently as Connie unfastened the jeans and helped her out of them and into the pants of the suit and then the top.

"It looks quite well on you," said Connie, eyeing her closely. "It's still too big but if it was any smaller it wouldn't stretch around your breasts."

The girl nodded, looking to see herself in the large mirror on the wall. "It is very nice," she said and began to unbutton the top.

"Don't you want to keep it on for a while?"

"Not now," said Mary firmly and began to work her way out of the jacket so determinedly that Connie came to her aid. She watched without comment as Connie walked into the bedroom with the suit in her hand and hung it in the closet.

Coming back, Connie drew the other clothes out of the bag and showed them to her. She accepted them with a matter-of-fact air and then went and sat down on the sofa. Connie, worried, said then, "As a matter of fact, Mary, I thought perhaps you would not want to be here when Sadie comes to clean tomorrow and you can't go out in the street with those things on."

The girl looked at her in quick alarm, her eyes wide. "Can't you tell her not to come? I can't—I can't go out. Somebody might see me and recognize me."

"That's the reason for the new clothes."

"They won't help."

Looking at her sitting perched sideways on the sofa, with the air of a bird on a tree limb, Connie was struck by the essential reality of her response. It would indeed be difficult to hide the identity of someone who was at the same time so small and so striking. No one would ever accept Mary as being a little girl—no one, that is, who had a glimpse of that severely beautiful face with its transparent white skin and coldly burning blue eyes. Perhaps that was the reason why she had worn that preposterous black felt hat—in order to have something to hide behind.

Dropping the subject for the moment, Connie asked then, "Did you listen to the radio today? I did not read the paper this morning. I left it here for you."

The girl shook her head and glanced at the newspaper that lay scattered on the floor as if she had sat down on the rug to look at it.

"I was afraid that someone might hear the radio," she said in her quiet little voice. "I didn't want anyone to think there was anybody in your apartment."

"I don't think the people next door can hear anything. Anyway, they're not there in the daytime. "But what *do* you want to do about tomorrow. I can tell Sadie that you're a friend who has come to stay with me for a while."

The sudden fierceness that she had noticed before burst out in Mary's glance and voice. "She mustn't come here!"

Irritated, Connie began, "Well, I—" when the phone rang, startling both of them. Mary stared at her intently while she answered it.

"Oh, Sadie!" Connie exclaimed into the phone. "What, you want to skip tomorrow? That's fine. The place can go another week. I can pick up after myself. You go ahead and take care of the old lady. Right-o, Sadie."

She looked over at Mary as she put the phone down. "That's lucky. Sadie wants tomorrow free to look after somebody who is coming out of the hospital and will need waiting on."

Mary visibly relaxed but said nothing.

When Connie came back into the livingroom from changing her clothes, she found Mary still sitting on the sofa, her head dropped forward as if in dejection. Connie, eyeing her in concern, said nothing immediately but sat down in the big armchair and switched on the radio. The newscaster was in the midst of an account of the latest developments in the post office bombing. The two suspects arrested still refused to make statements. The special squad that had been looking for human remains in the debris had as yet found nothing conclusive, but the belief persisted that a third person had been involved and had been killed in the blast. The police refused to make definite statements for fear of prejudicing their investigations. The news reporters, however, had learned that they now believed that this third person was a girl who was described as being unusually small, having long blonde hair and wearing jeans and a dark woolen cape or poncho and a black felt hat. It was surmised that she had not been able to escape from the building before the explosion, since the bomb, being of amateur production, had gone off prematurely.

Connie sat fixed in her chair as the newscaster went on to other news. At last she looked over at Mary and asked, apprehensively, "Did you hear what he said?"

Mary gave a little shrug. "That was in this morning's paper."

A slightly sick feeling took possession of Connie. "I suppose if they think you are dead, they are not looking for you."

Mary gave a sudden, unmirthful little laugh. "*Do* they think I'm dead? You notice that the police did not say so. The news reporter surmised it."

Her suddenly displayed acuteness made Connie uneasy. This was a different Mary, a Mary whose thoughts were not vaguely wandering far afield but were sharply focussed on the problem at hand. The little girl helpless with fear had vanished and in her stead was an astute woman weighing the circumstances dispassionately.

"You think the police are giving out a false impression on purpose?"

Mary answered after a slight hesitation. "It would be easier to catch somebody if he thought he was not being hunted, wouldn't it? Give him a false feeling of security, wouldn't it?" She added, after a little pause, "Do you see why I can not let anyone see me? Many people must have heard and read that description. Even if the clothes are different, I'm too small to escape notice. And the fact that I am supposed to be dead would only make them notice me more if they saw me."

"You're telling me the truth when you say you had nothing to do with the bombing? But if you knew what was going to happen, why didn't you give warning of it? It could have resulted in the killing and maiming of many innocent people. In fact, one man was taken to the hospital. You do have an obligation to society, you know."

Mary said with a crispness entirely new to her, "That's debatable."

"Do you mean you've opted out of society?"

Mary smiled at her ironically. "Society is a large term. There's one type of society I've opted out of."

"You mean ýour parents' type." Connie was thoughtful for a while. "There are a lot of things in our world that I don't care for. But I can't condone irresponsible actions that damage other people, no matter what the pretext. I don't go for violence for the sake of violence."

Mary said in a mild voice, "I would not commit violence myself. I have learned that in the last month. But I had to find out. I couldn't rely on what somebody else told me."

"So you'be been experimenting—with drugs and political protest and sex—"

"Not sex."

Connie looked at her sharply in surprise but decided not to pick up the statement. Instead she said, "But even if you draw the line at manufacturing and planting bombs yourself, you should have tried to prevent those boys."

"How? No, I could not have prevented them. They would not have listened to me. I wasn't a member of their group. They don't listen to anybody but each other. They have all their own arguments."

"So you went along out of curiosity, at the risk of getting yourself blown to bits."

Mary replied in the same soft voice she had used before, "I had to see for myself."

"Well, I advise you to keep your curiosity under better control. You've been lucky this time."

A trace of fear reappeared in Mary's eyes. "Yes—so far," she murmured.

"Well, cheer up. Though I admit I don't see how you are going to avoid an interview with the police indefinitely. According to the news stories, those two boys have not implicated you."

"They know I did not have anything to do with the bombing. And I'm not going to talk to the police. I'm not going to let them pin anything on me." A little shudder went through her.

Connie, to dispel her own uneasiness, said, "I'm going to fix supper. How do you like your steak—rare or well-done?"

She tried to keep up an easy flow of talk while she brought the silver and the china to the table in the livingroom and watched the steaks sizzling under the broiler. Mary answered only briefly and sometimes absently. Connie found herself lapsing into longer and longer silences, preoccupied in spite of herself with the questions that underlay their talk. The two men that Mary had said she feared—if they really existed, she should be able to describe them.

As they sat down to dinner and she was cutting Mary's steak into bite-size pieces, she asked, in a carefully casual manner,

"Mary, what about those men you say you're afraid of? What do they look like?"

"They dress like hippies. One of them has a beard and bushy red hair. The other one has a scar on his face."

Has she invented that? Connie wondered. "They dress like hippies but they are not hippies? Is that it?"

"Yes. They are not hippies. They are petty criminals."

"Petty criminals? What do they do?"

"They push drugs. I am sure they both push drugs. They try to make as many addicts as they can."

"Did they try on you?"

"Yes—the one I had met before did. The other one is new—I never saw him until Jasper brought him along."

"Jasper?"

"That's the name he goes by. He is the one that was hanging around the people I knew."

Does she mean to be so vague? Connie wondered. "Well, these friends of yours, the drug pushers—"

Mary said vehemently, "They are not my friends!"

"Well, anyway—you could turn them in to the police."

"It wouldn't do any good. It would just get me into trouble."

Connie gazed at her, speculating. "Or have you tried to turn them in and that is why you think they are after you—out of revenge?"

Mary shook her head and then brushed her hair out of her face with her bandaged hand.

"Then why is it that you think they are looking for you to kill you?"

"I heard what they said."

"You heard what they said? You mean there in that house?

Mary nodded.

"And you think they want to catch you to keep you from going to the police?"

"It's worse than that."

"It could scarcely be." Connie thought for several moments before she said, "You know, Mary, the newspaper story said something about a woman who was sitting on a bus at the traffic light on the corner where the post office is. She said she noticed you standing at the door and thought you must be funny because it was a whole hour before the time when the post office is open for business. I gather the police think you were acting as a look-out for the two boys who planted the bomb. What were you doing there?"

"Trying to see into the post office. I saw the boys go in at the back of the post office. I didn't want them to see me, but I wanted to watch them."

"Could you see anything?"

"No, I couldn't."

I haven't got very far with that, thought Connie.

They finished eating in silence and Connie cleared away the dishes. When she returned from the kitchen she found Mary seated again on the sofa, idly playing with the buttons in the uphol-

stery. Since she seemed disinclined to talk, Connie took up a novel and tried to absorb herself in the story. When ten o'clock came
she turned on the news roundup, but though the newscaster referred to the post office bombing, he merely reiterated what they already knew. The man who had been taken to the hospital was im-
proving. The identity of the girl who was supposed to have been
blown to bits in the explosion was still unknown, though she was
assumed to be a college dropout who had been living with the boys.
The boys, however, denied any knowledge of her.

"Is all that true, Mary?"

"It is true that I'm a college dropout. But it is not true that I
was living with the boys."

"Whom have you been living with, then?"

"Nobody," said the girl emphatically.

Chapter Seven

She did not know how long she had been asleep when she was roused by Mary's sudden move. She woke to see the compound glow of the city lights shining into the bedroom, making everything in the room faintly visible. She felt the girl beside her stir and turn over towards her, with a low cry that was half a sob. Before she was fully roused she felt the girl throw herself on top of her and found herself gripped in a frantic embrace. Mary's face was in the pillow by her head. Mary's bare stomach was pressed against her body, her thighs straddling Connie's hips. She was gasping wildly into Connie's ear, "Don't let them find me! Please! Please don't!"

Connie struggled to free herself from the frantically clinging arms. "Mary! Calm down! You've been dreaming! You've had a nightmare! You're scaring yourself out of your wits! Quiet down!"

The girl continued to cling to her, continued to plead. "Everything I've told you is true!" She was sobbing now as she pinned Connie down with an amazing strength. "Those men are looking for me! They will rape me! They will kill me! They will torture me! You're the only one who can help me! Please! Please!"

Connie, half choked by her grip, stopped struggling against her. Putting her arms around the small, tense body, she said as soothingly as she could, "Of course, Mary, of course. Now quiet down. Nobody can hurt you in here, with me. You're perfectly safe. There, darling, don't be so frightened."

She hugged the girl to her, stroking the back of her head, deliberately relaxing her own body in order to prompt Mary to do likewise. Gradually Mary's sobs subsided and her grip on Connie loosened. They lay then a long time quietly in each other's arms. As Mary's body sank closer against her own, Connie grew once more drowsy.

Presently she felt Mary stir. "There," she said gently, "Are you better now?"

Mary raised her head and rubbed her cheek against Connie's.

"Do you want me to turn on the light? Do you want to get up?"

"No," said the girl, rubbing her face against Connie's again. "No. I like it better this way. I can feel you better."

She sounded like a contented child, comforted by the feeling of security induced by the warm closeness of their bodies. After a while she rolled down beside Connie, lying along the length of her body, her head on Connie's pillow. She gave a little sigh and shortly fell asleep.

When morning came and she raised herself on her elbow to look at the bedside clock, Connie leaned over the still sleeping girl. Mary stirred and sleepily lifted her bandaged hand to stroke Connie's cheek.

"I've got to get up now, Mary."

"Yes," said Mary drowsily and did not move when she got out of bed.

When she returned from the bathroom she found Mary lying on her bed gazing at the ceiling. "You certainly had a wild nightmare last night."

Mary brought her gaze down from the ceiling but said nothing.

"Do you often have these frights?"

Mary contemplated her. "It doesn't take much to get me keyed up."

"Is it something you've suffered from as a child?"

Mary turned her gaze back to the ceiling. "I've always had a hard time sleeping quietly. I've always been afraid when I am alone at night. I never seem to feel quite safe. Having a light on doesn't help. It's just that I'm vulnerable at night. It was heaven to have you beside me last night."

"I was very glad to be able to comfort you. You slept very quietly afterwards."

Mary's eyes came down from the ceiling and smiled at her. "Dear Stantia."

Connie, irresistibly drawn, sat down on the bed beside her and took her in her arms as Mary nestled close to her. She said into Connie's neck, "But I wasn't imagining things. I am in danger. Please believe me."

Giving herself a shake, Connie looked at her. "Well, you're safe here. Do as you did yesterday and I'll come home as early as I can this evening."

The thought of Roger suddenly crossed her mind and she let go of Mary and stood up. Mary lay back on the pillow.

When Connie turned on the radio they found that the post office bombing was no longer in first place in the news. The fighting in Vietnam had been stepped up, a serious earthquake had taken place somewhere in the Middle East, and two prominent United

States senators had accused each other of malfeasance in office.
Perhaps, thought Connie, this evening I can get Mary to tell me
more details.

In the office she found it no easier than she had the day before
to concentrate on her work. The night's experience came back to
her again and again, each time reminding her of the emotions it
had aroused. Her heart grew tender whenever she thought of Mary
—little, confiding Mary, at once artless and unfathomable. Mary
was someone unique in her experience, someone who in three
short days had come to hold sway over her innermost thoughts
and feelings in a way no one else had ever remotely done. In the
two years of her intimacy with Roger he had never achieved this
dominion over her heart and mind. There was now, in the center
of her consciousness, a hidden spot, like a secret glade in a forest,
full of sunlight, that was filled with Mary. And how, she wondered, did Mary feel about her? She found it impossible to judge what
Mary really thought of her.

Connie started at the sound of her office door opening. Roger's
secretary stood there, her eyes bright with interest in the message
she brought. "Mr. Wellington wants to know if you can join him
right away. He is in Mr. Clay's office."

Mr. Clay. The senior partner. Bryanston had been dead long before she joined the firm. Mr. Clay did not concern himself with
any but the most important clients. Connie hurried down the cor-
ridors to the suite of big rooms on the front of the building.

As she entered, Roger, who was leaning over the big bare desk
behind which Mr. Clay sat, said, "Hi, Connie." Mr. Clay nodded
briefly to her. He was a florid, white-haired man clutching a cigar
in a bony, wrinkled hand adorned by a large signet ring. The other
men in the room, two of the older partners, likewise greeted her
and one of them gestured to a chair beside himself. She sat down.

Mr. Clay said, as if he were continuing with something he had
been saying before she came in, "Of course, Roger, I realize that
this isn't the sort of thing we normally handle. But Christeson is
not an ordinary client of this firm. He is not willing to confide his
personal affairs to other lawyers. We'll have to take care of this
matter."

"My objection, sir," said Roger, deferentially, "is that perhaps
we are not equipped to give him the very best advice, since his
problem is not within our normal practice."

"It is a very delicate matter," said Mr. Clay. "That is precisely
why he wants us. We'll have to do our best, Roger."

Roger nodded. "I've looked into the present situation of his family, sir. I know that we have been counsel for the Christeson interests ever since the time of the present Henry Christeson's father—"

Mr. Clay interrupted him with a dry smile. "H.B.'s father and I graduated from Harvard in the same class. He was the first major client Bryanston and Clay acquired. Yes, you know all about the Christesons, I've no doubt. It is an old fortune—industry, mining, railroads and various other enterprises through several generations in American history. H.B. is the responsible member of that family now. He is well aware of the importance of his interests to the national economy."

"Well, sir," said Roger, "I've made a general survey of the family. Mr. Christeson has been married twice. The daughter is the child of the first marriage. He has two sons by his present wife. They are minors. He has them in a school in Scotland. He keeps them well guarded. He takes every precaution, since a family like that lives under the threat of kidnaping. But, of course, with the daughter it is more difficult. She is no longer a minor and apparently refuses to be controlled by him."

Clay nodded. "She is a problem, a serious problem. H.B.'s first wife was unstable. I think her daughter inherits some of that instability."

"Does she control her own money?" one of the other partners suddenly asked.

"Yes and no," said Clay. "There is a certain amount of property and assets that she inherited from her mother and also from her maternal grandmother. The rest is income in a trust her grandfather set up for her. H.B.'s father did not believe in letting the girls in the family have too free a hand with their inheritance. He was afraid of fortune hunters."

The old man glanced suddenly at Connie and smiled sweetly. "He was afraid their husbands would dissipate it," he explained, speaking directly to her.

Connie automatically smiled back but did not reply. Mr. Clay was well along in his eighties and she did not think he was open to new ideas as far as women were concerned. He had been reluctant to accept women lawyers into the firm. He turned away to speak to the men.

"Well, I think you understand the situation. I agree that it is a good thing to have Miss Norton do that research in the newspaper files. Roger, you can explain to Miss Norton what we want her to do."

It was a dismissal and Connie, observing that Roger was gathering up the papers he had laid on the desk, stood up, ready to go out of the room with him. The old man at the desk courteously rose and bowed to her as she turned to go.

Roger, walking closely behind her, said, "Come to my office, Connie."

He followed her into the room and closed the door behind them. "Sit down, Connie. This is going to take some time."

She said, "What is the problem with Christeson? I thought at first he wanted us to get him a divorce. Is it something to do with his daughter?"

Roger fiddled with the papers he had put down on his desk. "The fact is that H.B. Christeson has received a communication threatening harm to his daughter. He is in touch with the police, but they told him to take no action until he knows more about the situation."

"Has she been kidnaped?"

"We don't know." Roger picked up a piece of paper from the pile. "The note Christeson received says, 'You don't know what has happened to your daughter. We do. Want to find out?' "

"Is that all?"

"Yes. I suppose this is meant to soften him up—as a preliminary to a demand for money. The real problem is that Christeson doesn't know his daughter's whereabouts. He has not heard from her for several months. He says that for the last two or three years, since she has come of age, he has had only a general idea of her activities and associates. Now he has hired detectives to have her traced. But in the meantime, your job is to go to the Public Library and search through the New York papers for the last twenty years to see what you can pick up about her. The ordinary news columns may make some mention of her, simply because she is H.B. Christeson's daughter. But I think the society news will be your chief source."

"Is she married? Or divorced? What name does she go by?"

"She is neither married nor divorced. Her name is Charlotte— Charlotte Christeson. I don't know anything about her interests or avocations. That is for you to find out. All I know is that she and her father don't get along harmoniously. Apparently there is considerable antagonism between them."

"If months go by and he doesn't even know where she is—what was this about her mother being unstable?"

Roger grinned. "That's the old man's euphemism for the fact that H.B.'s first wife was an alcoholic. It was probably the reason for the break-up of the marriage. I don't know the details. If you spend the afternoon in the newspaper room of the Public Library, I expect you'll be able to fill me in. I've got to get back to another case for a while."

Connie left him already absorbed in the files piled on his desk. Half an hour later she sat in the high-ceilinged reading room of the Public Library, scanning the big bound volumes of newspapers the attendant had brought her. There was not a great deal for her to note. The Christesons shunned publicity. But here and there, on the second or third pages, tucked in between items about the recent presidential inauguration, the President's golfing activities, the war in Korea, she came upon short paragraphs. The passage of fifteen years since these events made it seem all like ancient history.

The Christesons had been married in the middle of the Second World War. She found pictures of them at the time of their wedding, Christeson in the uniform of a Navy captain, his wife in that of the WAVES. Connie read carefully the captions that identified them — H.B. as the scion of a family whose industrial empire had provided great wartime support for his country, his bride as the daughter of a well-to-do Virginian family. There were other pictures of the wife, a woman in her late twenties, wearing a Chanel creation at a charity ball, or in riding clothes at a fox hunt in Virginia. There was something familiar about the rather haggard-looking face. Connie looked at it more closely and referred back to the wedding announcement. It gave her name, Connie read it first casually and then read it again, slowly: Charlotte Mary Gilray.

For some minutes she read and reread the name and examined the pictures of the woman. Mary. Mary Gilray. Charlotte Christeson. The daughter of Charlotte Mary Gilray Christeson.

Seldom in her life had Connie felt the inner perturbation that now assailed her. Until that moment Mary had been someone remote from her own daily preoccupations, someone whose existence had nothing to do with Bryanston and Clay, with the day to day problems that confronted her in her office. Mary was someone entirely separate from all this — like a princess in a tower, she thought wrily — a forlorn girl to whom she had given the shelter of her apartment, a girl without parents, without money. Now she was revealed as someone who had all these things in abundance. She felt absurdly as if she had suddenly been bereft of something of enormous value — that the Mary who had become interwoven with her innermost self was snatched from her.

Then she told herself that this was all nonsense. Of course, Mary was just someone of whom she knew very little, someone whose

life history and background it was her job to discover. Grimly she
set about the task of tracing the activities of Charlotte Christeson.
Gradually, out of many casual newspaper items, she began to e-
volve a picture. Charlotte had been ten years old when her parents had been divorced. They had shared custody of her—a few
months with each parent in turn. Then it appeared that she was
often with her maternal grandmother, when her mother had died
in a sanatarium and her father had married a second time. After
that there were occasions when her presence in the United States,
at Junior League functions and such affairs, was noted as taking
place on visits from the schools she attended in Switzerland. Once
she was pictured as a bridesmaid in a fashionable wedding. Connie,
eagerly scanning the smudged photographs, tried hard to see clearly Mary's features. In the end she gave it up. The girl in the bridesmaid's dress could have been any other girl similarly clad.

Connie at last finished with the newspaper and looked at her
notes. She doubted that they would be of any value to Roger. Obviously, what he wanted to know about, Charlotte Christeson's
activities during the last six months, were not to be discovered in
newspaper files. She had not attended any public social functions.
She was not involved in any of the doings of the jet set. She was
not mentioned, as a suspect or as being under arrest—at least, by
her right name—in any account of student demonstrations or protest rallies. If there was any information to be obtained about her
life in the last few years, it would have to come from another source.

Or from Mary herself. She could ask Mary. Suddenly the full
force of her own situation struck Connie. It was true: If the girl
living in her apartment was in fact Charlotte Christeson, she could
ask her questions about the things they wanted to know. She, Connie Norton, held in her hands the key to the information that was
vital to the firm, to the firm's client. What was she going to do a-
bout it? There seemed to be little doubt about that. With a sinking heart she thought, I must tell Roger at once. I must explain
that this girl has taken refuge with me and that I am sure that she
is the woman you are looking for.

She sat and contemplated this decision for several minutes. It
was the logical, the right, the inevitable decision. But as she sat
and thought about it, as she remembered Mary, as she remembered all the little nuances of her dealings with Mary, she discovered
that this was not the decision she was in fact going to make. She
would not tell Roger about this, at least, not until she had told
Mary what she knew. To do otherwise was a betrayal of Mary.

As this resolution hardened in her she got up and closed her briefcase. As she walked back to her office she faced the fact squarely. She was not going straight to Roger to tell him where the Christeson heiress was at that moment. And as a consequence she would have to bear the self-reproach, the sense of responsibility for the consequences that would inevitably follow. But though she presented this idea to herself in as harsh a light as she could, she found that her resolution stood.

She found it difficult to go through the small tasks that must be done before she left the office for the day. Roger was out of his office. He did not expect to return until much later and he had left word that he would appreciate it if she gave her notes to his secretary. When he got a chance that night he would give her a ring at her apartment. As she prepared the notes to give them to the secretary, she stared for a while at a slip of paper on which she had written, for her own guidance, the biographical data: Charlotte Mary Gilray Christeson, daughter of Henry B. Christeson and Charlotte Mary Gilray, born April 20, 1943. On an impulse she folded it across and put it in her handbag.

On the bus on the way home, she stayed wrapped in a dense cloud of preoccupation. Her mind still tried to shy away from the coming encounter with Mary, what she would say, what further information she would demand from Mary, what she would do if Mary refused to tell her, or denied the truth of what she said.

Chapter Eight

The sound of her key in the lock must have caught Mary's ear, for Connie heard the small voice say at once: "Stantia, is that you?"

"Yes. Turn the other lock, will you?"

When she stepped into the apartment she heard a man's voice singing a Schubert song. It was barely audible, for though Mary had mustered the courage to turn on the record player, she obviously feared that the music might be heard beyond the walls of the apartment.

Mary stood a little way from the door, watching her as she put down her handbag. They looked at each other, without speaking. Connie found it suddenly difficult to find something to say, and the girl seemed, as always, to wait for her to begin the conversation. The penetrating blue eyes stayed fixed on Connie's face for a while and then, as if Mary sensed there was something different about their meeting this evening, she turned away and walked back to the sofa, where she obviously had been sitting when she had heard Connie at the door.

"I see you've found out how to operate the record-player," said Connie, for something to say.

The girl looked at her for a moment and then replied, "I didn't think anybody would hear it if I turned it low. It takes such a long time for the day to go by."

The odd little note of sadness in her voice reached into Connie's heart and the confused mood of the afternoon suddenly cleared. She saw now that, unaware of this herself, she had been trying to build up a barrier between herself and Mary, a barrier that would make it possible for her to deal with Mary as a stranger, someone who had no special call on her loyalty. Now Mary had demolished that attempt to create a distance between them, had demolished it with the mere tone of her voice.

Connie said tenderly, "It must be pretty dreary in here by yourself all day."

Mary replied in a patient little voice, "I don't mind being by myself. But I don't feel safe if you're not here." She glanced around the apartment with an air of distress. Connie started to step closer to her, eager to put her arms around her. But she stopped herself and said abruptly, "I'll go and change my things."

A few minutes later she returned to the livingroom wearing shirt and slacks. Her nerves in a jangle, she said half-beligerantly, "Do you mind if I have a drink? I need one tonight."

She was opening the door to the liquor cabinet as she spoke and she saw the quick expression of distrust pass over Mary's face. Of course, her mother was an alcoholic. No wonder she had a decided reaction to the sight of whiskey bottles. The children of alcoholics, Connie had heard, usually went in one direction or another —followed their parents down the drunkard's path or were total abstainers. Mary was obviously the latter.

But the fact that she now had this clue to Mary's behavior cut through Connie's defenses. Throughout the afternoon she had debated with herself about whether or not she would confront Mary with the information she had gleaned from the newspaper files. She shrank from doing so. But could she maintain silence? Could she really sit and judge Mary's behavior from the basis of this secretly held knowledge? And did she want to? A great uneasiness of spirit troubled her. It was not fair to Mary to watch her thus and Mary still ignorant of the fact that she knew the real situation. And yet how much deception did Mary intend to use on her?

Connie poured a drink and took it over to the big armchair and sat down. The record had come to an end and Mary got up to choose another.

"You can turn the thing up now," said Connie, "since I'm home. It doesn't matter if anyone hears it now. I often play music for myself at this time of day."

Without a word the girl, who was kneeling in front of the record-player, reached up and turned the knob to increase the volume. Standing up, she put the record on and returned to her seat on the sofa, still without speaking.

Connie sipped at her drink. She was baffled by her own feelings. Since she had entered the apartment she had alternated between an aching longing to get as close to Mary as she could and a sore feeling that arose from the fact that Mary was someone other than the forlorn girl who had sought refuge with her. The suspicion that Mary might have deliberately assumed her air of helpless innocence to gain her own ends hung there between them.

Mary's silence began to get on her nerves. "I'm sorry you have to be here by yourself all day. But if it is dangerous for you to go out, I don't see any alternative." These men whom the girl feared. Perhaps they were the ones who were threatening her father, even though they had lost control over her. But perhaps they thought that was only temporary. Perhaps they were merely biding their

time till she showed herself. In that case, she should solve her
difficulties by applying to her father for help, for protection.

Connie looked up to find Mary's cold blue eyes fixed on her.
Probably the girl had been watching her for some time. It was
uncanny. Under the stare of those vivid eyes she felt as if every
thought, every feeling of her own was revealed, that she was unable to hide anything that was going on in her mind.

"What is it, Mary?" she demanded.

Instead of answering, Mary dropped her eyes and sat in dejection, her fair hair falling over her face. Connie sat and looked at
her for several moments, at once uncertain. At last she put down
her half-empty glass and moved over to sit down by the girl.

"Mary," she said gently, "please tell me everything—who you
really are, what the trouble really is. I can't help you if you keep
me in the dark."

Mary raised her eyes. They were not bold now. She leaned toward Connie and passed her good hand behind Connie's neck.
"Why are you so impatient with me tonight?" she asked in her
small voice.

"I'm not impatient. I suppose I'm really worried. You can't go
on like this for long. I can't hide you here in this apartment indefinitely."

Mary drew back and gave her a more considering look.

Connie asked, "Couldn't your father help you? Couldn't you go
to him for help?"

Mary drew away from her, eyeing her with suspicion. "No. He
is the last person I would ask."

"But why? Even if you are not on good terms with him, he would
surely protect you in these circumstances."

A contemptuous smile crossed the girl's face. "That's only an
assumption. What makes you think I'm not on good terms with
him?"

"Just the way you act. Of course it is an assumption but I'm sure
it is a valid one. In a case like this your father would want to help
you."

Mary's smile grew more indulgent. "Who has been talking to you
today, Stantia? Have you been discussing me with your precious
Roger?"

Stung, Connie bit her lip and did not reply.

"Because if you have, you're nothing more than a cheat, like all
the rest of them." Mary's eyes blazed and her face went white with
anger. "Have you told him about me?"

"No, no, I haven't!" She hesitated for a moment and then, making up her mind, got up and crossed to the table where her handbag lay. She drew out of it the slip of paper on which she had written Charlotte Christeson's birthdate and parents' names. Coming back to the sofa she stood in front of the girl and offered it to her silently. When Mary took the slip, she turned away and walked back to the armchair. She sat down and took a sip of her drink. Raising her eyes she met the blue stare.

"Where did you get this?" If she had been pale before, she was livid now.

Connie, a little frightened in spite of herself, said in a low voice, "Out of the New York Times—from the accounts of your parents' divorce."

For a moment the girl could not speak. Then she poured out a stream of invective, so vivid, so vehement that Connie sat amazed.

Abruptly Mary came to a stop. "And will you tell me what prompted you to go snooping?" she asked in a suddenly calm voice.

"Mary," said Connie desperately, "if you'll be quiet for a few minutes, I'll tell you what has happened."

She thought at first that Mary was going to refuse to listen to her but presently she said angrily, "Well, what is it? What has happened?"

"You probably don't realize that the law firm I'm connected with are your father's legal advisers." She paused to see if the girl would respond but Mary kept silent. "This morning I was sent to the Public Library to look up information about you in old newspaper files. That is, I was sent to find out what I could about Charlotte Christeson, Henry Christeson's daughter. That is how I discovered that you were using part of your own name—that you and Charlotte Christeson are one woman."

"I should not have used any of my own name," the girl burst out in a vexed voice. "I should have used something entirely different. Why did they send you to do this? Why do they want to know about me?"

"Your father wants to find you. He has received a threatening letter about you—the sort of letter kidnapers send."

The girl did not reply but her eyes widened in alarm.

"That is why I asked you why you don't let your father know where you are and let him protect you."

A slight shudder went through Mary's body. "No! And you must not let your law firm know about me."

"Now, look," said Connie earnestly, "This is ridiculous. It's my responsibility to disclose the fact that you're Charlotte Christeson, that you've taken refuge in my apartment,—I suppose, from these men who are threatening your father. Besides, your father is really concerned about you. It is cruel to keep him in ignorance of where you are. In good conscience you should let him know that you are safe."

"What do you know about it?" the girl demanded contemptuously, "I am not going to let him know where I am and I forbid you to tell anyone."

"Oh, you do!" Connie's temper flared for a moment. "And why do you think I have to do as you say?" Even as she spoke her momentary anger sank. Of course I am going to do what she wants and I can't for the life of me think why that is. She got up impatiently and said, "I'm hungry. Will you eat some spaghetti?"

The girl nodded carelessly and got up and went to the record-player to put another record on. They ate in silence, except for an occasional remark, the music filling the gaps. When Connie got up to clear the table, the girl followed her into the kitchen, carrying dishes in her sound hand. When Connie had washed and dried them she put them neatly away in the cabinet.

The phone rang as they returned to the livingroom. Connie was conscious of the girl's eyes on her as she went to answer.

"Hi, Connie," said Roger's voice. "Sorry I couldn't see you this afternoon."

"That's all right, Roger. Have you seen my notes?"

"Yes. Not much help there, is there? I'm talking to the detective—his name is Fairchild—in the morning. Maybe he will be more helpful."

"Will you be by this evening?"

"Lord, no! I'm still at the office. I think I'll be here till the wee hours."

"Well, I'm sorry. See you tomorrow, then."

As she put down the phone, Connie glanced over at Mary. "Well, are you satisfied now?" she asked crossly.

Without a word the girl got up and went again to the record player and renewed the record. It was a Beethoven trio and they sat silently throughout it, the convolutions of the music weaving through their thoughts. When it came to an end, the girl did not move, and Connie, wrapped in the intricacies of her own problem, did not realize how long a time passed before a sound from the girl roused her. She looked over and saw that Mary was weeping, her head hung forward and the tears dropping onto her lap. Connie was struck by a kind of horror. She had seen other people weep and though her impulse was to try and comfort them, she had not been deeply stirred. Now she had a sense of catastrophe at the sight of the girl's tears. She jumped up and went to sit by her.

"Mary!" she cried, putting her arm around her.

The girl did not move. Her body was very tense and the fingers of her unbandaged hand gripped her knee, white-knuckled. Her bare feet were placed close together and the toes were drawn up tautly. If only I knew what exactly it is that upsets her, thought Connie.

"Mary," she said in a quiet voice," don't cry. You break my heart."

The girl raised her head and wiped away some of the tears with her fingers. "It all looks so hopeless," she said in a very small voice.

"It can't be that bad," said Connie with false heartiness. "I've told you one thing you can do. You can get in touch with your father. Even if you're afraid the police will question you about the post office bombing, he can probably help you there, too."

Mary straightened up and her tears stopped flowing. "I tell you, I have no intention of going to him." She turned slightly towards Connie and said in a firm voice, "Stantia, it's you who are going to help me. It's you I need."

Connie, disconcerted, said uncertainly, "Mary, I will do everything I can, but there are definite limits to what I am able to do. Your father is wealthy and powerful."

The girl did not answer. She leaned against Connie and put her head on her shoulder. She gave a little sigh as she rested her bandaged hand on Connie's arm. They sat in silence for some minutes. Connie felt the tension ease in the girl's body.

Chapter Nine

After a while, just when Connie was about to suggest that she had better go to bed and sleep, the girl stirred beside her. On a sudden decision, Connie said,

"Mary, I suppose there are reasons for your attitude towards your father. Evidently you don't like things he did. But you shouldn't harbor resentment like that. You're a grown woman now and you should be able to see things that happened in your childhood in better perspective."

The girl did not answer at once. Instead she raised her head so as to lay her cheek against Connie's. After a moment she kissed her on the lips, a soft, lingering kiss that had something possessive in it. Connie sat still, unable to move. She had never received a kiss like that. Roger, even in a tender mood, had a harder, more perfunctory way of kissing her. She had no impulse to draw back, no wish to stir at all. She wanted simply to sit quiet and accept this insinuating, tantalizing caress.

Presently the girl drew back and looked at her. Her gaze was tranquil, half abstracted. She said then, "He was unkind to my mother, but not in a way anybody could see—except me."

The sudden explanation, introduced out of the blue, astonished Connie, even though she was gradually getting used to these lightning changes of mood. The girl went on.

"My mother drank too much. It began before I was born. When I got big enough to notice, I used to see her sit in a chair and gradually sink into a stupor. I didn't understand about alcohol then, of course, or not until the very end, when I was ten years old. But I knew she had a bottle of something that smelled nasty and that she kept putting some of what was in it into her glass. Most of the time she just fell asleep in the chair, but sometimes she would fall out of it, onto the floor."

Connie, shocked, protested. "Didn't somebody take you away when she was like that? Didn't you have a nurse?"

"Yes, I had a nurse. More than one—a whole series of them. But they didn't stay long—none of the servants did—because my parents quarreled so violently. My mother was always at least a little drunk and she'd get mad at them and curse them. I always knew when she was that way, because she was always gentle and kind with everybody when she was sober. I'm sure she did not realize how her manner changed when she was drunk."

"Didn't anybody—your father—try to do something about her?"

"Oh, yes. She was sent away to a sanatorium several times, but as soon as she got home it would start all over again. My grandmother told me later that she could not help herself. My grandmother said it was an inherited tendency and then when she was a young girl it was wartime and everybody drank a lot. And my father drank too much then, also, whenever he was home on leave. I suppose that is one reason they began to quarrel. After a while he stopped drinking so much and then he was impatient with her. He thought if he could do it so could she. He didn't try to help her, except to put her in the sanatorium whenever she got too bad."

A brooding look had appeared on the girl's face. The train of memory had caught up her imagination.

"It must have been pretty difficult for him," said Connie, hesitantly.

The girl's eyes glowed with indignation. "He stopped loving her. In fact, I've come to believe he never really loved her very deeply. I don't believe people fall in and out of love. If you can stop loving somebody, then you never really loved them in the first place. If you love someone, you love them forever, whatever happens."

Connie said softly, "Some people have the gift of killing love. They turn love into hate."

"Then that's a gift my father has."

Connie started to protest again but left off. Mary went on talking. "I think my parents got married just because it seemed the thing to do. It was wartime and everybody was getting married before going off to war—that sort of thing. Everybody was wound up to a sense of impending doom. It was what was called a suitable match—my father's money and my mother's family. But I'm sure he ended by hating her, when the war was over and he settled down and she didn't. And I'm sure she knew how he felt and it drove her to drinking more, to escape from it. He would say very cutting things to her—he has a genius for sarcasm, the barbed remark. She did not know how to answer him. Very often she was too muddled to understand, really, what he said. But he was just as sweet as pie whenever anybody else was around. He never noticed me, because he thought I was too young to understand. We lived in a big house that had an enclosed porch, full of hot-house plants—my mother liked to look after plants, and she mostly sat

there, in a big wicker chair. When he came in there and found
her half-drunk, sitting there with a whiskey bottle, he'd fly into a
rage and call her bad names. When he left she'd just pour herself
another drink."

The girl fell silent, wrapped in the remembrance of that childhood passage. Connie said,

"You should not have been left with her when she was like that."

The girl gave a quick little jerk of her head. "I was happy with
her when we were alone. She'd just sit there quietly and I'd play
make-believe games. I didn't know she was drinking herself to
death. Everything seemed peaceful and I knew she loved me."

There was a short pause and Connie asked, "Was she as small
a woman as you?"

Mary's eyes flashed. "Oh, no! That was another thing. Even before I was born she drank a lot and took sleeping pills and afterwards she blamed herself because she thought that is what made
me so little. I was a very small baby, my grandmother said. I don't
know whether there is medically any real explanation. But that
is the way my mother felt about it and I think it was just one more
thing to make her miserable."

"Your grandmother told you about this?"

"Yes, after my mother died and I went to live with my grandmother. I overheard some friends of the family saying how sorry
they were for my father, having such a hard time with a drunken
wife, what a dreadful life she had led him, and I questioned my
grandmother. She said that there was something to be said on my
mother's side, that he hadn't been very kind to her. In the end,
you know, he made her agree to a divorce. My grandmother
hoped that when she was separated from my father she might stop
drinking. But I guess it was too late. In the end she killed herself.
The last time she was in the sanatorium she took an overdose of
something. She told my grandmother she could not bear the idea
of coming out and starting all over again. She said she was afraid
that she would be a bad influence for me while I was growing up.
She loved me."

"You lived with your grandmother after that?"

"Until she died, when I was fifteen. I was sent to school in Switzerland then. My father was married again and he didn't want me
around. Besides, I didn't want to be with him and I told him so."

"Perhaps that was just as well. You don't sound as if you were
very compatible."

"That's putting it mildly." The girl leaned back against the sofa back with an air of fatigue. "My mother called me Tottie. That's why I don't seem to answer to Mary."

They sat in silence then until Connie glanced at the clock and saw that it was almost midnight. She said, "I think I had better change the bandage on your hand before we go to bed—Tottie." The girl looked at her sharply but only nodded. Neither of them spoke while Connie changed the bandage. Then Tottie got up from the stool on which she had been sitting and waited while Connie helped her off with the jeans and shirt.

"Your hand is much better, Tottie, and the bruises are almost gone." Connie touched lightly the discolorations on her thigh and buttock.

"They are not really sore any more." said Tottie, patiently waiting while Connie's hands gently moved about her.

She is so little, thought Connie. The top of her head just comes to my shoulder. But she is lovely. The very details that might have spoiled the symmetry of the small body—the full, soft breasts, the narrow buttocks—seemed to add up to a different sort of perfection. If she weren't so thin. I can count all her ribs. I wonder what she would think if she knew how the sight of her affects me.

Alarmed by the idea that Tottie might guess her thoughts and take offense, she glanced up quickly, but Tottie's gaze was still calmly attentive. She waited for a few seconds longer for some further attention from Connie, and when Connie turned away, she walked naked into the bedroom and got into bed. Connie, perturbed, finished in the bathroom, mechanically brushing her teeth and hanging the damp towels up to dry. She realized, in a sort of misery, that she was delaying going to join Tottie in bed. Perhaps if Tottie was already half asleep, she would be less aware of the invitation of Tottie's body. Yes, that was what it was, an invitation, to feel the warm, soft flesh of Tottie's breasts, Tottie's smooth little hams, to hold the small, frail body in her arms, against her own flesh. She had never before experienced this demand, this anticipation of pleasure in the rounded softness of a body so like her own.

But when she finally went into the bedroom, Tottie was lying on her back in the bed, watching her as she took off her bathrobe and put on the shortie nightgown. Connie, her nerves a-tingle, paused to look at her, to challenge her watching eyes. Do you have any idea, Connie asked her silently, what you are doing to me? Do you have the least suspicion that you have walked into my life and taken possession of me as casually as you might rent an apartment or hire a maid?

Tottie answered her silent inquiry with the same calm gaze as before. She lay with her bandaged hand resting on her bare stomach. She said nothing as Connie turned away to hang the bathrobe over the back of a chair and place her slippers under it. It seemed to Connie impossible that she could sit so close to the girl and not betray the tumult in her body. She had no idea what Tottie would think if she knew. It has been years, thought Connie, since I've felt this diffidence before another person, this eagerness for acceptance.

Tottie stirred behind her and she held her breath, unwilling to turn and look at her. She felt Tottie's hands creep under the nightgown and around her bare body. Tottie pressed close to her and lay her cheek against her bare shoulder.

Connie, startled by the sudden touch, sat quite still. All the nerve ends in her skin had been brought to a high degree of tenderness and the touch of Tottie's hands was like fire. Tottie's breath tickled her ear as she said, in a murmur, "I love you, Stantia. I love you so much."

For a moment Connie continued to sit motionless, unable to speak. Then she turned her head to look down into Tottie's face as the girl tried to look up into hers. Tottie's lips were slightly puckered and her eyes were troubled and pleading, as if she sought reassurance. A sudden shiver passed through Connie. She felt Tottie's hands, the whole palm of her sound hand and the fingers free of the bandage on the other, gently stroke her skin, as Tottie's cheek moved against her arm. The girl's touch had catalysed the undefined longing that had filled her when she had bathed and dressed her, a longing that seemed to flow all through her body, a longing which the tentative, hesitant motions of the girl's hands raised to an almost unendurable pitch.

Slowly Connie turned and lay down in the bed, pulling Tottie down with her. "Tottie," she murmured, "Tottie."

The girl stretched herself out beside her. She bent over Connie's face and covered it with kisses, soft, swift, eager kisses. When she finally paused, she said breathlessly, "Love me, Stantia, you must love me. I will die if you don't love me!" Totties legs and arms sought urgently, clumsily, to find their natural lodging in the curves and hollows of her own. Connie, driven beyond the power to withhold herself, seized her in her arms wordlessly. The small, soft body, with its slender bones and transparent skin, which had seemed so tantalizingly beyond the reach of anything except the merest glimpse of her eyes and the briefest touch of her hands, yielded eagerly under her grip, pressed against her as if it sought to amalgamate with her own flesh. They lay locked for a while in each other's arms, the pulse of the blood in their separate bodies beating each against the other. Connie was aware, as if in a delicious dream, of Tottie's body growing taut under her hands, until the intensity of her trembling entered into Connie's own body.

Presently Tottie nestled closer still. "That has never happened to me before," she murmured into Connie's ear, the depth of her contentment apparent in her scarcely audible voice. Connie, still caught up in the transport of their joint emotion, was mute.

After a while, slowly, hesitantly, Tottie's hands moved about her, as if seeking to put in practice a newly learned caress. Connie lay still, luxuriating in the response of her own body to Tottie's touch. Oh, Tottie, you can take me anywhere, far away where no one else has ever taken me before. And she felt herself swept down a swift stream into a great space empty of everything except the presence of Tottie.

She came slowly back to the reality of the tumbled bed, the lamp-lit room. Tottie lay clinging to her in comforting drowsiness. As she stirred, Tottie, nuzzling gently at her neck and face, murmured, in a plaintive little voice, "I thought you would never love me. You were so kind, so gentle—and so impersonal—just like a nurse with a child. And I wanted you to kiss me and hold me close, as your very own. I love you so much."

Connie held her tighter, talking into the long hair that had fallen over her face. "I think I must have loved you from the very beginning. You stole my heart when I opened the orange soda bottle for you."

Tottie raised her head to look down into her eyes. "But you never looked at me again that evening. I thought you did not like me. I was very unhappy."

"Oh, Tottie." Connie brushed the long hair gently aside. "I'm such a stupid creature. I had no idea, until later, after I had left that apartment, how deeply you had affected me."

Tottie clung closer to her and rubbed her cheek against Connie's shoulder. "I've never been in love before. I've always heard about it—how it feels to love somebody. I've always wanted to love somebody—deeply, with all of me. But it had to be somebody who loved me the same way. The way you do, Stantia. Stantia, you mustn't love anybody else the way you love me. Have you ever loved anybody like this before?"

The question was asked in an artless, childish voice. Connie tightened her arms about Tottie, as if by doing so she could shut out the importunate, unwanted images of the past that beset her, images of episodes so pale in contrast with the present reality.

"Not anything like this—never anything like this. Oh, my darling, my little love!"

And they lay locked together again, aware that their separateness had melted away between them, that they were one in a new world.

It was daylight when Connie awoke to find the bedside lamp still palely alight in the sunny room. She lay passive, aware of the comforting warmth of Tottie sleeping beside her. The night's experience permeated her, so that she had still the sense of remoteness from her surroundings, from her usual routine. She was still in that distant place with Tottie, far from the consciousness of other people, sure now that Tottie was as aware of that island of apartness as herself. She raised herself on her elbow and leaned over Tottie. The sleeping face was serene, the long lashes quiet on the transparent skin. She had often wondered how one came to know that one deeply and truly loved someone. Now it was abundantly clear to her that she loved Tottie, that she would always love Tottie, that she could no more deny her love for Tottie than she could still the beating of her heart.

The girl beside her stirred and she hung over her, so that her lips were suspended within an inch of the soft, narrow mouth pursed a little in sleep. The vivid blue eyes opened into hers, instantly aware, instantly inviting. Tottie raised her head and lifted her arms to pass them around Connie's neck. She pressed her lips on Connie's.

"Dear Stantia," she said softly and lay still, Connie's head still clasped to her. "My own Stantia."

Connie, ready to get out of bed, sank back again with a delicious sense of luxury. The world beyond Tottie seemed remote and without substance.

Chapter Ten

It was some time later that she roused herself again and with more determination got up and swung her feet to the floor. In a sudden panic she looked at the small clock on the bedside table. It said eight-thirty and she jumped up.

"Good Lord, Tottie! It's late! I'll put the kettle on to boil while I get dressed."

As she went swiftly through the motions of bathing and dressing and making the coffee, her mind flew faster yet through the problems the day promised. All at once she looked at Tottie, still lying in bed, and was aware that Tottie's eyes were following her every move with an intense attention. She paused in fastening the zipper of her dress and Tottie, seeing her hesitation, put out her arms. Connie sat down on the edge of the bed and gathered her into her arms again.

"Stantia," said Tottie, putting her arms around Connie's neck, "I miss you so much when you go away."

"I can't think of anything but you all day long," Connie confessed and released her. "Now, let me go and get the coffee."

Unwillingly she drew herself away and went to the kitchen. As she was pouring the coffee, Tottie padded in barefooted, wearing the short bathrobe that on her reached halfway down her legs. She perched herself on the kitchen stool while Connie stood and sipped her coffee. At last, ready to pick up her handbag, Connie said, "Tottie, Roger is going to talk to a detective this morning. He's a man your father has hired to trace you."

Tottie, still drinking coffee, looked up at her with a little frown but did not answer.

Connie said, vexed, "You know, Tottie, I'm in a spot, knowing where you are."

Tottie, the soft vagueness of first awakening gone from her face, said sharply, "Why? You don't need to admit knowing anything about my whereabouts."

"I've never been any good at lying."

"Why should you believe I am the girl they are looking for?"

Connie gave her a wry smile. "They would have to think that I'm a lot more stupid than I am, if I didn't put two and two together. They know I know that Mary Gilray is part of your name. Like everyone else who reads the papers and listens to the radio, I know the description of the girl they are looking for."

"You can forget that I told you my name is Mary Gilray. You know me just as Mary. How many millions of Marys do you think are in the world? You met me at a party and you befriended me because I was down on my luck. Do you have to tell everybody everything about your private life?"

"Of course not. But, Tottie, you forget Roger. And you forget that I'm a member of the law firm that has been retained by your father to give him confidential advice on finding you. How can I in good conscience withhold information?"

Indignation flashed in Tottie's eyes. "You mean to say you haven't any conscientious feelings about betraying me?"

"No, Tottie, no! I don't mean that and you know it. But I am committed to furnishing information that is vital to a client's interests and your father is our client."

"I don't give a damn about my father's interests. He can look out for himself. But you're going to look out for my interests, do you hear? You just forget that I am anybody but just—Mary. When you're in your office you concern yourself with Charlotte Christeson, whom you've never met and don't know anything about, except what you've read in the papers."

Connie began to protest once more but the words died on her lips. Tottie stepped closer and put her hands on her arm.

"Stantia, nobody must know that I'm here with you," she said, looking up into Connie's eyes. "Nobody. Don't let anyone—anyone —make you give me away."

Connie, a few minutes later boarding the bus, thought wrily, Nobody. Of course she means Roger. Indeed, nobody must know. At least, until she could resolve her own dilemma, nobody must know.

It was still in a haze of preoccupation that she answered the greetings of the people she encountered as she entered the offices of Bryanston and Clay. She was seldom late and now she was aware that the receptionist and the girls in the outer office followed her with their eyes as she responded to their greetings and hurried down the hall to her own cubbyhole. She knew that they speculated about her and Roger. Because most of them liked her personally, they forgave her the extraordinary good fortune that made her Roger's choice. She often felt uncomfortable under this friendly patronage, but accepted it as inevitable. A man as attractive as

Roger necessarily was claimed by the women who came in daily contact with him as their own for purposes of fantasy and gossip. Roger himself paid little attention to them. But he rarely failed in the courteous gesture, the polite if absentminded response. He was a very popular man.

At a quarter of ten Roger sent for her. She hurried down the hall to his office.

"Oh, there you are!" he said. "I asked you to come because I want to tell you what this man Fairchild said. He's the detective, you remember. I went over your notes, but there wasn't much help there."

"I'm sorry. But I can't very well manufacture information that doesn't exist."

"Oh, of course not! Well, let's get down to what he told me. To begin with, Fairchild has never had any personal contact with Charlotte Christeson, but he had several pictures of her and he has been told a good deal about her background. He says that she left college during the Christmas break and did not go back. Her father did not know about this right away. He hasn't been in direct touch with her for some time. But the college authorities wrote to him and asked for an address for her and that's how he found out she wasn't there."

"He doesn't pay her bills?"

"No, she has her own income."

"Well, then, she must have a bank account. Couldn't she be traced through the bank that handles her money?"

"That's one of the peculiar things about this. Yes, she has accounts with the First National Bank—a checking account and a savings account, into which her trustees pay the income due her from the property her mother and her grandmother left her. But she hasn't drawn any checks since January. And she hasn't picked up any of her mail. She hasn't written to anyone about having it forwarded. That doesn't sound very good."

"You mean, something may have happened to her?"

Roger nodded thoughtfully. "Fairchild went to her college and interviewed some of her friends. He found out that she had got interested in some of these youth protest groups. First, she joined a Quaker group that was protesting the war in Southeast Asia. Then she got in with some anti-draft protesters."

"Was she ever arrested?"

"No. At least, if she was, it was under an assumed name and her identity was not established. I think that is pretty good evidence

that she kept shy of the law, because the FBI has investigated these
protest rallies and riots and they have records of anyone charged
with even a misdemeanor. I think they would have uncovered her
real name, if she had been arrested under an alias."

"You said she was involved with the Quakers. They do not engage in violence."

"Yes, but she didn't stay with them. The people Fairchild interviewed said that she became involved with several boys who were
arrested for burning their draft cards. He located a couple of them
—in jail—and they told him the names of some others with whom
she associated—people who lived in common lodgings—people
who were on drugs and that sort of thing. It seems that she has got
something of a reputation as a poet. She writes lyrics for protest
songs. Some of them have been used by singers on popular records."

"Doesn't she get paid for this? And if so, can't she be traced
that way?

"Well, naturally, she hasn't been using the name of Charlotte
Christeson. She has been using the middle part of her name—Mary
Gilray. I suppose payments made to her have been made in that
name. I don't suppose she has bank accounts as Mary Gilray. It
must be a pretty hand-to-mouth existence,—that is, if she is still
alive."

"Still alive!"

Roger cast her a glance of mild surprise at the alarm in her voice.
"Fairchild considers it very possible that she is dead—that the
people who sent Christeson that threatening letter may already
have liquidated her. And besides, haven't you noticed the descriptions of the girl that was supposed to have been at the site of the
bombing? The police still don't know whether she was blown up
in that post office and it seems the descriptions given of her could
fit Charlotte Christeson."

Connie sat very still, afraid to speak. Roger went on.

"She is unusually small, I'm told, and dressed in some outland-
ish fashion that would call attention. You realize that this possibility— that the girl is dead—may have some pretty serious consequences for her family. She is an heiress to a very large share of an
enormous estate. Whoever can provide evidence of the mode and
time of her death has valuable information to sell."

"Do you mean these people who are trying to extort money
from her father?"

"They are the first who spring to mind." Roger was thoughtful
for a few moments. "Does it strike you, Connie, from what you
could learn from those old newspaper files, that the Christeson

girl would embark on a career of terrorist bombing?"

"How can I answer such a question, Roger? I have no impression of the girl from the newspaper accounts, except that she is the daughter of a wealthy man. If I were to imagine something of what she is like, it would probably be quite false."

Roger looked at her speculatively. Uneasily, Connie tried to avoid his gaze. If I have told him nothing now, she thought, I cannot hereafter admit to any knowledge of Tottie. Do I blurt it out now, that H.B. Christeson's daughter is at this moment in my apartment, that she has been there since Saturday and that since yesterday I have been fully aware of her identity? Of course not. There was no impersonally known "missing girl". There was only Tottie and Tottie was not to be betrayed. She had the curious feeling, as she returned to her own office, that she and Tottie with her hovered disembodied in the wings of this drama that involved Charlotte Christeson.

She was startled out of her preoccupation by her secretary, who opened the door and said, "Oh, I just want to remind you that it is time for your lunch appointment."

Connie stared at her for a moment before she remembered. Of course, this was Wednesday and on Wednesdays the women lawyers in the office lunched together, in a gesture of solidarity.

"Oh, thank you!" Connie said hastily. "I'm late, aren't I?"

She hurriedly took her handbag from the drawer of her desk and ran down the hall to the ladies' washroom. In the mirror over the washbasin she gave herself a hasty glance, smoothing back the fine glossy hair from her forehead, checking the state of the pale lipstick she wore. Without her willing it, Tottie's face appeared before her, with its violet-shadowed eyes and small, prim mouth. Oh, Tottie, she thought, if you only knew what you cost me!

The lunch went much as it always did, at the usual table in the usual restaurant. Today there were five of them, two of the women being, like herself, associates in the firm, both senior to her. The third was a girl not yet through law school and the fourth was the librarian. Connie, feeling out of step with the usual routine, entered only casually into the conversation. Some of it was shop talk and she could let it pass by her without calling attention to her failure to enter in. But presently she was aware that she had been spoken to directly and that her woolgathering had been noticed.

"Connie, you are certainly 'way off in the blue somewhere," said one of the lawyers, Ruth Price. "Are we justified in surmising something from this? Is Roger working himself up to a declaration?"

"You've seen as much of Roger as I have lately," said Connie
in as light a tone as she could manage. She was perfectly aware
of the fact that the imminence of a wedding announcement for
herself and Roger was a constant topic of conversation amongst
the women in the office, who watched with discreet intentness
for any sign of a climax or a decline in their affair.

"I must say," said Ruth, "that Roger is the firm's fairhaired boy.
He gets all the plums. He's been handed half a dozen major cases
in the last year. Of course, he works like a dog. Now he's been
handed H.B. Christeson's daughter. Well, not the girl, of course—"
She broke off, glancing at Connie. "That's a queer business. Can
you tell us anything about it, Connie?"

"About the Christeson case?" Connie played for time. "Well,
I know very little. I've done some research into the girl's background. That's all."

"Is she really a hippie? And was she blown up in that post
office? You hear all sorts of things on the news." Ruth was still
looking at her with great interest.

"You'll have to ask the experts," said Connie. "All I know is
that she can't be found—"

"And that her father has received a threatening letter," the
second lawyer, Dorothy Sloan, supplied. "We all know the arms
and legs of the case, Connie, so you needn't be so discreet. The
point is: has she disappeared willingly or has she been kidnaped—"

"Or liquidated?" Ruth Price broke in.

Connie, outnumbered, laughed shakily. "I can't tell you!
Really I can't!"

All four of the women were watching her face. Ruth said, "Oh,
we just thought you'd have a little inside dope, since you work so
closely with Roger." As if to change the tone of the conversation, she added, "He's bound to be the next partner to be made."

"Not a doubt of it," Dorothy agreed.

"I'd just as soon it was Roger," Ruth said. "He's got plenty of
brains and a sense of responsibility."

"Lucky you," said Dorothy. "He's good looking, too."

"I'm glad you all give him a passing grade," said Connie flip-
pantly. "It's such an endorsement of my good judgment."

"Oh, you're doing all right, Connie," said Ruth, with a kindly
air. "Don't let us ride you. You've got a winner in Roger. But you
might as well get used to sharing him with the clients. You won't
see any more of him when you're married than you do now."

"The trouble comes when your schedules conflict," said Dorothy. "If he's working, you're loafing, and vice versa."

"It sounds a little like Russia," said the librarian. "The wife works in the day while the husband works at night."

"Must cut down on the population increase," said Ruth. "Not much opportunity for marital bliss. But maybe it is a good thing. Not so much familiarity to breed contempt."

"Unless it leads to familiarity away from home," said Dorothy.

"I wouldn't say you had to go to Russia for that," said Ruth.

Their bantering talk flowed past Connie. She was thankful that they had dropped the subject of Christeson's daughter. Again her inner thoughts shut out their voices. What was Tottie doing for lunch? she wondered. Probably nothing. Tottie couldn't be bothered to prepare food for herself. Perhaps this evening she had better stop again at the delicatessen and see what she could find for supper—

Dorothy's voice cut into her thoughts. "Are you off in the clouds again, Connie? It can't be that you're in love!"

"Well, why not?" Connie retorted defensively. "Isn't that a normal state for someone in my position?" Oh, Tottie! she thought.

"Oh, now, really!" cried Dorothy. "After all this time?"

Her tone was mocking and Connie, to her own vexation, knew she was blushing, because the young law clerk gave her a sympathetic glance.

"I don't see that the length of time has anything to do with it," she replied, miserable from a compound of feelings. She knew that the woman who jibed at her had been married and divorced and was the veteran of a number of affairs. Dorothy was discontented, suspicious of freely offered friendship, prone to seek ulterior motives for any act of kindness. Yet she was a good sort, ready to offer a helping hand.

"Time—and availability," Dorothy seemed to linger purposely over the phrase—"generally dissipate romance." Her brilliant eyes behind the exaggeratedly large round glasses were fastened on Connie's face. Connie did not answer her.

Connie was relieved when the waitress came to bring their checks and take their money. Her emotions were still in turmoil and she was thankful that throughout the afternoon she was left in peace to pursue the research on which she was engaged. At least, to outward appearance that was what she was doing, sitting at her desk with books and papers before her. In reality, her mind kept straying to the apartment and Tottie, and half an hour would pass without her realizing its passage. It was with relief that she finally noticed that five o'clock had come. In half an hour she could go home to Tottie.

She boarded the bus absentmindedly, preoccupied with what she might find at the delicatessen for supper, wondering what mood she would find Tottie in. Only as the bus neared her corner did she realize that she had overlooked a vital matter. She had made no effort to check with Roger about his plans for the evening. She had not even asked his secretary if he had arranged to work after dinner. He would certainly become aware of her lapse before the evening was over. Her heart sank at the thought that he would phone, or worse still, come in person to the apartment to find her. Pray God that his mind would be so securely fastened on his professional problems that he would give her only a passing thought. And that he planned to work on into the night, as he had the night before.

Chapter Eleven

At last she arrived at her own door. When she inserted the key she found that this time the second lock was not fastened and the door opened easily. Alarmed, she looked quickly about the livingroom for Tottie. Her heart gave a bound of relief and joy when she saw Tottie's small figure seated at the table near the window, her back to the door. The heels of her bare feet were hooked on the rung of the chair as she sat hunched over a litter of sheets from a yellow scratch pad which Connie recognized as one of a supply she kept for use on nights when she brought work home from the office. Tottie must have found it on the bottom shelf of the bookcase.

Tottie did not turn around and Connie said eagerly, "Tottie, what are you doing?"

The girl at the table turned slowly towards her. The blue eyes were vague. Tottie seemed lost in some inner contemplation. Connie put down her handbag and went over to her. Impulsively she put her arm around Tottie's shoulders. Tottie, in a sudden gesture tossed down her pencil and leaned against her, turning her face up to be kissed.

"Stantia," she murmured.

Connie looked down at the sheets of yellow writing paper. A few disconnected lines appeared on them, obviously poetry. She turned her eyes to Tottie.

"Have you been doing that all day?"

Tottie gave a vague glance around. "I suppose so," she said and got up from her chair.

Neither of them spoke as Connie went into the bedroom and changed her clothes, though Tottie followed her and perched on the end of the bed. As Connie took off her bra Tottie slipped off the bed and came to her. She put her hands on Connie's round, firm breasts and laid her cheek against her.

"I get so lonesome when you are not here," she said in her small voice. "I get frightened. I keep imagining that I hear people coming to the door."

"There's no reason to be frightened, Tottie," said Connie gently. "If anybody should come—the resident manager, for instance—she's a woman—it is not strange that I should have a friend staying with me. You can tell her that you've got a cold and don't want to go out. There is nobody else who would come here in the daytime."

Tottie drew away. Connie saw that she was unconvinced. They were silent again until Connie, still preoccupied with the problem she had been struggling with all day, said, "Tottie, please tell me what you have been doing since you dropped out of college."

"Why are you so anxious to know?" Tottie's voice and glance were coolly suspicious.

"Because I am in a dangerous situation. I've told nobody that you are here, that I know where you are. People have talked about you all day to me. Everyone assumes that I am as baffled as they are, as your father, Roger, the police are about your whereabouts. Can't you see, Tottie, that the least you could do would be to tell me all you know so that I can protect myself, so that I won't give myself away by saying something in ignorance. It is possible that this detective your father has hired to find you will be able to trace you here to this apartment. What would we do then?"

The desperation in her voice reached Tottie. Tottie shook her head. "No. He won't trace me here. There is no one who can tell him where I am."

"What about those men you ran away from? You are certain they could not have followed you?"

"Yes, I am certain."

Connie thought for a moment. In a worried voice she asked, "Tell me, Tottie, are you a member of the SDS or the Weathermen or any group of that sort?"

"No, and I've never been. I'm not really an activist, Stantia, and the people I've been going with know that. They would not allow me to take part in any of their really important things."

"You mean they didn't trust you?"

"Yes. They recognized the fact that I wasn't committed to the same ideas they are, that I was just hanging around them because I was curious."

"Well, your activities are very peculiar. You put yourself in considerable danger for no real purpose."

"I had a purpose."

"What purpose?"

Tottie sighed. "It's so hard to explain things. You *must* understand, Stantia. Nobody else does, but *you* must."

"I must understand what?"

"Me," Tottie said succinctly. She thought for a while before she went on. "Stantia, I just got sick and tired of my life. Everything was so cut and dried, so much in a groove—and so meaningless. I was just a type, not an individual, just the daughter of rich people. It seemed to me, all at once, that there was nothing ahead of me except to become just what my parents were—do the same stupid things, marry the same sort of man as my father, be just as unhappy as my mother."

"Lots of young people feel something like that at one time or another," said Connie severely, feeling middleaged. "It's probably a phase—like all the others you go through, growing up."

Tottie gazed at her but made no comment on her statement. Instead she said, "The reason I decided to go to college after all was because I thought perhaps, if I studied something systematically, I would find greater satisfaction. I like to study. I've always liked to write—things."

"Poetry?"

Tottie nodded. "I spent most of my time in college studying literature and sociology and philosophy. But then after a while I began to distrust what I was reading, to distrust myself, my own reactions—"

"What do you mean by distrust?"

"I distrusted the reality—that's not a very good word—the reality of it all and then I knew that I didn't know enough at firsthand about people and what prompts them to act the way they do. I've never had any intimate friends, anybody I could talk to about how I felt about things, except my grandmother when I was little. I've always had to make up in my mind the sort of friend I wanted." She stopped and gazed at Connie for a while. "I never thought I'd meet you."

"Tottie," said Connie gently.

Tottie went on. "The end of the first semester, last year, I made up my mind that I had to get out of my prison—the prison of my life. I had to get out where I could see people as they really are, all sorts of people, not just the ones who were surrounded by all the things money buys, with people who wouldn't know that I am H.B. Christeson's daughter."

"So you went out and got yourself mixed up with some real radicals."

"Not mixed up with them, Stantia, " Tottie said reprovingly. "I've explained that to you. "They were all real activists. Some of them were draft resisters—yes, maybe I would have joined a group of pacifists. I hate war—and violence."

"You've chosen some funny companions, then, lately," said Connie drily.

Tottie frowned at her. "I wanted to see what they were like. They want to demolish everything so that they can start fresh. I had a job for a while in a settlement house in a city ghetto. I can see why some people get discouraged at the idea of ever making a real change in such conditions."

"Yes, but if you knock everything to bits, the job of rebuilding is just bigger."

"But it breaks the pattern. You can begin fresh, without a pattern to hamper you. That is the idea. It's easier to start fresh, instead of tinkering with an unworkable system."

"Unworkable? Some people would say that the sort of society we've been brought up in has worked for quite a while."

"Worked for whom? I know a lot of people who would say it has never worked for them. And I wanted to break away before the pattern of my life became petrified and I was imprisoned forever."

"Well, what did you do then?"

"I just left college at the midterm break, but I didn't go to my father. He isn't open to reason—at least, to my sort of reason. I didn't want to spend every day justifying my opinions. It's exhausting to deal with somebody like my father. The way things are, that's the way they are, and he doesn't want to hear about anything else. Ever since my sophomore year in college I've spent my summers on my own. Once I took a trip to South America and saw all the slums. I spent some time with a welfare agency looking after migrant workers in the south here at home. But that wasn't altogether satisfactory."

"So what did you do when you left college?"

"I didn't want anybody to know who I was, so I just gave away all my clothes and things and I went to California, to Berkeley, where I heard there were a lot of students' communes. I realized I couldn't draw money from my bank accounts without giving away my whereabouts, but the trustees pay over my income by quarters, so I just took a lump sum, enough to last me for a while, and I would get jobs of some sort if I ran short. I didn't want any chance that my father would find out what I was doing or where I was."

"What did you do in California?"

"I tried to live in a couple of communes. One was in an apartment house in San Francisco. The people in that commune were supposed to be able to do just what they wanted. Everybody was supposed to buy food and contribute to the rent. Some of them took drugs and they would lie around all day and never have any money to contribute. And you weren't supposed to have to accept a man if you didn't want to. But when one of them—a big fellow who thought everybody needed at least one orgasm a day—tried to rape me, I left."

"Tried to?"

"He couldn't catch me." said Tottie with a triumphant smile.

"And what about the second place?"

"That was a shack in the Sierra hills in southern California. It was just a desert camp. There were six or eight women there with a tribe of children. I suppose the women knew their own offspring but I don't think anybody knew who the fathers were. About half of them were permanent but most of them were drifters, just people who stopped by and stayed for a while. I tried it for a while but then I decided that none of them knew what they were doing or what they wanted to do. As for the sexual set-up. I'd as soon go back to the city and make some money by standing on the street corner and soliciting. I didn't want to be a slave-drudge for a lot of lazy, dirty men. So I started hitchhiking my way back East. I stayed at all sorts of pads I was told about. Some of them were weird, with religious overtones and very rigid rules about sleeping and eating and working. And some of them were just places to flop, full of dirt and bugs."

"You're lucky you weren't raped or murdered. Don't you know how dangerous it is to hitchhike?"

Tottie smiled a cold little smile. "I had to jump out once. Anyway, I got as far as Chicago in time for the demonstrations at the Democratic convention. After that I joined some sit-ins at several schools."

"Were you ever arrested, Tottie?"

"No. I always managed to run away in time."

"Then you don't have a police record. That's more important than a lot of people realize."

"Yes, I know."

"The detective who has been tracing you knows that you have been using the name of Mary Gilray. But he says he has lost track of what you were doing for the last month or so. He says you apparently stopped associating with the people you were with before that."

"Yes, that's true. That was because about that time I went to Boston, with some of the people I had met in Chicago. They were planning a sit-in at City Hall and some of them were arrested. I realized then that I might run into some people I had known before, even before I dropped out of college. This was a different thing from California and Chicago. I decided the situation was too dangerous for me, so I left and came here."

"Phil Quinn knew you as Mary Gilray. It was Phil who identified you to me."

"I met him at somebody's pad, where a rock group were playing some songs I had written the words for. I wasn't glad to see him because I didn't want anybody to recognize me as Mary Gilray. He had seen me in Chicago with some people he knew. He told everybody there at that pad that I was Mary Gilray and that I had written the lyrics to those songs. I was very mad at him, though I didn't tell him so."

"But he never knew you as Charlotte Christeson?"

"Oh, no, though there were times when I was afraid he would find out. If he gets interested in somebody, he has a way of concentrating on them. There was another fellow there also who I was afraid of. He said his name was Jasper. When he found out I was Mary Gilray he came over and starting talking to me. He said he had seen me somewhere else. He was a bright-looking boy with long red hair and a very smooth manner. But his eyes were too bright and he kept too close to me all that evening. He was always turning up after that wherever I was and I began to wonder why. Sometimes you meet people who seem to have their own reasons for joining a group, a reason that doesn't have anything to do with what the group is all about. I finally decided he was pushing drugs —heroin, that is. He always had plenty of money and he was too friendly with everybody and his eyes were always wandering about, as if he was watching for something. He found out where I was staying and he kept turning up there and he followed me about. I got scared. I didn't know why he was so interested, but I began to think he might suspect who I was besides being Mary Gilray. Anyway, I just left. I just went to the bus station one morning, when I had managed to shake him off, and got on a bus and came here."

Connie, watching the play of feeling on her face as she relived what she described, thought, You are really frightened. It would be so easy to trace a little thing like you anywhere. There can't be two of you.

"I met those two boys on the bus. They had been arrested in Chicago and spent a few months in jail. So when we arrived here they told me about a lodging house where I could stay. I slept there but I spent a lot of time with them. That's how I came to go to those friends of Phil's where I met you."

"You weren't living with them?"

"No. I've told you I wasn't. The second time I went to that apartment I saw Phil and of course he recognized me as Mary Gilray. I didn't tell him I didn't want him to identify me to people because I didn't want to make it seem important. But then the next time I was there Jasper turned up. He had met Phil and Phil had mentioned me. Jasper had come there looking for me."

"Well, why did you go back there after that, if you knew he would be there?"

Tottie hesitated before answering. "Well, I was hungry and those people always have sandwiches and things spread out for anybody who wants food. I knew he would be there anyway. He had followed me to the place where I was staying and I knew he was always around, watching me anyway. And then that evening when you were there, there was another reason. I didn't have anywhere else to go. The woman who keeps the lodging house where I was staying got mad because I didn't have any money left and I owed her rent. She told me to go on the street and get some and I told her that I wasn't about to. So while I was deciding what to do I went there, where I met you. I hoped Jasper wouldn't be there. But he came in a little while later and he had this other man with him. Did you see him?"

"You mean Jasper—the fellow you describe as having a lot of red hair? No, I didn't see him."

"I mean the other fellow, who was with Jasper. He was a real brutish type. I was certain they were into something together."

"Did they bother you?"

Tottie nodded. "They wouldn't leave me alone. I wanted to get away from that place but I knew they would follow me. I tried to think of some way to get rid of them. I thought perhaps I could ask you to let me go with you. But you didn't even look at me again and I got very discouraged. After a while you and Phil left. But Jasper and his friend stayed and stayed. They were waiting for me to go. Finally those two boys I was with left and I managed to slip out with them, hoping Jasper wouldn't notice. I went with the boys to the pad where they were staying. They let me stay, though I didn't tell them why. In the morning, when the boys went out, I decided I would follow them. They didn't know I did."

"You mean, you realized that they were going to bomb the post office and you followed them to watch?"

"I was curious. It made me excited—to imagine what it would be like."

"Did you see what they did?"

Tottie shook her head. "No. I couldn't see what they were doing. I can't even swear that they were the ones who set the bomb. That's just circumstantial evidence, isn't it? They made bombs, the post office was bombed, they were arrested at the scene."

"Yes, that's circumstantial evidence. But it is pretty strong evidence. Why did you get involved with Jasper and his friend after you ran away from there?"

"Because I was so frightened by then that I didn't know what to do. They had followed me to the pad where I spent the night and they waited to follow me when I left there in the morning. So when I started to run away from the post office, they stopped me and said I'd better go with them, because the police would catch me otherwise. I was afraid not to go with them. I expect I was pretty tired and I wasn't thinking straight."

"You must have been exhausted. You've told me that you went with those men to a house from which you escaped after you overheard some plans they had for you. What was it you overheard?"

A little shiver went through Tottie's body. "Jasper had found out that I was Charlotte Christeson. He and the other man planned to kidnap me and demand a ransom from my father."

"I see. I suppose you know that there is a federal statute on kidnaping. It is a very serious offense and it takes a pretty tough criminal to try it."

"They weren't concerned about returning me safe and sound. Jasper's friend said it would be easier to kill me and then clear out of the country as soon as they got hold of the money. That man is a sadist. He talked about some other things he would do to me while they waited, just to amuse himself."

"Oh, Tottie! How could you get yourself into such a mess?"

Tottie gave her a wan smile.

"Well, the detective thinks that you were the girl who was blown up in the post office. He thinks the men who are trying to extort money from your father know you're dead and they have information to sell about how you died."

"There wasn't any girl blown up in the post office," Tottie retorted. "I was the girl who was supposed to be there and I wasn't blown up."

"Only you and I and your would-be kidnapers know that for certain. And I should inform Roger, so that he can tell your father. Tottie, your father would see to it that you have police protection."

Tottie frowned and her eyes were angry. "You shall not do that, Stantia. I'm safe enough right here in your apartment—so long as nobody knows I am here. I'm a great deal safer than I would be if the police knew where I was."

Connie eyed her. "You say you've never been arrested. But do you realize that the FBI are probably looking for you? They are certainly investigating the bombing of a United States post office."

Tottie glared at her. "And you want to turn me in to the police? Stantia, how could you even think of that?"

Connie said stubbornly. "I still think you should rely on your father to help you."

Tottie turned away from her in silence. Before either of them spoke again the telephone rang. Connie jumped up in alarm. It must be Roger. And was he downstairs, on his way up?

Chapter Twelve

"Oh, you're home!" said Roger's voice. There was a faintly in-jured tone in it, which Connie instantly noticed. "I thought some-thing must be wrong. Are you all right?"

"Why, I'm fine, Roger!"

"You left the office so early, without saying anything to me," he said, still with the faint note of complaint. "I thought certain-ly something must be wrong."

"Oh, no. I just wanted to come home early. You weren't in your office. I know you're so busy you wouldn't appreciate an inter-ruption that wasn't vital."

There was a slight pause at Roger's end of the wire. Then he said, "As a matter of fact, I thought I'd take a break tonight, I'm getting stale. How about dinner and a quiet evening at my place with some music?"

Connie, her heart sinking, said hesitantly, "Roger, I don't feel up to it. Could we postpone it till tomorrow? I thought I'd go to bed early."

"What's the matter, Connie?" The tone in Roger's voice was sharp. The dawning of suspicion, thought Connie. "Aren't you feeling well?"

"There's nothing definite," said Connie, desperately. "I told you yesterday that I thought I was catching cold. I must have some sort of bug."

Again there was a slight pause at the other end of the wire and then Roger said, "Well, I'm sorry, Connie. Are you sure a little conviviality wouldn't help?"

He doesn't believe me, thought Connie. He must not come here to see me. "I'm quite sure it wouldn't. I'm going to get into bed as soon as I have had a snack. I've taken some antihistamine and you know that always makes me dopey. I think if I go bed I can sleep it off. So don't call me. I'm sure I'll be all right in the morning. See you in the office, Roger."

She knew she was speaking with a decisiveness that was unfam-iliar to him and she could guess his surprise. But at last he indicat-ed that he accepted what she said, though his tone was one of dis-satisfaction. As she put the phone down she thought, I've never told so many lies in such a short space of time before.

When Connie turned around she saw that Tottie was looking at her with a curious little smile on her face. She did not wait for Connie to speak but said, "It's a funny thing, but I've seen it happen again and again. A man always seems to know when your attention wanders from him. He seems to smell it in the air."

Connie said defensively, "Of course Roger would guess that there is something wrong. I'm never sick. I practically never have a cold. And I don't know what possessed me to leave the office without leaving him a message." That's not true, she thought. I do know what possesses me. It's you, Tottie.

Tottie's smile grew more scornful. "Do you have to account to him for everything you do? Just because you sleep with him?"

The sting in her voice reached Connie's tenderest spot. She answered hotly, "No, that's not so."

Tottie sat up and stretched her legs, moving her bare feet on the seat of the sofa. "Well, he seems to think you do—and should. Which amounts to the same thing," she said disdainfully.

Connie, shaking with anger and dismay, kept silent. Her feelings were such a mixture of self-reproach, guilt, annoyance with Roger and anxiety over her own situation, that she found it impossible to sort out what her reaction to Tottie's jibe really was. She did not want to quarrel with Roger, with Tottie. She hated to quarrel, and yet she knew there must be a limit to what she would allow anyone to impute to her.

After a moment, she said as calmly as she could, "It's perfectly normal for him to want to know why I came home so early and why I won't go out with him. It's just a pattern that he is used to. And I do go out with him every evening he is free."

"Are you in love with him?"

Connie stared at her, shocked. Did she love Roger? The sudden question threw her into worse confusion. No, she did not love Roger. The fact was perfectly plain to her now. Yet for months she had been acting as if she believed she did. At least, she had accepted Roger's assumption that she did. She had given him every reason to suppose she did, since she had never disputed his right to absorb her time and attention.

"Tottie," she said, humbled by her retrospective view of her own conduct, "you know I don't. After last night you must know."

Tottie had got off the arm of the sofa and now she came over to Connie and stood looking up at her. "If you don't love him, why do you act as if you do? Are you that anxious to have a man?"

Connie flushed hotly. "We're supposed to get married some time in the near future. I suppose we're just—anticipating."

"Anticipating!" Tottie flashed the word back at her angrily. "You don't love him and you're getting ready to marry him! Why? Because it is the thing to do, I suppose."

The scorn in her voice prevented Connie from answering at once or looking up to meet her gaze. Tottie walked away, her bare feet padding softly across the floor to the window.

"Tottie," said Connie after a moment, "Tottie."

The girl at the window glanced around at her briefly.

"Tottie, I didn't have any real idea of how I felt till you came here. I was just going along with the stream. Now I'm caught in a box. I can't tell Roger I won't see him, just like that, because then he would be certain something is wrong. If he gets really suspicious, it will not take him long to find out about you. And where would we both be then? You can get out of this mess whenever you want to. All you have to do is let your father know where you are. But I don't think I'm going to get out of this without losing a great deal. In fact, I think I'll be ruined."

While she was speaking, Tottie turned away again, to look out at the darkening view beyond the window. Looking down at the little figure, Connie felt an overwhelming ache in her heart.

"Tottie," she pleaded, in desperation, "don't you have any idea of the change you've made by coming here, the difference you have made to me?"

Tottie turned around again and put both her hands on Connie's arm. "Stantia, you don't have to be afraid. Nothing bad is going to happen to you. You're mine now and don't forget that." She lifted her arms suddenly and put them around Connie's neck and rested her head against Connie's shoulder. Connie drew her close and they stood together, gazing out at the street where the street lamps were beginning to glow brightly in the fading daylight. After a while Tottie said, "Stantia, you're not going to marry Roger. He is going to have to know that some time. You can't marry someone you don't love. That's immoral—it's obscene. It's one of the dreadful things people do to each other. It's—it's a sin."

Connie was prodded into saying, "A good many people have done it—are still doing it every day—for a variety of reasons, some of them very sound, from a practical point of view."

Tottie turned her head back to look up into her eyes. "It's a form of prostitution, if you ask me. Do you have a 'practical' reason for marrying Roger?"

Connie, flushing again, retorted, "There are a lot of people who contend that human society can't be anything but materialistic, since we are only highly sophisticated animals."

"But you don't believe that."

"No, I don't. I think there must be something more than that."

A sweet smile appeared on Tottie's face. "Of course. You wouldn't love me, if that was not the case. You'd stick to Roger otherwise. He has a lot more to offer—status in the world, money, all that. But you don't feel like that, Stantia, so how could you possibly marry him?"

Connie defended herself. "I'm sure that is what everybody thinks —that I'm marrying Roger because he is a good catch. But it wasn't I who started it. In the beginning it was Roger who sought me and I—well, I like him and after all, I have to do something with my life."

"You just went along with him because he is more positive than you. You're altogether too pliant, Stantia. You'll do anything anybody asks you to, because you don't want to hurt anybody's feelings."

"That's not true, Tottie! But I can't get all excited about things that don't seem to be important after all."

"Like refusing to marry somebody because you don't love him," Tottie snapped out.

Connie, vexed, bit her lip. "That's not so at all. I like Roger and there didn't seem to be any use waiting around for the great love of my life to come along. When I met Roger I liked him better than anybody I'd ever known, except Phil. And I think it is a good thing I didn't try to marry Phil. I don't think we'd suit each other very well now."

"How do you know that ten years from now—or sooner—you wouldn't find the same thing was true with Roger?"

"I'm more aware of my own nature now. I can make allowances for myself and for Roger, too."

"In other words, once upon a time you would have married Phil for love, but you're marrying Roger now as a calculated risk. That's really not fair to Roger, Stantia."

Connie gave a short little laugh. "I don't think Roger would ever marry except on the basis of a carefully calculated risk. If he ever acted on impulse, he would be miserably unhappy with the results. He would deeply resent whoever it was who had led him into such a situation."

"Then, of course, you're not marrying Roger! You're much better off with me. I like impulses—your kind, that is." Tottie laughed up into Connie's face. "Hug me, Stantia."

Connie put her arms around her once more and said, speaking into the top of her head, "Tottie, I love you. I'm happy here with you in spite of everything."

Tottie did not answer but put a kiss on her throat.

They spent the rest of the evening in companionable semi-silence. Whatever tomorrow will bring, thought Connie, I'll not think about it now. Sufficient unto the day is the evil thereof. Tottie seemed to relapse into the abstracted mood she had been in when Connie arrived. Connie, carefully gathering up the sheets of yellow paper on which Tottie had been writing, thought, How suddenly and completely she can change her mood! No doubt it was the poetic temperament.

When they went to bed, Tottie at once moved close to her. They lay together in warm relaxation, making love with a gentle fondness that was so near dreaming that they slipped easily into slumber and it was morning before they knew it.

"Tottie!" Connie looked with dismay at the bedside clock. "I'm late again! I'm going to have to set the alarm after this!"

She dressed in a hurry, making the coffee as she did so. Tottie, slower to stir, said sleepily, "Do you always have to be in such a rush, Stantia?"

"Bryanston and Clay expect me to keep regular office hours. Tottie, I may have to do something with Roger tonight."

Tottie turned over on her back to look up at her, her small mouth pinched shut. "What?" she demanded, her eyes angry.

"Go out to dinner with him, probably. I must not let him guess there is anyone here with me. So we may go to dinner from the office. I'll call you when I find out what arrangement I make, so listen for the phone. I'll let it ring twice and hang up. Wait for me to call again right after that. That way you'll know it's me."

She waited, anxiously watching Tottie's face. Finally Tottie nodded briefly, without a word.

On the bus the day's prospects began to press upon Connie with redoubled effect. She dreaded her impending interview with Roger. If I were only a better liar, she thought. She hurried to her office, anxious to appear well started on the day's work, if Roger should come to seek her. Whether he did would depend on the amount of pressure he was under or the strength of his resentment the evening before. She felt an inner disturbance, compounded of a tender shrinking from the infliction of pain on Roger and a sense of the irreversibility of the development of her emotions in the last few days. Because, she realized, she had irrevocably chosen Tottie, as Tottie had chosen her. The choice had been accomplished before she was fully aware of it. She was Tottie's and Tottie was hers.

Chapter Thirteen

She was startled by the sudden rap on the door of her office and its instant opening. Roger walked into the room. One glance at his face told her that he was angry, perturbed and anxious. He held the morning paper in his hand.

"Well!" He threw the paper down on her desk. "That settles Fairchild's theory."

Connie looked at the paper and then at him. "What?" she asked, stupidly.

He gave her an irritated glance. "Didn't you hear the news on the radio this morning?"

"No. I overslept again and didn't have time to bother with the radio."

"Fairchild thought that Charlotte Christeson might be dead, that she might be the girl who was believed to have been blown up in the post office," he said, more patiently. "Well, she is not dead, if she was that girl. The police and the fire marshal have declared that they did not find any human remains in the ruins of the building. Now they are looking for the girl. There is a warrant out for her arrest. Destruction of the United States mail is a felony in itself, aside from the matter of planting bombs. And that postal clerk in the hospital isn't doing so well. If he dies, there'll be a murder charge besides. Those two boys who were arrested at the scene have already been charged. The girl is wanted as a material witness. Here, the paper has the details."

He picked the paper up impatiently and thrust it at her. She took it and read the items on the page he had turned back. It was front page news again, she noted, with a sinking heart. Tottie's description appeared again. The young men who were under arrest refused to implicate anyone else. The police, working with the description of the girl who was seen standing at the post office door shortly before the explosion, had questioned a number of young people who had recently been involved in student demonstrations. The girl had been identified by one of them as Mary Gilray, a writer of protest songs, who had taken part in a number of sit-ins.

Connie looked up from her reading. Roger stood near her desk, waiting for her comment. She could think of nothing to say.

"You notice she is identified as Mary Gilray," he said. "This bears out Fairchild's suspicion that she might be Charlotte Christeson."

Connie, her mouth dry, said, "I should think she would make every effort not to be found, under the circumstances."

"Yes, but how would she do that? How would you go about eluding the police—and the FBI?"

"Do you mean me or a metaphorical you?"

He was impatient with her apparent lack of seriousness. "I mean anybody, of course. How does one go about evading the police, under these circumstances? Well, I suppose one way would be to get out of the country—like some of these draft dodgers."

"She would have to have a passport," said Connie, eager to encourage his supposition.

"She may well have a valid passport and she may have decided to get out of the country before the immigration people are alerted to be on the lookout for her. On the other hand, it is possible for people to cross the border into Mexico or Canada illegally. Or even stow away on a vessel—going to Cuba or somewhere else where they would be allowed to land."

He was thinking aloud and Connie did not interrupt him.

"This is all speculation," he went on, after a moment's silence. "The first thing to do is to find out if Christeson's attention has been called to the fact that the police are looking for a girl who may be his daughter. I'd better go and see about that."

When he had gone she sat quiet, trying to bring her mind to bear on the problem, in search of a practical solution. It seemed as if she and Tottie were now sitting in the middle of a net whose meshes were drawing tighter around them. A feeling of panic threatened to take possession of her. She believed Tottie when Tottie said she had nothing to do with the bombing, that it had been curiosity that led her to the scene. She believed this because it seemed in fact something that Tottie would do. But Connie doubted that her own intuitive faith in Tottie's truthfulness would carry over to police interrogators. They would certainly be convinced that a girl who had spent several months associating with radical students and protesters, who was known to have been on the scene of other major civil disturbances, would in fact be implicated in the bombing of the post office.

And now there was a warrant out for her arrest. A cold shiver passed through Connie. If Tottie was traced to her apartment, she could scarely claim ignorance of the fact that the girl who had taken refuge with her was the girl who was being sought as Mary

Gilray. Tottie must be persuaded to give herself up. Connie's heart failed her. A profound conviction seized her that in this she would never succeed. And on top of that she had a sudden horrified revulsion at the thought of Tottie—little, uncompromising, unwary Tottie—in the hands of the police, lodged in a jail cell, subject to interrogation. Connie sat in a sweat of passionate denial of that possibility. At last she determined that, if Tottie was to be arrested, her father must first be told where she was, so that he could give her what protection he could.

"I'm not going to tell anybody till I find out what he is prepared to do," said Connie aloud. Hearing her own voice she was startled and glanced hastily at the door of her office.

But no one intruded on her and she spent the morning in a state of apprehension and speculation. There was no point, she decided, in calling Tottie until she knew more. She considered wildly for a moment the idea of going home and telling Tottie what was happening. But she decided against this, as being useless and possibly dangerous. She did not want to arouse curiosity by unusual actions. And perhaps Tottie had listened to the radio and had heard the news herself. Tottie would know then what the situation was and would come to some solution herself.

When the door of her office opened again she started in alarm. But it was only her secretary. The girl exclaimed at the fact that she had not gone to lunch and Connie realized then that it was already almost two o'clock. To satisfy the girl, she agreed to have a sandwich sent in and when it came she ate mechanically. She was sure that sooner or later she would hear again from Roger. It was three o'clock when he sent to ask her to come to his office.

"I talked to Mr. Clay," he said, looking up as she came in. "He says that Christeson already knew that the police had a warrant out for the girl under the name of Mary Gilray. He seems to be ready to believe that she is his daughter. Now he says he is going to make an appeal on television and the radio to his daughter this evening, asking her to get in touch with him and promising to give her any support he can under the circumstances. If the girl has any sense, she will respond."

"But, Roger, if she has been kidnaped, how could she? She might not even hear the appeal."

"That's a possibility. But the supposition is that she was not, and is not now in the hands of the extortionists who sent that threatening note to Christeson. If she is the girl who was seen at the post office and she was not blown to bits, then she is presumably free."

"Why are you so certain of that, Roger? These men may in fact have kidnaped her right after the bombing."

Roger was silent for a few moments, considering what she said. "Well, yes. In fact, we just don't know where we are. That's obvious. If she doesn't respond to Christeson's appeal, we still won't know whether she intends to evade arrest or whether she is unable to respond."

"If she is free and does respond, she will be under arrest, won't she?"

"Yes, of course. But she will probably be released on bail at once, if her father puts up the money, and she'll be free until a hearing is held to determine if there is enough evidence to hold her as a material witness or on a more definite charge."

"Out on bail," said Connie, in a bemused voice. "Then you don't think he will refuse to put up bail for her?"

"No, I don't." The undertone of anxiety in her voice caused him to focus his attention on her. "What is the matter, Connie? You seem upset."

"I hate to think of a girl like that being put in jail. She isn't a hardened offender."

Roger studied her for a moment. "From what I've heard of this girl's chosen associates and mode of life during the last few months, I wouldn't say a jail term would do her any harm. I wouldn't say the police handle people with gloves on, exactly, but some of the people she has been living with aren't Sir Galahads or Robin Hoods. I don't think you need waste your sympathy."

"I expect I'm just edgy. Well, are we to do anything before Christeson makes this appeal?"

"There is nothing we can do." He was silent for a few minutes and she did not interrupt his thought. Presently he said, in a different tone of voice, "Connie, how about going out with me this evening?"

She wanted desperately to say No, and the idea occurred to her that she could still claim lack of energy or a headache, the remnant of her cold, to excuse a refusal. But an uneasy caution prevented her. Roger seemed to sense some other reason for her unwillingness. She must avoid a misunderstanding with him.

She looked up to see him watching her. "All right, Roger. But I'm afraid I'll not be very lively company."

He became once more buoyant. "Oh, a good dinner and some entertainment will pep you up. We can play it by ear and do just what you feel like doing."

"If you don't mind, Roger, I shan't bother to go home and change. I'll just wait for you here in the office till you're ready."

"Just as you say," he agreed heartily. "We can go to that Italian place to eat. It's nice and relaxed."

When she was back in her own office Connie thought quickly of what she should do. She must call Tottie and explain to her. Uneasily she wondered how Tottie would take the situation. She must also warn Tottie of the warrant that was out for her and of her father's projected appeal. It would be like Tottie to ignore the radio, to close her ears to the newscast, if she did have the radio turned on.

But now she must call Tottie and obviously not through the office switchboard. The possibility that a stray word, an incriminating phrase, might catch the ear of one of the operators was too obvious a danger. So she told her secretary that she had a headache from eating lunch at her desk without a real break in the day and that she was going to the corner drugstore for some aspirin.

As she left the office she was aware of fear. She found she was terrified by the idea that even a slight deviation from her usual routine might cause comment by some of her daily associates. All at once, in the course of a few days, she seemed to be living in a glass house. Her protection from curious eyes was of the flimsiest sort. She was so overwhelmed by this feeling that before entering the phone booth she made a quick survey of the drugstore. There was no one there whom she recognized.

She remembered her instructions to Tottie and followed them carefully, letting the phone ring twice on her first call and hanging up before calling again. Fervently she hoped Tottie would remember what they had arranged, that Tottie would not be too abstracted to answer or suddenly frightened.

The phone rang again and again and panic welled up in Connie. She felt an immense relief when at last she heard Tottie's small voice say "Hello."

"Tottie, listen to me carefully. I'm calling from the drugstore, so there's no chance we'll be overheard. Did you listen to the news on the radio?"

"I heard it."

"Tottie, there's a warrant out for your arrest. If you give yourself up, you'll probably be released on bail for a hearing later. Your father says he will put up the bail. Tottie, you must get in touch with your father. He is going to go on radio and television this evening to make a public appeal to you to cooperate with the police, at eight o'clock."

At first there was dead silence on the other end of the line. Then Tottie said calmiy, "I'm not letting anybody know where I am."

"Can you think of some way of getting in touch with your father without telling him where you are?"

"I don't intend to get in touch with him," Tottie declared adamantly, and then she asked quickly in a different tone of voice, "When are you going to be home?"

Connie took a deep breath and said, "Tottie, I have to go out with Roger this evening. I mustn't let him suspect anything. I told him that I would wait here in my office till he is free, so that he would not come to the apartment. We are going to have dinner and then I'll tell him I want to go home. You'll have to stay out of sight somehow."

For a long moment there was silence at the other end of the line and Connie began again urgently, "Tottie, I can't help it. If I refuse to spend the evening with him, he'll be certain that something is wrong. He seems suspicious already. I can't explain anything to him without giving you away. He knows the description of you that the police have been circulating."

Still there was silence at the other end of the line.

"Tottie!" Connie was desperate. "Say something! Are you listening to me?"

"Yes. Are you going to his apartment?" Tottie's voice was no longer small and soft.

Connie pleaded with a sinking heart, "I'm going to try not to. Tottie, don't be mad at me. There is nothing else I can do."

Tottie threatened, "If you go to bed with him, you needn't come back here."

"Well, I haven't anywhere else to go," Connie retorted sharply.

"You can jolly well stay with him!"

"Oh, Tottie, please! We can't talk like this on the telephone! I've got to go out with him this evening. I'll get home as soon as I can. And make sure there isn't anything of yours left lying around for him to find when he brings me home."

After a moment's silence Tottie said in a less belligerent tone, "All right."

"I'm going to have to hang up, Tottie. Kiss me, Tottie," said Connie in a coaxing voice.

"All right," said Tottie again, in a softer voice, and then with a flare of anger added, "But remember about tonight."

The afternoon dragged through endless hours. Connie tried in vain to give her attention to her work. At last it was six o'clock and most of the office staff had gone for the day. How long, she wondered, would she have to wait for Roger?

Shortly after seven o'clock he rapped briefly on her door and came into her office.

"Goodness, Roger! So soon?"

He gave her a sharp glance. "Aren't you pleased?"

"Why, of course!" She tried to sound warmly welcoming.

His gaze lingered on her speculatively. "I'm sorry if I seem to have been neglecting you lately, Connie. I've got a hell of a load of work to carry."

She nodded casually, anxious not to give her imagined complaint an undue importance. The Italian restaurant he had proposed was an unpretentious place and the waiter gave them a small table in a corner, with no very close neighbors. The small shaded lamp on the table gave out only a rosy glow that shone up into their faces. The conventional lovers' seclusion in a public place, thought Connie. They ordered their meal and the waiter brought them a bottle of chianti and filled their glasses.

"Well, Connie," said Roger, pleasantly, lifting his, "here's to us."

Automatically she responded and he reached over to place his longfingered, well-manicured hand on hers. "It seems an age since we did this, Connie."

Oh, God! thought Connie. Aloud she said, "So it does, Roger."

"We have some serious talking to do. I've been postponing it till I could see daylight. I think you know what I mean."

Connie, her heart sinking further, made no reply.

"You do, don't you?" he demanded, looking at her over the little table lamp.

Connie answered slowly, "Suppose you go on and tell me, Roger. Tell me what you've got on your mind."

He continued to look at her somewhat doubtfully. "Well, I think it's time we were setting up house. I'm pretty sure I'm going to make partnership by the end of the year. What do we do first?"

"Get married," said Connie, striving for a flippant manner. "At least, that's the conventional requirement. I don't think it really matters, but your parents might prefer their grandchildren to be legitimate."

He refused to be amused. "You know very well it's something we've just been postponing for convenience."

Connie, recognizing the strain of puritanism that seemed to lie just below the surface with Roger, said in a softer tone, "Of course. But why should you feel the need to act just now?"

He looked at her as if her coolness shocked him. "This isn't a sudden idea. It's been bothering me for quite a while. Well, I don't think it will ever be more convenient than it is right now."

Poor Roger, thought Connie. The slightest change in daily habits caused him such annoyance, and even a minor anguish. She said quietly, "You speak of convenience, Roger. But aren't you overlooking the fact that you're considering only your own? I believe that we originally thought of it as our mutual convenience."

He stared at her in amazement. "Why, Connie, of course! But I assumed—"

He hesitated and she finished for him crisply, "You assumed that your convenience would naturally be mine, that I've just been waiting for you to say the word."

"You don't need to distort the situation," he replied in an offended tone. "If you have some reason for waiting longer, just say so."

She did not answer at once. Then she said in a cool voice, "Roger, let's begin at the beginning. *If* we are going to get married."

She sat quite still for a moment. When he spoke there was suppressed rage in his voice. "What are you talking about? That's not the question. It's never been."

"Wait a minute," Connie retorted, speaking with a new sharpness. "I think you are overlooking something. Or your memory is at fault. Please think back for a few months. You said then that you wanted me strictly to understand that, no matter how intimate we became, we were going to keep the door open and if one of us wanted out, the other would be ready to accept the fact. You said we were to operate as absolutely free agents, otherwise we couldn't come to an honest decision. Or did you mean that was just for yourself?"

He was too angry to reply promptly. Then he said, "You know perfectly well that what has happened between us since then has changed all that. We're not experimenting now. You know that."

Connie gave a little shrug. "I don't remember you saying anything like this until this evening. How could I 'know' anything like that if you haven't mentioned it?"

"It wasn't necessary for me to talk about it. You usually understand me better than that. You've certainly been acting as if you took it for granted that we were on a permanent basis."

So that's the tactic, thought Connie. Because I put everything and everybody aside to suit your convenience, then I am staking out a claim. I wonder how it would be if, instead of talking about marriage plans, you had chosen this evening to announce to me that you wanted out. I suppose then you would have remembered quite clearly that we were not committed to each other.

She said aloud, "It's dangerous to be tacit about something like this."

He threw his napkin down with a gesture of disgust and said, "This isn't something we can talk about in a public place. Do you want any dessert? If you don't, let's get out of here and go to my apartment."

I could, thought Connie, just refuse to go and then we would quarrel and it would be over with. But like Roger, she disliked quarreling in a public place. And besides—yes, it was true that, though she did not love Roger, she was fond of him and in good conscience she did not want to break off with him forever after a few wounding words exchanged in a restaurant. So she waited while he called the waiter and paid the check and stood aside for her to go ahead of him to the door. They rode in silence in the cab.

Chapter Fourteen

The door of Roger's apartment was opened by the servant, who was not altogether able to disguise his surprise at their early arrival. Roger told him to bring them coffee and liqueurs to the library and then to leave for the evening. Connie walked without haste into the big, luxuriously furnished room and sat down in one of the armchairs beside the fireplace with its cold gas logs behind the oldfashioned summer screen. Roger busied himself at the tray the servant placed on the corner of the wide mahogany table. He brought her a demitasse of coffee and a liqueur glass, which she put down on the ornate little side table at her elbow. Then he sat down opposite and took out the pipe he only smoked in moments of leisure.

Presently he said in a thoughtful voice, "Let's begin all over again, Connie. I've been thinking more and more lately that this is an awkward business, you living in one place and I in another, and that it would be a good deal better if we just came to terms and got married."

He waited to see how she would take this statement. Connie, with a strange sense of remoteness, instead of meeting the invitation in his words, parried with the question, "What is it, Roger, that has prompted you to raise this just now?"

He gave her a level glance, as if to show that he intended to keep his temper. "Just the realization that time is moving on. It's easy to get into a rut and not notice that the days and months are passing—especially when you're kept busy trying to meet deadlines." He paused for a moment. "Maybe it was the trip to Chicago. That seemed to point up the fact that it sometimes looks as if I just leave you dangling—not that I intend to. Things just come out that way."

As if I wouldn't dangle just as much if we were married, thought Connie. Aloud she said, "I really do think, Roger, we had better begin over again, as if the last few months did not exist. Let's look at things with fresh eyes. We might come to a different conclusion. You're not really committed to marrying me, you know. I haven't supposed that at any time."

Though he kept his voice even, his irritation showed in his eyes. "I'm not talking about commitments. I'm talking about reaching a decision. I want to marry you, Connie, and the sooner the better."

"Yes, but I'm not sure that I want to marry you—or anyone—just now."

His real astonishment showed in his face. "But, Connie, I don't understand." He paused, as if another thought had come into his mind. "Are you interested in somebody else?"

In spite of herself Connie hesitated in her reply and she could see the suspicion harden in his eyes. "Is that the only reason you can think of for me to say I don't want to marry you?"

He turned his eyes away and drank off his coffee and emptied his liqueur glass. It was obvious that his suspicion had become a certainty in his mind. "I think you owe it to me to give me a straight answer. Will you marry me now, as soon as we can make the arrangements?"

He looked up directly at her as he asked the question. She met his gaze. "No," she said firmly.

He looked away again. "Well, that's that. At least I know where I stand. As you say, we'll begin over again. I'm entitled to another try. We'll ignore the past. From now on it's understood that I start even with anybody else in your life."

Oh, Lord have mercy! Connie cried inwardly. Why can't he blow up and order me out of his life? But she knew the answer. He doesn't believe that I will give him up. He is certain that this is only a female aberration, a woman's contrariness, and that all he has to do is be patient and cajole me out of it.

"I don't promise anything, Roger. You'll just have to let things take their course."

It was the course he was least capable of adopting, but with some effort he refrained from saying so flatly. "I believe in taking positive action, as you know. Not in letting things go by the board."

His tone was dry but his determination was plain. Connie said, "You know, Roger, I'd like to go home, right now," and she stood up.

He was as quickly on his feet and stepped across the space between them. "Connie!" he said urgently, seizing her arms. "Stay for a while! I don't want you to go yet!"

Connie strove not to flinch from the touch of his hands. Her flesh shuddered away from the bodily contact. "No!" she said, more vehemently than she intended. "No! I'm not going to bed with you! Please let me go, Roger."

Staring into her eyes he seemed to realize that her withdrawal was genuine and he reluctantly dropped his hands.

"You don't have to come with me. Just get me a cab."

But he insisted on accompanying her and again they rode in silence, until they reached her apartment building. Then she said,

"I'd rather you didn't come up."

His first response was to contradict her and insist, but again he restrained himself, unwillingly. He told the cab to wait and walked to the door of the apartment. But before she went in he seized her suddenly in his arms and kissed her violently on the mouth.

"I'll see you tomorrow, Connie." His words were spoken in a tone more of threat than of promise. She opened the door and fled inside.

At the door of her own apartment she became aware, as she fumbled in her handbag for her keys, that her hands were trembling. But she knew that Tottie would not answer the doorbell if she rang. Finally she got the door open and stepping inside she closed and double-locked it with an enormous sense of relief. Fleetingly she smiled to herself at the thought that it was Roger she was fleeing from.

The livingroom was in darkness except for the reflection on the ceiling of the street lamps outside. She stood still for a moment, listening. The apartment was as quiet as if it was indeed empty. She crossed to the door to the bedroom, which stood a little open. The bedroom also was dark except for the glow of outside lights.

"Tottie."

There was no answering sound and she repeated. "Tottie."

Still there was no response and she said, with rising anxiety, "Tottie! It's me, Connie. I'm by myself. Where are you?"

She was crossing the room as she spoke and now she turned on the bedside lamp. As the light bloomed she looked about to see that the room was empty. Nonplussed, she started for the bathroom. Before she reached it, she was suddenly seized around the waist from behind. Two small hands were clasped tightly over her stomach.

"Tottie! Where were you hiding? You had me scared."

Tottie let go of her and she turned around to look down into the other girl's face. Tottie looked up at her with a mischievous smile.

"You didn't expect me to be anywhere in sight, did you?"

"Tottie," said Connie softly, reaching down to hug her. The negative feeling of relief from pursuit that she had felt a few moments before turned into a more positive feeling of happiness at being welcomed. Tottie, her face buried in Connie's neck, nibbled gently at her skin. Then she drew back to say, "You've got an awful lot of clothes in that closet. I didn't think anybody would go poking behind them except you and even you wouldn't find me behind that hamper you've got your laundry in."

Connie laughed and let go of her. "Good heavens, Tottie! You haven't spent the evening in there!"

"Of course not." Tottie perched on the end of the bed to watch her undress. "I had picked out the spot and I dived in there when I heard your key in the door. What did you do with him? Drown him?"

Connie sobered as she watched Tottie's face. "I told him that I wouldn't marry him and I wouldn't go to bed with him tonight. He is very angry with me."

"I see. That's why you are home early."

Connie did not answer at once but went on taking off her dress. As she pulled it over her head a flood of recollection poured over her and she exclaimed, "Tottie, the radio! Did you listen to your father?" She stood staring at Tottie in consternation. Neither she nor Roger, in the heat of their argument, had given a moment's thought to Christeson and the appeal he was to make.

Tottie nodded calmly but said nothing.

"What did he say?" Connie demanded, standing in her pantie girdle and bra with the dress in her hands.

"He said," Tottie replied slowly, "that he wanted me to come forward and tell the police what I knew about the people who made the bomb, that if I didn't have anything to do with making the bomb or planting it, I didn't have anything to fear and that he would stand by me."

Connie watched her face as she reported this. There was nothing in Tottie's voice or expression to give a clue to her inner feelings. "Well, Tottie, what are you going to do? Are you going to get in touch with your father?"

Tottie's eyes grew angry and contemptuous. "Of course not."

Connie, distressed, said nothing as she hung up her dress and took off her slippers. Tottie sat silent, with brooding eyes. Finally Connie said, "Tottie, remember, there is a warrant out for your arrest. If you don't do as your father suggests, you're going to be subject to imprisonment without bail. I'm sure he will put up bail for you now and you can clear yourself at the hearing. Tottie, you don't really have any choice. Besides, you know, you've got me involved. If you're found here in my apartment, I'm liable to be charged as an accessory. I couldn't hope to convince anyone that I didn't know who you are or that you are wanted by the police."

"Nobody is going to know I'm here unless you tell them."

"Any little accident could result in somebody finding out. I was able to keep Roger away this evening, but I may not be so successful next time. The resident manager might find out. Sometimes she comes to check on things in the apartment. Tottie, we're both in a very dangerous situation, and you're the one who can act to get us out of it."

"I'm not going to, if it means letting people know where I am," Tottie said emphatically.

Connie took a deep breath and said, "You told me, Tottie, that you had nothing to do with planning any of these affairs in which you've been involved, that you didn't even endorse the reasons' why these were done, that you were just indulging your curiosity. You said—"

Tottie smiled grimly as she interrupted, "Do you suppose the police would believe that for a moment? And if they don't believe it, where do you suppose I would be? I'm not that childish."

Connie frowned in her anxiety. "But you've got to do something. You can't live as a fugitive indefinitely. Your father has offered an out—the only out, really, under the circumstances. If you don't take it, you're certainly going to have a hell of a time. But my situation will be even worse."

Tottie's eyes glowed brilliantly and she said disdainfully, "You're really frightened, aren't you, Stantia? Scared out of your wits."

Connie, stung by her tone, retorted, "Jails aren't very nice places. In fact, some of them aren't even decent. I think you would be very sorry if you found yourself in one."

Tottie dropped her eyes and, with the sudden change of mood she so often showed, said quietly, desperately, "It would be even worse than you think. I have claustrophobia. I'm sure I'd have a fit of some kind if they locked me up in a cell—if I heard a key turning in an iron door."

A shudder went through her small body. Connie, seeing it, felt a pang of loving concern. "Oh, Tottie!," she cried, putting an arm around her, "what *can* we do, if you don't get in touch with your father?"

Tottie leaned against her and rested her head on her shoulder. "Stantia, it will work out all right. But just us together. You're the only person I trust. I won't put myself in anybody else's hands. Oh, Stantia, hold me tight! I get so frightened here by myself. I begin imagining things. I begin thinking about those men who wanted to rape and kidnap me. Stantia, I'd die if anything like that happened to me!"

Her body, pressed tightly against Connie, was shaken by the imagined horror. Connie tightened her embrace and said into the top of her head, "Tottie, I can't protect you if you don't help me. If the police should discover you here and come to get you, I couldn't prevent them from taking you away. I don't even have money enough to go bail for you."

Tottie stopped trembling and relaxed in Connie's arms. Lifting her head she looked up at Connie and raised her hand to stroke her cheek gently. "They're not going to know I'm here because we won't tell them," she said with a childish seriousness.

"And these men you're afraid of? Jasper and his friend?"

"They are more likely to find me."

"Why do you think that?" Connie demanded, resisting the chill that Tottie's manner had conveyed to her.

Tottie drew away from her and replied, "They just might."

"Is there any possibility that they traced you here? That they followed you when you came here?" Connie frowned down at her in alarm.

Tottie shook her head thoughtfully. "They could not have. I've told you that. It's just that I am so afraid of them."

She spoke with the same childish earnestness as before. Her head hung down now and the long blonde hair hid her face.

Connie gave herself a slight shake to dispel the effect of her foreboding. "Well, if you won't get in touch with your father, I suppose we'll just have to await the consequences." I can't persuade her now, she thought. I'll have to coax her into it by degrees. Thinking this, she paused in putting on her robe to contemplate the self-absorbed Tottie. What an extraordinary little person she is. And how she has insinuated herself into my very being. It is as if I had known her all my life. She is part of me now and she knows it.

Tottie suddenly brushed the long hair away from her face and looked up. She was no longer preoccupied or fearful. Instead there was a mischievous light in her blue eyes as she said, putting her arms around Connie's waist and pressing against her bare stomach, "I like you better without your clothes on."

"Oh, do you?" Connie responded, smiling down at her. "Well, you'd better let me put my robe on and get you something to eat. I'll bet you haven't had anything."

Tottie released her and said, "There was some cottage cheese in the icebox. I ate that."

An hour or so later, as they lay in bed in the dark, Connie tried to sort out her own emotions. She should be thinking first of her situation in the firm, of the consequences for her professional life if she and Tottie should become entangled with the police. She should be feeling remorse and a sense of loss over herself and Roger. Yet lying here, with the half-asleep Tottie in her arms, their legs intertwined, she could not summon a spark of genuine concern for any of this. Tomorrow would do for all that. In the meantime, the bliss of feeling Tottie's warm, confiding little body pressed against hers spread through her and presently she sank into deep slumber.

It was morning when she was roused by Tottie's small, sweet voice, singing. She opened her eyes to the sunlight in the room. Was it late, she wondered? Had she overslept again? But, reluctant to move, she closed her eyes again and listened to Tottie's singing.

"All day in the rain," sang Tottie, "my eyes were blind, Till over the hill you came, my love."

The gentle, beguiling tune and words took the urgency out of even the thought of duty. This was a new experience, awakening to the pleasure of the presence of the beloved, with the memory of the evening before's bliss hanging in the air like perfume. There was nothing businesslike about Tottie, nothing that savored of love-making reduced to its set time and place, put out of mind once it was concluded lest it should interfere with the more important demands of a workaday world.

Tottie, as if awakening to her veiled scrutiny, looked over her shoulder. She was sitting at the foot of the bed, naked, her back to Connie, her legs drawn up and her arms clasped around her knees. The cool blue eyes stared at Connie through the curtain of pale blonde hair.

"Is that one of your own songs, Tottie?"

Tottie nodded.

"Is it one of those that have been recorded?"

Tottie shook her head. "I made up the words just now."

Shaking off her bemused state, Connie swung her legs off the bed and got up. A shower helped dissipate the sense of no-hurry and she turned the radio on to listen to the news. Tottie, she discovered on coming out of the bathroom, had put on her shirt and jeans and had gone into the kitchen.

The voice of the newscaster filled the bedroom as Connie dressed. He began with news about the Vietnam war and then the next item was about the appeal made the evening before by H.B. Christeson, the multi-millionaire father of the girl being sought in connection with the bombing of the post office. So far, said the newscaster, there was no information concerning a response to the appeal. The police had agreed to take no steps until the girl had had an opportunity to communicate with her father. Any further news would have to await events.

Going into the kitchen, Connie found the kettle boiling and

Tottie putting cups and saucers on the counter. She seemed absorbed in her own thoughts and oblivious of the sound of the man's voice on the radio. There is no use my tackling her now, thought Connie. She won't listen.

They sat amicably mute while they ate the toast and drank the coffee Tottie had prepared. Connie, watching her, saw that her mind seemed totally occupied by her own thoughts. Perhaps it is the creative mood, thought Connie. But when they had finished their first cups of coffee Tottie seemed aware of the fact and jumped up to replenish them. As she stood at the stove pouring the hot water into the cups, Connie saw that the pink skin of her bottom was showing through a frayed hole in her jeans.

"Those jeans are really worn out," she said, reaching over and poking her finger through the hole.

Tottie paused in what she was doing to twist around and glance down where Connie's finger was.

"I did buy you some clothes. Why don't you wear them?"

"I'm saving them for best," said Tottie primly and turned back to what she was doing.

A few minutes later, getting ready to leave, Connie hesitated again. But she glanced at Tottie's face and said instead, walking to the front door, "Tottie, if anything comes up today, I'll call you as I did yesterday. You remember? I'll call and let the phone ring twice and then I'll hang up and call back again right away."

Tottie's vivid blue eyes dwelt noncommittally on hers as she nodded.

"And, Tottie," Connie went on, "I think you had better pay attention to the radio. There may be more news about your father or what the police intend to do."

She looked anxiously at Tottie, who merely nodded again. With her hand halfway to the doorknob Connie stopped and leaned over to kiss her. Instantly Tottie put her arms around her neck and clung there for a moment. She was smiling tranquilly as Connie closed the door.

Chapter Fifteen

Connie arrived at the office at her usual time, a little ahead of most of the staff, and her appearance aroused no special interest. Back in the familiar surroundings of the office she was at once aware of a certain apprehensiveness concerning Roger. She hoped his work would keep him fully occupied and unable to give more than   passing thought to their joint affairs. As the first hours of the morning passed and she did not hear from him, she began to feel less tense and tried to absorb herself in her own work. But her composure was suddenly shattered by the telephone. She picked the instrument up to hear her secretary say, "It is Mr. Wellington, Miss Norton."

"Connie," said Roger's voice. "Come to my office right away, will you? We have a new problem."

He hung up as she said Yes. There was no mistaking the note of alarm in his voice. She left her own office at once and hurried down the hall to his.

"Connie!" he greeted her as he caught sight of her. "Come in here quickly and let me tell you what has happened." He gestured to a chair and went on at once. "Things are going from bad to worse in this Christeson business. Christeson has received a ransome note, demanding $250,000 for the return of his daughter. The kidnapers say they will send instructions later about how and where the money is to be delivered. And they say they will kill the girl if the police get into the case."

Connie moistened her suddenly dry lips and asked, "What has he done besides calling us?"

"Oh, he's informed the police. We advised him to do so, on the understanding that they'll keep out of it until he has had a chance to pay over the money and collect the girl."

Connie was silent and he went on. "As a matter of fact, Connie, he is pretty cool about the whole thing. He thinks she laid herself open to this. The principal reason he wants to get her back is because of the threat to his family interests. He says so in almost so many words. Well, I suppose he is right there. She must have realized that she was endangering herself by associating with all sorts of riffraff. She must know that there are plenty of people who would seek to profit from the fact that she is H. B. Christeson's daughter. She has grown up being guarded against the threat of kidnaping."

Connie ventured, "She probably isn't very sophisticated."

Roger cast her a satirical glance. "Not sophisticated? I'd scarcely think that could be true, considering her career in the last year." His manner became more professional. "However, there is another aspect of Christeson's attitude that is more serious. He says he will pay out this money and do everything necessary to get her back out of the hands of the kidnappers. But he is also determined to entrap the criminals. He is fanatical on this point. This can be dangerous. Men like that won't hesitate to commit murder to protect themselves."

Connie suppressed a shudder. "Surely you can persuade him to be careful. If the police have agreed to hold back—"

"He's not a very persuadable person, from what I've seen. Well, I just wanted to let you know where we stand."

"There's nothing more going to be done right now?"

"We have to wait for the instructions about paying over the cash. That's when Christeson may really throw a monkey wrench into the works." Roger paused for a while, thoughtfully. "I'll let you know when I hear anything more."

Connie got up. "You're still going on the supposition that Charlotte Christeson is the girl they call Mary Gilray—the girl involved in the post office bombing?"

Roger's face showed a slight surprise. "Why, yes. The girl at the post office was not killed, so I suppose these men have abducted her. They must have recognized her as Christeson's daughter. They must be people who have associated with her in these radical groups."

Seeing him absorbed in his own speculations, Connie turned towards the door. Her movement roused his attention. He said, "Connie," in a different tone of voice, and she stopped unwillingly. "Connie," he said again, "how about this evening? We could go to a show."

"No, thank you, Roger," she said firmly. "Not tonight. I'm going to spend the evening at home. I'm not in the mood for company."

He had got to his feet and was leaning now against his desk with his arms crossed, eyeing her closely. "You're not in the mood for company, or is it mine you're talking about?"

Connie's temper rose. "If I say I'm not in the mood, I mean I'm not in the mood and that's that."

Roger, seeing the angry flush in her face, said with a touch of formality, "Well, I'm sorry. I'll try another time."

Going down the hall to her own office Connie thought, He is
certain there is someone else I'm interested in. And she was dismayed at the certainty that her own manner had confirmed his
suspicions.

She arrived at the apartment earlier than usual, for she made
no pretense of working beyond the regular office closing time.
She was anxious to talk to Tottie, anxious to tell her of the latest
news and to learn what Tottie's reaction would be. It would be a
relief to discuss the difficulties of her situation. It was only Tottie
with whom she could do so.

The livingroom was empty when she got the door open.

"Tottie!" she called. "Where are you?"

Almost at once Tottie appeared in the door to the bedroom.
She came padding quickly across the room in bare feet and put
her arms around Connie.

"You've been gone such a long time," she complained softly,
rubbing her head against Connie's shoulder.

Connie, her heart melting with delight at the soft little caresses,
said as briskly as she could, "As a matter of fact, it has been a
short day."

"Not for me," said Tottie, following her into the bedroom.

"Then you haven't been composing, You would not have noticed
the time if you had been."

"I didn't feel like it. I felt uneasy. You shouldn't go away and
leave me when I feel uneasy."

Connie looked at her in astonishment, half expecting to find
that she was mocking. But Tottie's face showed only a wistful
melancholy.

"Well, darling, I can't help it. I've got my job to attend to."

Tottie made no response but sat contentedly on the end of the
bed as Connie took off her dress and put on a pair of slacks and a
shirt. The weather had turned warmer and the air conditioning
was on, but Tottie had opened the windows and the sound of the
fountain came up to them from the park. She could not talk about
the day's events and dispel the tranquil pleasure of the moment,
thought Connie. Not just now.

Tottie followed her into the livingroom and they sat on the sofa
together, Tottie punctuating a rambling tale of her days in the
Swiss boarding school with little pats and caresses. There was a
carefree quality to Tottie's manner that transported both of them
back to the timeless happiness of childhood. She never spoke of
people as an adult would, of their shortcomings and misdoings.
Instead, like a child, she reported them as figures in a drama sus-

pended in time, their actions, however inexplicable, accepted for what they seemed to be. Watching her face and the play of the light of her imagination on it, Connie was enthralled by this undisguised projection of her inner life. Tottie's spirit seemed to glow through her physical presence, unchecked and unaltered by any selfconsciousness.

They ate their supper in the kitchen, lit by the last rays of the June evening's sun.

"It's almost the longest day, Stantia," said Tottie, as Connie picked up their empty plates and put them in the dishwasher.

"In another couple of weeks."

And the interchange reminded Connie that time was running by. As they went back into the livingroom she decided she must now tell Tottie about the ransom demand her father had received. Tottie had given no hint, throughout the evening, of whatever it had been that had cast down her spirits during the day. Even if Tottie had listened to the radio she would have heard nothing. Roger had said that Christeson had succeeded in keeping the ransom note from the press.

Connie stopped in the process of putting records on the record player and said, "Your father has received a note demanding ransome for you. It was sent by some people who say they have you in their hands and that they will kill you if the ransom is not paid. Tottie, it must be Jasper and his friend."

Tottie stared at her without speaking.

"Apparently, Tottie, whoever sent that note intends it to be believed that you are their prisoner. Tottie, could it be anyone else?"

"Anyone else than Jasper and that other man? No, I don't think it could be. So if they found me—"

She did not finish the sentence, but Connie spoke hurriedly, to try and dispel the look of fear in her eyes. "Your father is going to pay the ransom. But he says he intends to catch the men who sent it. Of course, he is going to make sure you are released first."

Tottie's eyes sparkled with anger. "You're so sure of that!"

"Tottie, you can't let him go on thinking you are in danger of your life in these men's hands. It is cruel to keep him on tenterhooks like this!"

"Is he on tenterhooks?" Tottie asked, disbelievingly.

"Naturally he is upset. He's your father."

"We'll pass all that by. He's not going to lose any sleep over it, I assure you. But I'll bet he is as mad as the devil over the idea that I'm going to cost him more money."

"Tottie, you mustn't—"

"He thinks this is all my fault—that I got myself into this jam
through my own stupidity and that it serves me right. He's chiefly
concerned about protecting the Christeson interests. Stantia, I've
heard all my life about the sacredness of the Christeson interests.
Of course, he wouldn't come out and say this now. He always
knows how to put up a good front. You can never fault him on his
public behavior. He takes people in like that. I know that right
now what he is chiefly thinking about is how he is going to get
back the money he is paying out as ransom."

Connie said persuasively, "If you let him know now that you
are not in danger, he would not have to pay out the money at all.
I—I could go and tell him."

"And let everybody know that you've been aiding and abetting
a fugitive from justice? I thought that was what you're so scared
about. And besides, don't you know what he would do? He'd try
to set up a trap here in your apartment to catch these men who
are trying to do him out of some money. If I got caught in the
cross-fire, it would be just too bad."

Connie said stubbornly. "It would not have to be like that at
all. You could go to your father's house. You would be safe there.
He has guards."

"And the police would know all about it. I'd be turning myself
in.".

"You'll have to surrender sometime. Your father is going bail
for you."

The telephone ringing made them both jump. They stared at it
jointly while it rang several times more.

"I'd better answer it," said Connie, unhappily certain that it
was Roger. She quailed at the thought of carrying on a conversation with him while Tottie listened.

But when she lifted the receiver and said Hello, it was a woman's
voice that said graciously, "Good evening, Connie. This is Marcia
Wellington. How are you?"

Connie stammered a response and the voice went on, "Roger
told me that you're not feeling up to scratch. I hope you are better."

"Oh, I just had a cold. It seems to have gone." So he has got his
mother to call me, she thought.

"Well, I'm glad. I've been wanting to have you over and tomorrow evening seems like a good time for me. Is it convenient
for you? We haven't seen you for an age. I've had so many things
on my calendar lately and house guests besides, but I'm sorry to

have been so neglectful. Can you come to dinner tomorrow evening?"

Connie stared for a moment at the little painting of Paris that hung over the telephone stand. She knew she must say yes and at last she did so. She listened then as patiently as she could to Mrs. Wellington's flow of talk, aware that Roger's mother was making a special effort to be cordial and warm. At last she was able to put down the phone. She stood for a moment longer before turning around to face Tottie.

Tottie's voice demanded, "Who was that?"

"Roger's mother. I've got to go to dinner with them tomorrow evening."

"I don't want you to."

"I can't help it. They're my future inlaws—or so it is assumed. She invites me over there every so often—partly, I think, because Roger asks her to and partly to keep her finger on the pulse of his private life, shall we say."

Tottie looked at her speculatively. "She doesn't like you.

"Oh, I don't think she has anything against me personally. She would be a little jealous of any woman Roger said he was going to marry."

"But you are not going to marry him."

"She doesn't know that—unless Roger has already told her and I don't think he has. I think he has asked her to have me over to help change my mind again. Bringing up the reinforcements, you know." She smiled bleakly.

"If you're not going to marry him," Tottie said dogmatically, "you don't have to go there."

"She would know right away that there is something wrong, then."

"Well, the sooner she knows the better."

"That wouldn't be fair to Roger."

"Why not?"

Connie hesitated, searching for the explanation in her own mind. "Well, if he hasn't told her that we have broken off, he would hate for me to be the one to let her know."

"You mean, he doesn't believe that you mean it when you say you won't marry him?"

"He believes it—at least, I think he does. But he thinks he can convince me that I'm just having a mental aberration of some kind. He thinks—"

She stopped and Tottie watched her closely for a few moments.

Then Tottie said, "He thinks you're interested in somebody else."

"Yes," Connie admitted.

"Did you tell him he was right?" Tottie's eyes blazed.

"No, of course I couldn't!"

"Yes, I can imagine how you told him no. It just convinced him he was right, didn't it?"

Connie did not answer.

"So now he thinks if he gets his mother to invite you to their house, you'll be reminded of all the things you'll be giving up if you don't marry Roger. He wants to buy you, Stantia."

Connie tried to smile. "Well, that will be a change—for him. He has always thought he could have me for the asking before this."

"It must be a shock to him," said Tottie, coming over to put her arms around Connie.

When Connie woke the next morning, to find that a grey sky had succeeded the week of sunshiny days, she remembered first that it was Saturday and second that she had accepted Roger's mother's invitation. Saturday, with its relaxed office schedule. And this evening, with its demand for a polite disguising of her rejection of Roger. She would have to remind Tottie of this evening and warn her to keep out of sight. She remembered Tottie's hideaway in the closet and smiled to herself.

Tottie was good-humored as they ate their leisurely breakfast, sitting on the high stool in the kitchen swinging her small bare feet and humming snatches of song in between their bursts of conversation, while Connie fried bacon and eggs.

As she sat down at the table, Connie said, "I'm coming home early this afternoon, Tottie, unless something happens about your father. You haven't changed your mind about getting in touch with him?"

"No."

"I'll call you then, if I'm delayed for any reason. I expect Roger to come for me this evening about seven o'clock."

Tottie made no response. They neither of them referred to the evening again. Connie dressed and left the apartment, with a last glimpse of Tottie sitting in the armchair dangling her feet over the arm.

The offices of Bryanston and Clay had their usual Saturday air of half-desertion when she got off the elevator and greeted the receptionist. Mr. Wellington, the girl informed her, had arrived half an hour before and wanted to see her.

He was standing by the window, moodily gazing down at the empty street, as she came into his office.

"Oh, Connie," he said, stepping quickly over to kiss her.

She could not keep from drawing back. He was aware of her reluctance and a half-angry, half-offended expression came into his eyes. She said quickly, as if in genuine surprise, "In the office, Roger?"

He was mollified and said carelessly, "Well, it's Saturday."

"What is it you wanted me for, Roger?"

"I think we're going to have some news from Christeson this morning. You'll be in your office?"

"Yes, I'll be there."

She went down the corridor to her own office. There she had a sense of sanctuary, which she knew was false. About noon the door opened without warning, startling her from the half-reverie in which she had spent the last two hours. Roger came in, a small piece of paper in his hand.

"He's heard," he announced. "Christeson has heard from the kidnapers again. He sent for me right after I saw you this morning. I've just got back from his house. He has received instructions to leave the cash in small denominations in a car in an allnight parking lot on the other side of town. Christeson has talked to the police. They tell him it will be too risky to try to surround the parking lot. They're certain the car will be covered and if they try to interfere, they'll find themselves in an ambush. Either the money would not be collected or there'd be a gun battle."

Connie was unable to suppress a little shiver. "Roger, this is a pretty desperate business."

"They are pretty desperate men. I wouldn't like to be that girl."

"Is Christeson going to put that money there?"

"He is going to send the money there at the time indicated. You know it's amazing what a man will do for money. One of Christeson's own guards has volunteered to be the messenger—for a pretty large fee. He's willing to risk his life—willing to risk being gunned to death from ambush—just for a fistful of money."

"And how about the girl?"

"She is to be turned loose tomorrow. They don't say where or when exactly. I suppose that gives them a running start, right out of the country, probably. Christeson is pretty restive about the whole thing. The police keep warning him not to make any false moves until he gets his daughter back. But I'm convinced that, without consulting anybody, he has people out trying to track down these criminals. I just hope to God that they don't realize they're being sought until the deal comes off."

"So now we can only wait?"

"So now we can only wait," Roger agreed.

Connie left the office about four o'clock. When she put the key into the lock of her own door, Tottie's small voice said, "Stantia?"

"Yes. Open up, Tottie."

The door opened and she walked in. Tottie closed the door at once and locked it with both locks before following her.

Tottie came close to her and said, "I've been waiting and waiting."

Connie looked down into her face, turned up to her own. "Tottie, your father has heard from those men who say they have kidnaped you. They have told him to leave the ransom money in a car in a parking lot tonight, he has hired a man to do that—to take the money there and put it in the car. That man's life is going to be in danger—unnecessarily, really, since you could prevent the whole thing."

Tottie continued to look up to her without a real change of expression. "He's getting paid for it, isn't he? Quite a big sum of money."

"Well, yes."

Tottie turned away and said coolly, "I don't see why I should keep him from earning it, if that's what he wants."

Connie, with a sense of defeat, said, "But your father naturally thinks you are in great jeopardy. Really, Tottie—"

Tottie suddenly turned back to her and reaching up placed her fingers on Connie's lips. "I don't want to hear anything more about that. Now, kiss me, Stantia."

Connie obeyed, leaning down to reach her lips. Tottie rested against her and murmured, "Tomorrow is Sunday and you don't have to leave me."

Connie, guiltily conscious of Roger, did not answer. She went into the bedroom to change her things. When she returned to the livingroom she saw that Tottie had found the box of strawberries she had brought and was sitting eating them. Connie, watching her covertly, saw nothing on the pale thin face except the self-absorption of a child. The white, blue-shadowed skin, which had obviously never been tanned by the sun, seemed more transparent now, from a week's confinement in the house. Yet, in a moment, she knew, the vivid blue eyes could be raised to meet hers and she would be pierced by the realization that this was a woman with an infinitely greater capacity than her own for seizing upon the essence of an emotion. How extraordinarily quick and sure Tottie could be, in cutting through the welter of conventional thoughts and phrases behind which she herself sought to shelter. Tottie had a courage there that she lacked. Tottie might be afraid of physical assault. She was so little and so fragile that she knew she had no defense against it. But Tottie confronted by a moral threat was something else entirely.

"What are you looking at me like that for, Stantia?"

"How was I looking at you, Tottie?" Connie parried, flushing.

"As if you'd like to give me a piece of your mind. I haven't done anything bad."

Connie laughed briefly. "I'm just on edge, Tottie. I'm not looking forward to this evening."

She waited for Tottie to upbraid her about Roger. But Tottie, after giving her a long look, turned her attention back to the basket in her hand and chose another strawberry to place in her small mouth.

Chapter Sixteen

The night was still damp, with low white clouds reflecting the glare of city lights, but the rain held off. Now I'm in for it, thought Connie, as she and Roger walked down the drive of his parents' house to his car. Roger said nothing as he held the door open for her and then climbed in behind the wheel. As they left the spacious grounds and turned into the highway that led back to the city from the suburb she realized that he was not taking her to her apartment but to his own.

"Roger, I'd rather go straight home," she said sharply.

He stopped for a traffic light and said while they waited, "I haven't had a chance to talk to you all evening. Did my mother say something to you?"

"Yes. I gather you complained about me to her."

He defended himself instantly. "I didn't complain of you. I told her that you had suddenly got cold feet and that maybe she could say something to you to reassure you."

Her indignation kept Connie silent. Roger went on, "I suppose it isn't unusual for people to get scared at the idea of marriage when they are confronted with it as about to take place." He spoke in a slightly condescending tone. By "they" she knew he meant the irresolute of mind, for whom he had nothing but contempt.

But there was no use being angry and communicating her anger to him. She said, in as reasonable a voice as she could summon, "Roger, I object to your bringing your mother into this. It is something we have to deal with ourselves. Whether I marry you or not is my decision—a decision no one else can make for me, even you."

In spite of her resolve to keep cool, the decided tone of her voice irritated him. He said through his teeth, "You keep talking as if there was something to decide. You're just beating about the bush. I didn't bring my mother into it, as you call it. She just noticed that I was upset about you and thought she could give you some encouragement."

Connie's precarious restraint exploded. "There is something to decide! And I've already told you what I have decided!"

His attention was engaged by the traffic. Then he said, exasperated, "I'd appreciate it if you would wait till we get to my place to discuss this."

Fuming, she kept silent. In a few minutes they reached his street and he manuevered the car into the garage of his apartment building and into its slot. In the lighted garage, walking to the elevator, she saw he was scowling and tried harder to control her own temper. When they reached his apartment he let them in with his latchkey. It was already nearly midnight, she noticed by the clock in the vestibule, and his servant had gone for the night. A tray with bottles and glasses and covered dishes waited on the side table in the library. It all had the look of habitual arrangements and this somehow added to her vexation.

"Will you have a drink?" he inquired, in a half surly tone.

"No, thank you," she replied formally.

He proceeded to pour himself a double scotch, while she sat down in one of the armchairs. He was exaggeratedly elaborate about disposing his drink on the small table beside the other chair and in sitting down and crossing his legs.

Without further preamble he said, "I don't accept what you say about having to decide to marry me. That's all water under the bridge."

For the moment she was too furious to speak and then she wondered if he was deliberately goading her to lose her self-control. When she thought she could speak calmly she said, "Roger, that is not true. We've never actually discussed getting married before this."

He made an impatient gesture. "It's been assumed we'd get married when we got ready to."

Connie almost choked with indignation. "We've never assumed anything of the kind! Tacitly or otherwise! You've reserved your decision all along, to see if it really suited you to marry me! You've been telling yourself all along that you can make up your mind when and if you wanted to! That you are not bound to any woman and that no one could bind you without your express consent!"

He was looking at her now, as if alert to some new facet of her manner. "I don't admit what you say. But I'd say *you* assumed it all along."

She was almost crying with a sense of outrage. "Because I've been to bed with you, you believe that I intended to make you marry me, that you had to be on your guard against me in case *you* changed your mind."

There was an unpleasant smile on his face now. "That's ridiculous. But a woman—at least, the sort of woman I've always thought you are—doesn't live intimately with a man for months without some idea that their relationship is permanent."

She was so upset that she found it impossible to continue to sit quietly in her chair. She sprang up, moved to the other side of the room, with her back to him. In the turmoil of her emotions she was not aware that he also had got up and had followed her, until his voice spoke at her shoulder.

"Connie, I'm sorry I upset you. I couldn't help it. You mean a lot to me."

Instinctively she drew away from him. Trying to preserve objectivity, she thought, it is true. What he says is true. I did think he was the man I was going to marry. That did seem to make it all right for me to live with him.

He went on speaking close to her ear. "Connie, you know we've always assumed that we meant something special to each other. I know perfectly well you don't sleep around. I couldn't go for a woman that did that."

She raised her head to say, "But it is not true that you have always had your mind made up to marry me, Roger. What I don't understand is why you have suddenly decided that we should get married. What has prompted this now? You've not given me any hint lately that there should be a change in our affairs."

The reasonable tone of her question seemed both to surprise and irritate him. He countered with a question of his own. "Why should anything have prompted it? Aside from the fact that I'm tired of waiting."

She turned around to look at him. She was quite sure his decision had been prompted by an undefined feeling that her attention had been diverted from him to someone else. But she decided to say nothing. It was safer to accept his statement.

He went on. "As I said, this is all beating about the bush. What I want you to do now is tell me when. Then we can arrange the details."

The silence between them dragged on for some minutes. Finally she said in a completely composed voice, "Roger, I am not going to marry you." She was not looking at him, but she heard the quick intake of his breath.

In a moment he said, his voice hard and tense, "You can't mean that."

"I do mean it."

His answer was to seize her arms in an iron grip and bring his face close enough that she could feel his breath. "What the devil has got into you?" he demanded through his teeth.

Unable to struggle out of his grip, she said angrily, "Let me go, Roger! I'm going home."

He increased the pressure of his hands and drew her closer to him, so that she was forced to turn her head back to avoid contact with his mouth.

"You're not leaving here until you tell me this is all nonsense."

A surge of despair swept over her and it was only with a super-human effort that she was able to restrain herself from struggling frantically in his grip. She realized, in the fog of her own turmoil, that he was wrought up to a high pitch of excitement and that her efforts to escape him would only carry him beyond the point of control. She forced herself to lie passive in his arms and say pleadingly, "Roger, you mustn't do this. Please let me go. I can't breathe."

Slowly he released his hold, eyeing her all the while with a look of indignation mingled with perplexity. When at last he took his hands away, she walked back to the armchair and sat down, pressing the fingers of one hand against her lips. Roger, taking up his glass and finding it empty, walked over to the tray of bottles and put in more ice and more whiskey. When he came back he said belligerantly,

"I consider that you are treating me very badly. I'm making you a fair offer. It's time we got married. I'm sure you are as aware of this as I am."

"I don't see why you should be so sure of that. I have given you my answer."

Once started the argument ebbed and flowed, sometimes trailing off into ludicrous side issues, sometimes exploding into rancorous personal remarks. To Connie it began to seem as unending as it was soul-consuming. Again and again she declared her intention to return to her own apartment. Each time Roger refused pointblank to allow her to leave or ignored what she said in a new verbal assault.

He switched suddenly from hectoring to cajoling. "Connie, maybe I have been taking you too much for granted. How about beginning again from scratch? I'm willing to make a fresh start. How about it, Connie?"

He leaned over her, his manner both urgent and inviting. Yet in spite of the superficial air of supplication she saw that there was expectation of triumph in his eyes.

She drew back from him. "Roger, I'm not going to marry you and I'm not going to bed with you again."

He straightened up with a flash of anger in his eyes. "What have you got against me, all at once?"

"I haven't anything against you," said Connie and added despairingly, "How can I convince you that it is simply that I don't want to marry you?"

He stared at her hard for a moment. "You wouldn't say that unless there was somebody else. There is, isn't there?"

Connie bit her lip in consternation. "You don't have to leap to that conclusion."

"That's not answering my question," he said, not taking his eyes from her. "Who is it you are involved with?"

Connie flushed with anger and chagrin. "I don't have to account to you."

"God damn it!" he burst out. "Can't you be frank? It is somebody you met while I was in Chicago, isn't it? Who is he?"

Connie, her own temper hardening, said, "It's none of your business. I haven't inquired how you spent your free time in Chicago."

He flew into a rage and they spent the next half hour shouting angrily at each other. At last, when she declared once more that she was going, he did not try to stop her but followed her to the door and down the corridor to the elevator.

"I can get myself home, thank you," she said furiously.

He continued to stand beside her, waiting for the elevator.

"It's two-thirty. It's not safe for you to be out alone. I'll take you home."

Too angry to argue further with him she went with him to the basement garage and got into his car. They rode in silence through the deserted streets. When they reached her apartment building he waited at the curb until the night switchboard operator came and unlocked the door for her to enter.

Chapter Seventeen

She inserted her key in the lock of her own door as quietly as she could. Tottie had turned the second lock and it took her another moment or so to get it open. The livingroom was in darkness except for a low wattage bulb in a small lamp in one corner. She walked softly across to the bedroom door, which stood a little open, and pushed it back. The bedroom was dark except for the reflected glow of the city lights from the window. Tottie must have decided that she was not coming back that night, for she could see by the slight hump in the bed that Tottie was sleeping there.

She moved to the side of the bed and leaned over. She did not think she had made any noise, but some slight sound roused the sleeping girl. The hump in the bed suddenly erupted and a piercing scream shattered the stillness. Connie leaned down and grabbed the girl.

"Tottie! It's just me! I didn't mean to waken you. Oh, Tottie, forgive me for frightening you so!"

Tottie, shaking in terror, clutched at her desperately. Connie reached for the bedside lamp and switched it on. Tottie stared up at her blindly in the sudden light.

"Tottie, Tottie," Connie repeated, in a contrite voice, sitting down beside her and putting her arms around the small, shaking, naked body.

Tottie buried her face in Connie's shoulder and moaned a little.

"I had no idea I would be so late, Tottie."

"Why are you so late?" Tottie demanded, pushing away from her. Anger had taken the place of fright in her eyes.

Connie, conscious now of her own fatigue, felt her heart sink. This was not the Tottie she had been imagining as her refuge from the emotional buffeting of the evening. This was a resentful Tottie, nursing a sense of injury.

"It would take a lot to explain," she said tentatively.

Tottie, having drawn away from her, sat humped over, her knees under her chin, the lamplight falling on the white skin of her bare back and the long fine hair hanging over her shoulders. She rested her chin on her arms and watched with brooding eyes as Connie got up and began to undress.

To fill the silence, Connie said, "In the first place, Roger wanted me to name the date for our wedding."

"Did you give him one?" Tottie asked the question in a coldly hostile voice, lifting her head to look at her.

Connie, holding her dress in her hands preparatory to hanging it up, said, "No. I told him I won't marry him."

"Did he believe you?"

Connie said, with a wry grimace, "I've spent the evening trying to convince him of the fact."

Tottie dropped her head down on her arms again and continued to watch her with a brooding stare. Connie, casting a look at her from time to time, went on undressing. Then, unable to stand the scrutiny longer, she said, "He got his mother to say something to me about it."

"What did you tell her?" Tottie's question was whipped out.

"I told her that I wasn't ready to make up my mind—that right now I don't want to get married."

"Is *that* all you said, that you weren't ready?"

"Tottie, please remember, I've been going with him for more than a year. Everybody—everybody except Roger and I, that is, has taken it for granted that we were going to get married some time."

"Are you sure that he didn't assume that?"

"No. On the contrary, I am sure he didn't think he was committed. Roger never likes to pin himself down to anything ahead of time. Perhaps I did assume that we were going to marry eventually. It seemed the logical thing."

There was short silence. Then Tottie said emphatically, "I don't like it."

"You don't like what?"

"I don't like the idea that you'd even assume you were going to marry him."

"You'd rather I just thought I was sleeping with him for the luxuries he provides—like a call girl?" Connie asked bitterly.

Tottie gave her a resentful look in silence. Connie, standing naked, felt the warm damp wind blowing on her from the open window. Tottie was frowning at her and she turned away and went into the bathroom. When she returned to the bedroom Tottie was sitting as before, in the middle of the bed, her head now buried in her arms, so that her long fair hair hung down over her like a veil. Connie went to the side of the bed and said gently, "Tottie, I've had a dreadful evening."

Tottie raised her head and looked at her. There was a pinched expression around her mouth. "Did you go to bed with him?"

Connie stared at her for a moment. "No. I've told him that that's all over between us. I'm not going to marry him and I'm not sleeping with him any more."

She realized, when she saw Tottie's body relax, how tense the girl had been. Tottie straightened up and moved over so that Connie could get into bed beside her. As she lay down on her back, Tottie turned and hung over her. The ends of the long hair tickled her bare stomach.

"I missed you so much," Tottie murmured, her face close to Connie's. The lamp light shone into Connie's eyes and made them luminous. Tottie went on, "You didn't come and you didn't come. And then I decided you didn't intend to come home—that you'd rather be with him. You made me very unhappy, Stantia."

Connie swallowed and said with a trace of irony, "I had my hands full, Tottie." Suddenly with a sense of overwhelming necessity, she reached up and caught Tottie's head in her hands, "Tottie, do you love me?" she asked urgently.

Tottie relaxed into a little laugh. Without answering she bent down and pressed her lips on Connie's. Then she raised her head again and, propped up on her elbows, gazed down at Connie with a half-mocking smile.

"You silly Stantia," she said softly. "Why didn't you just tell him to go and fly a kite?"

Connie swallowed again. Her throat seemed tight and sore, from fatigue, she supposed. "It amounted to that."

"Well, it took you long enough."

"He would not believe me. He refused to believe me."

"Of course he wouldn't believe it. He is used to thinking you're just waiting round for him—everybody is just waiting round for him. All men think that, as far as women are concerned."

Connie gazed up at her uneasily. "But, Tottie, the trouble is, he wouldn't believe me until he came to the conclusion that I'm interested in somebody else."

Tottie gave a short laugh of derision. "So you are," she said, drily. "Somebody who loves you a good deal more than he ever did."

Connie raised her hand and stroked Tottie's head gently. "Tottie," she said, and was not able to say anything further. Tottie leaned down to kiss her again.

"Go to sleep, Stantia," she commanded, reaching over to switch off the light and settling herself down beside Connie in the dark. Her voice continued to murmur in Connie's ear, "Poor Stantia," and Connie felt soft little kisses on her face and neck and shoulders and Tottie's gentle little fingers probing around her body.

But it was Tottie who dropped off to sleep first. Connie, listening to her light little snore, sought vainly to find surcease from the images and thoughts that insisted on crowding her mind. Over and over again she rehearsed the words, the gestures, the meaning of the glances that she had received through the hours of struggling with Roger. And when she consciously drew her thoughts away from that, her mind sped on to the problem of Tottie, of Tottie's father, of the menace of the men who purported to be Tottie's kidnapers, of the police with their warrant for Tottie's arrest. Underneath it all lay the question of her own life, the upheaval that the last week had brought about. There was no reassurance, no comfort to be found in any of it. And yet, stronger then the dismay and uncertainty she felt, was the conviction that she had abandoned her old way of life, that she could never go back to it.

When sleep finally overtook her it was uneasy and full of strange dreams. Vaguely she became aware that day was breaking. Then all at once she was roused by a loud crash and a flash of light. Sitting up in bed she heard the thunder rolling heavily about. The sultriness of the night before had climaxed in a morning thunderstorm and the air outside the window was white with rain. She jumped out of bed to run and pull down the big window and her feet encountered the damp coolness of the already wet floor. When she returned to the bed Tottie stirred and looked up at her.

"We're having a thunderstorm. Maybe it will be fresher."

She lay down again and then remembered. This was Sunday. She raised her head to look at the bedside clock. Quarter to nine. By this time she was usually on her way back from church.

Tottie said at her elbow, "What is the matter?"

"I've overslept. I've missed communion."

"You didn't go to sleep till after daylight. I didn't intend to wake you up."

"Wake me up! Why, you were asleep before I was."

Tottie nodded. "But I woke up again after you were asleep. Do you want some coffee?" I'll get it."

Tottie got out of bed and padded off to the kitchen as she was, without bothering to find the bathrobe. Connie sank back gratefully on the pillow and was not aware that she had once more lapsed into sleep until she roused to find Tottie standing beside her with a tray on which were two steaming cups. Hastily she cleared a space on the bedside table for Tottie to put the tray down.

Tottie sat down on the edge of the bed with her legs dangling and her back against Connie. She had brought toast with the coffee and munched contentedly. Connie, watching her, thought, how like a child she can be, unselfconscious, concentrated on the moment. And yet—

All at once Tottie turned and looked at her, "What are you thinking about, Stantia?"

"I'm trying not to think," said Connie, aware of the returning clamor of the inner debate from which sleep had rescued her for a short while.

"Not to think?" queried Tottie, drawing her legs up onto the bed and leaning against Connie. Her small body fits so easily against mine, thought Connie. There was a comforting warmth in the touch of Tottie's nakedness that seemed scarcely, at this moment, erotic. It was like a prolonged kiss, the sort of kiss that spoke of loving concern.

"I hate to think of tomorrow in the office," Connie fretted. While she had been with Roger the passions of the moment had absorbed all her attention and undoubtedly all of his. But in the cold light of Monday morning, after ample time for reflection and a reconsideration of everything that had been said, in anger and recrimination—Connie shuddered at the thought of the penalty that she must pay in feelings of guilt, embarrassment, resentment, self-justification. She had always envied those, whom she considered fortunate, who could speak their minds, give free rein to their emotions, without suffering the pangs of remorse afterwards.

Tottie ran her fingers over Connie's face. "Worry, worry, worry," she said, as if chiding a child, "Why do you worry about Monday morning in the office?"

"Things have changed considerably in the last twenty-four hours. It won't be very easy for me to confront Roger in the office after last night."

"Do you have to?"

"I work with him a lot. Especially since I'm involved now in your father's affairs and he is too."

"Will he make trouble for you in the office, Stantia?"

"Roger? Well, I don't know. I don't really think so. Or at least he would not do so deliberately. He makes a very sharp distinction between his personal and his professional life. But he is very resentful. And I'm afraid he will want revenge of some kind, because I have rejected him. And revenge will involve finding out who else it is that I'm interested in. He wants to know what sort of a rival he has. He can't really believe that I would choose anybody in preference to him. He can make my life pretty miserable, Tottie."

Tottie's eyes were fixed on her with a gravely cheerful expression. "Well, then, you'll have to make a complete change. You must get another job."

Connie gave a little sigh. "It's not as simple as that. If I resign from Bryanston and Clay, it would be very difficult to find another connection that is as good. It's a pretty competitive profession, Tottie, and women aren't welcome in it."

A little smile began to form around Tottie's narrow mouth. "Stantia dear, it is hardly the profession for you. You let people bully you. You shouldn't."

"I don't do anything of the sort!" Connie cried, angrily.

"Oh, yes, you do," Tottie insisted equably. "All anybody has to do is to make you think that you're not doing right or that you're being unkind or unjust and you knock yourself out to prove the contrary. You shouldn't rise to that sort of bait, really you shouldn't, Stantia."

"That sounds as if you think that I don't have any guts at all," said Connie bitterly. "I don't think that Roger had that impression last night."

But Tottie went on in the same calm, judicious tone. "It isn't a matter of not having guts. It's a matter of selfconfidence in deciding what you want to do and going ahead and doing it. People get used to expecting you to do what suits them best. You always give in. I know."

Still smiling, Tottie arranged herself comfortably so that she lay between Connie's legs and pillowed her head on Connie's breast.

"I'm not really all that much of a push-over," said Connie, at the same time shifting her own body to accommodate Tottie.

"Well," said Tottie, evenly, "do you want to be some man's wife and play second fiddle to him for the next twenty or thirty or forty years?"

"The question is at the moment academic."

But Tottie insisted. "But did you ever, really, want that? Or did you simply not face the fact?"

"Yes, I faced the fact. I thought what really mattered was whether I loved him enough so that I wouldn't mind all the compromises I'd have to make."

"Compromises he wouldn't even be aware of or if he was, would think were quite justified," Tottie interjected. "Stantia dear, you must not suppress yourself that way. In the end, you know, you'd feel sold—oh, perhaps, years from now, when it would be too late to do anything about it."

Connie was silent with her inner struggle to refute Tottie's statement. Finally she said, "I'm really mixed up. I thought I had it all worked out. But I haven't."

Tottie received her confession without comment. After a while she said, "The answer is that nobody should have to give up like that to anybody else—especially not just because she is a woman."

Connie sighed. "I'm beginning to think it is all impossible."

"What is?"

"Making any sort of success of my life," said Connie humbly.

Tottie said with quick firmness, "That's nonsense. You're just going about it the wrong way. I'll show you."

"You'll show me? What do you mean?"

Tottie raised herself on her elbows in order to look into Connie's face. "Stantia, if you are going to make any compromises for anyone, it's going to be for me. Because I can make some compromises for you. And I will."

Connie did not speak for a while, but gently stroked Tottie's head. At last she said, "I don't know what you have in mind, Tottie, but I do know one thing. If anybody finds out that you've spent the last week here with me, I'll be ruined. Are you really aware of that?"

"The answer to that is that nobody must find out."

Connie gave a mirthless laugh. "I've a feeling somebody is bound to find out. Shall we call it a premonition of disaster?"

Tottie, pushing aside the long hair hanging over her face, said with a slight frown, "You're still upset, Stantia. Nothing is going to happen to us."

"Does that mean you still don't mean to do anything about it?"

"I don't intend to do what you're talking about," said Tottie, settling down again. She took Connie's face between her hands and began to place soft little kisses on her lips and cheeks and eyelids. Gradually Connie set aside all the dire possibilities that seemed to menace. The moment became what it so often did when she was with Tottie—a timeless and untroubled oasis in a frightening world, in which Tottie and she, alone and wishful of nothing beyond themselves, enjoyed the warmth and comfort of each other. Connie's arms encircled Tottie's slight hips and soft little buttocks. For a while there was nothing in the world except Tottie.

It was nearly noon when they finally got out of bed. Connie put on her robe and helped Tottie into her shirt and jeans. Tottie's injured hand had almost healed. Only a wide piece of adhesive tape over the palm remained as a bandage. But she still demanded Connie's attentions with the curiously childish imperiousness that was not really childish at all. Tottie, by instinct or experience, knew well how to subjugate a lover.

Struggling with the balky zipper on the jeans, Connie said impatiently, "Tottie, these things are in tatters. They're not going to hold together much longer."

Tottie giggled and, catching her around the waist, hugged her close.

Chapter Eighteen

The rain had cleared the air and it felt fresh and cool blowing in at the open window. Connie, going into the livingroom, turned on the radio, saying as she did so, "It is almost time for the twelve o'clock news."

She went on into the kitchen to consider the question of a meal. When she returned she found Tottie sitting close to the radio, absorbed in the newscast. Surprised by such attentiveness in the usually indifferent Tottie, she paused to listen.

The newscaster was speaking of a mass murder, an execution murder, he called it. The police, he said, were trying to identify seven people whose bodies had been found in a house in a slum area of the city. Two men and five women suspected by the police of being involved in heroin traffic had been shot in the early hours of the morning. The two men, who were white, had been tied to their chairs, One of them was a young man wearing a sleeveless leather jacket. He had long red hair and a beard. The other was older, blackhaired. The police reported that this was the first such murder, the outgrowth of a war between rival narcotics gangs, to take place locally. It was believed that the two men were involved in peddling drugs to young people adrift from their families. Neighbors had reported that the big, rundown three-storey brick house had been occupied for about a month after standing vacant for many years and that many young men and women had been seen going in and out. In searching the premises the police had found hand guns and instruments used by heroin addicts.

Absorbed in listening, Connie had not noticed Tottie. Now when she turned to speak to her, she saw that Tottie's eyes were wide open and that she was deathly pale.

"Tottie! What is the matter?", she demanded, talking hold of the terrified girl.

"Jasper!" Tottie gasped. "That's Jasper. The other man is the one who said he would kill me and rape me first."

Connie paused to listen again to the newscaster. But he had gone on to talk about the negotiations in Paris with the representatives of the Vietnamese government. She turned back to Tottie, whose head was hanging down now so that her long hair cascaded over her face.

"Tottie," said Connie, brushing it aside and lifting Tottie's chin with her fingers, "what was it the man said at the beginning? I didn't hear all of it."

"He said that the police had been alerted by some people in the neighborhood that there had been some shooting at that house. Stantia, that is the place those men took me to. I told you that Jasper was pushing drugs—that I was sure that that was his reason for being with the group I was with—looking for kids to get them hooked."

She was trembling as she spoke and her speech was jerky. Connie tried to soothe her but Tottie was so nervous that all she could do for several moments was to hold her and await the gradual relaxation of tension.

After a few moments Connie said, "Tottie, if these men are dead—and they are really the ones you say tried to kidnap you—you don't need to be afraid any longer. They can't harm you now."

Tottie did not answer at once but continued to cling to her, shuddering. Then she said, miserably, "I know they can't harm me now, but I've been so frightened, Stantia. It—it—"

She was not able to finish and Connie said comfortingly, "It's the reaction, darling. Now quiet down and be thankful."

"Yes," said Tottie, obediently. "Stantia, I would have died—or gone out of my mind—if either of those men had touched me."

Connie, glimpsing the source of her anguish, said quickly, "Now forget them, Tottie. It was all just a bad dream."

With an added briskness Connie tried to dispel the atmosphere of violence that seemed to have invaded the apartment, by discussing what they would have to eat. By maintaining an air of cheerful fondness, she was able to coax Tottie out of her state of terror. When they had finished eating, they sat together on the sofa, listening to music, carrying on the desultory, intimate sort of conversation that had become their custom. Occasionally, in a moment's silence, worrisome thoughts came up in Connie's mind, doubts about the accuracy of the news report, the fear that after all the murdered men might not be the men from whom Tottie had fled. But she kept these recurrent doubts to herself, unwilling to revive Tottie's distress.

It was after two o'clock that the telephone rang. Surely, thought Connie, this could not be Roger. Her mind cast rapidly over those of her friends who might call her.

But when she lifted the receiver and answered she found that it was Roger. He spoke hurriedly, as if prompted by some event that overrode embarrassment or anger.

"Connie, can you get down to the office right away? We have an unexpected development in the Christeson case. I am down here with Christeson and Greig and Blythe."

"Why, yes, of course. I'll have to dress, Roger. I'll be there as soon as I can."

"All right. Make it as quick as you can," he said and hung up. Connie set the receiver down and stood for a moment staring at the phone. She was roused by Tottie's voice.

"What is it?"

She looked up to see Tottie staring at her with alarm in her eyes. All the tension had leaped up in her again.

"I've got to go down to the office, Tottie," said Connie, as matter-of-factly as she could. "Your father is there, with some of the lawyers."

"Roger. He's there. He called you."

"Yes."

"What for?" Tottie demanded, frowning angrily.

Connie hesitated. "He didn't tell me, really, Tottie. But he said your father is down there with him and two of the partners. Tottie—"

She stopped, uncertain exactly what she wanted to say. Tottie offered no comment and finally she plunged on. "Tottie, this is the time for you to make your whereabouts known to your father. There is nothing more for you to be afraid of. He can help you out of all your difficulties now."

Tottie's grimace was hardly a smile. She replied, in a voice full of scorn, "What do you mean, make my whereabouts known? I thought we agreed just a little while ago that nobody was to know I've spent the week here with you."

"Yes, but you don't have to tell him that. You can tell the truth, that you never were kidnaped, that you've just been hiding because you were afraid of what might happen to you."

"Do you suppose he—and the police—would believe just that? If everybody thinks I've been in the hands of kidnapers for the past week or so, it won't be easy to convince them that I haven't. They'll want to know all the details, especially if they find out that I know something about Jasper and his friend. The police aren't going to be easy about this thing. They'll want to trace the drug possession chain and I'm going to look to them like a link in it."

"Well, you should help them with all the information you can provide."

Tottie made an impatient gesture. "I will, but on my own terms. Stantia, if I show up now, they'll find out in no time at all that I have been here with you the past week. Where will you be then?"

A chill went through Connie and she said nothing.

"You see?" said Tottie, with a note of triumph in her voice. "I don't want you going down to that office."

"Tottie!" Connie exclaimed, in despair. "I've got to go down there!"

Tottie's expression was stubborn. "Why?" she demanded. "Because your darling Roger called you?"

Connie looked into her furious eyes, dismayed. "Tottie, you can't mean that! Not after what I've told you. No, I'm not going down there because of darling Roger. I've got to go down there because it is my professional responsibility to do so. Besides, if I refuse, it will look very suspicious."

Her remonstrance seemed to have no effect on the other girl. The vivid blue eyes were burning with anger. Tottie said in an enraged voice, "How do I know he just doesn't want to get you alone again and has made up this story about my father being there?"

Connie, indignant, rejoined, "Tottie, Roger wouldn't do that. He would not act that way, I assure you. If he wanted to see me again, he would come here. He would think he could see me alone here. Don't you realize that?"

The force of this statement seemed to penetrate Tottie's anger and for a moment she did not answer. Then she said, "I don't see why you have to go there. Call him and tell him you won't go."

Connie took a deep breath and said patiently, "Tottie, I cannot. I must go down there. Besides, don't you realize? This must have something to do with that radio broadcast we heard. The police must have informed your father of something that had to do with the men who were murdered."

Tottie seemed to weigh what she said. "How could they know that those men were Jasper and his friend—that they were the ones who claimed to have kidnaped me?"

Her question baffled Connie. "I don't know," she said, uncertainly. "It just seems to me that there must be some connection."

Tottie pounced on her perplexity. "And so, if they get you down there, you'll give everything away. You'll find yourself telling them all about me. They'll trip you up in any kind of story you tell. You couldn't deceive a child. I know my father. If he's there, he'll get it all out of you in five minutes. And then where will you be with your precious Roger?"

Connie stared at her in silent consternation. Tottie's eyes blazed as she returned the stare. Finally Connie said as calmly as she could,

"Tottie, I object to this. I've got a job to do. Roger has nothing to do with it—except for the fact that he is the lawyer in the firm that I have most to do with professionally. Any personal relationship with him is out, as far as I'm concerned, after last night. You must believe me. You believed me this morning. Why are you acting like this now?"

Tottie turned away from her and buried her face in her arms crossed on her humped up knees. Connie went to her and, dropping down on her knees beside the sofa, put her arm around her.

"Tottie, dear," she murmured into Tottie's ear. "Tottie, I can't bear to have you talk to me like this."

Tottie raised her head a little. She made no attempt to draw away from Connie's embrace. "If you think you've seen the last of Roger," she said bitterly, "I can tell you, you're wrong."

"Well, what does it matter if he tries to see me again? I've told him that as far as I'm concerned our affair is over."

Tottie raised her head the rest of the way in order to turn and look at her. Their faces were on a level and very close. In spite of the clash of wills between them, Connie was aware of a degree of intimacy she had never encountered with anyone. It was like struggling with some suddenly strange, unfamiliar element in herself.

"If you do what I want," said Tottie, uncompromisingly, "you won't go down there."

"Well, I've got to," Connie declared and jumped to her feet. She was all at once aware of the passage of time. She had said she would be at the office in half an hour. "I've got to dress."

She went into the bedroom and, snatching up clothes, hastily dressed. Before she had finished the telephone rang again.

"Connie!" Roger's voice was full of angry indignation. "Where the devil are you? We're waiting for you."

"I'm coming. I'm sorry. I was held up by something. I'll be right down."

"Held up by something!" Suspicion entered into Roger's angry voice. "God damn it, Connie! This is vital!"

"Yes, yes. I'm on my way now. I hope I can get a cab in a hurry."

She hung up and finished fastening her dress. As she frantically transferred keys and money from the spangled pouch she had carried the night before to the leather purse she used for the office, Tottie, watching her, said, "So you are going down there anyway."

Connie gave her a hasty glance. There was a hint of a threat in the blue eyes fixed on her. "Yes, I have to."

She picked up her handbag and paused close to Tottie, who

stood by the door. But Tottie moved away from her with a taunting smile and put her arms behind her back.

"We'll wait till you get back," she said coolly.

Connie, half angry and half chagrined, ran out of the door down the corridor to the elevator. As she entered it she heard Tottie close and lock the door of the apartment.

It seemed to take endless time to find a cab and reach the office. Once inside the outer door of Bryanston and Clay it was apparent where the conference was being held, for the reception room was darkened and silent, while the sound of male voices came from the direction of Roger's office. She walked quickly down to the lighted glass door and opened it. The men seated around Roger's desk all looked up as she entered. Two of them were partners of the firm. The third must be Christeson, a tall muscular man clad in a brown lustrous jacket, his closely cut grey hair setting off his deeply tanned face. She sat down in the chair offered her.

"Mr. Christeson," said Roger, "this is Miss Norton."

Christeson gave her a brilliant smile. "How do you do, Miss Norton? Too bad to make you practice law on Sunday."

She murmured an appropriate response and glanced at Roger. Roger was immaculate in office attire, as if Sunday for him was not a day dedicated to tennis and shorts and gin tonics. He was studying some papers on the desk in front of him. He looked up as if conscious of her eyes on him.

"Connie," he said, "I don't have to remind you that Mr. Christeson has been threatened by some extortionists who claimed to have kidnaped his daughter."

Connie nodded and said nothing. The men all looked at her.

"They've saved us a lot of trouble," said Christeson.

"What do you mean?" Connie asked.

"They've been found," Roger explained. "Or, at least, their bodies. They are both dead."

Connie looked at Christeson. "But what about your daughter?"

"Ah, now," said Christeson, "that is why I told Mr. Wellington to send for you."

Connie looked back at Roger. "You'd better tell me what has happened."

"Well," said Roger, "you recall what I told you about the arrangements that were to be made to pay the ransom—that the money was to be left in a car in an all-night parking lot over on the other side of town and that we had to go along with the kidnapers' demand that the police should not be on the scene."

"Yes, you told me that."

"This was done. Mr. Christeson paid a man to take the money there and place it, in a kit bag, in the car indicated. When the police investigated early this morning, the bag was gone. The kidnapers hadn't said how they were going to return Miss Christeson. We assumed that they would just turn her loose to find her way home."

"And you haven't found her?"

"No. We're pretty worried about her."

"In fact, Connie," said one of the partners, in a kindly tone, "We may be in for an unpleasant surprise. She may be dead, too, you know."

The other partner said, "In fact, she may have been dead before that ransom note was sent. The police think that is a definite possibility."

Connie looked at Christeson. Any distress he might be feeling did not show in his face or manner. Then she glanced around at the other men.

"Early this morning," said Roger, accepting the role of spokesman, "the police were alerted to a shooting over there in a house near that parking lot. They raided the place and found the bodies of five women and two men who had been shot to death. The police call it an execution murder by one set of drug peddlers of another set, the cause being probably revenge for some double-cross transaction involving the proceeds of drug distribution in that area. I'm told that this sort of thing is common enough, though it doesn't always make front page news."

Connie said, warily, "I heard that news story on the radio this morning."

Roger ignored her statement. "Presumably the murderers made off with the drug supply these people had. But they overlooked something—something they did not expect to find there and didn't look for. When the police searched the place they found, in a closet in the room where the bodies of the two men were, the kit bag containing the ransom money that had been left in the car in the parking lot. It hadn't been disturbed. So we surmise that the kidnapers did not have time to examine the money before they were interrupted by their rivals. One of them hid the bag in the closet and then they were both shot."

Connie was unable to speak. So Tottie was right, beyond a shadow of a doubt. She had recognized the description of the men, who must have decided to demand ransom money even though she had escaped from them. They must have gambled on the chance that she would not seek refuge with her father. Or perhaps they thought she would not reveal her whereabouts through fear of the police, fear that the police would arrest her in connection with the post office bombing.

The partner whose name was Blythe said to her, "Buck up, Connie. What's a little violence before breakfast?"

She gave him a weak smile and asked, "Are the police now looking for the girl?"

The men exchanged glances. Blythe said, "The police want to broadcast a description of her. Mr. Christeson objects to this and he has sought our advice. He is afraid of this sort of publicity. There may be others who would seek to profit from Miss Christeson's disappearance. We certainly don't want to jump from the frying pan into the fire."

Christeson nodded in agreement. Roger said, "The police have already circulated her description, under the name of Mary Gilray." He held up a circular. "She is described here as very small, blonde hair, probably wearing blue jeans, sandals and a large black felt hat and black woolen poncho. That is the description given them of the girl who was at the scene of the post office bombing. She has not been seen since. Yet she would hardly pass unnoticed, I should think."

There was a moment's silence. Each man present seemed to be pursuing his own line of thought. Connie asked, "Why do you want me?"

Roger looked up with a frown. "Mr. Christeson wanted you here. He has something he wants to discuss with you."

Christeson was looking at her as Roger spoke. He said, "Miss Norton, I want your help. I disagree with these gentlemen. I don't believe my daughter is dead. I think she has refused to come forward because she won't deal with me." There was a satirical twinkle in his eyes. "Oh, yes, I won't disguise the fact. She and I have had some pretty acrimonious arguments. She's very stubborn and I'm inclined to think that she would refuse to do anything I might suggest, out of contrariness. That's always been her attitude."

He paused and gazed at Connie. Connie, uncomfortable under his scrutiny, looked down at her hands. If only she did not have such a vivid impression that Tottie was standing behind her chair, looking over her shoulder. The tone of Tottie's voice when she spoke of her father—"you can't fault him on his public manner"—the expression on her face—. Connie made an effort and looked up to find Christeson still watching her.

"My idea, Miss Norton," he said, "is to ask you to be a go-between, to see if I can get Charlotte to respond to an appeal to get in touch with you, rather than with me directly."

Connie stared at him in dismay. "But how do you propose to communicate with her, if you have no idea where she is?"

"On the supposition that she's alive—and until her dead body is found, I'll go on the theory that she is alive—I'm having Fairchild, the detective, look for her again. He has been in touch with some of the people she has been associating with recently. I think if he talks to these people, he can get a message transmitted to her. Somebody is sure to pass the information along. We'll just have to hope she acts on it. The message will be that she is to get in touch with you. How about it, Miss Norton?"

Connie said hesitantly, "Why, yes, of course, Mr. Christeson. I cannot refuse to help you. What do you expect me to do if your daughter does get in touch with me?"

"Persuade her to act like a rational human being," Christeson replied readily. His smile grew wider at the sight of her dismay. "You see what confidence I have in the capacities of a woman! These gentlemen here—" he paused and glanced around at the men in the room—"are all competent lawyers, I know, but this is a job that needs a woman's touch."

Connie murmured something, but Roger interrupted, with an edge to his voice, "The first thing to do is to persuade her to come forward and surrender under that warrant. You're standing bail for her, aren't you, Mr. Christeson?"

Christeson nodded again. "Yes, of course. If she gets in touch with you, Miss Norton, you can judge best how to handle her. You don't have to tell her all the details of what may happen, if you think it better not to. She is pretty ignorant about some things. Use your own judgment."

He got up, bringing the conference to an end and inviting the two partners to join him in a drink at his club. Connie found herself alone with Roger.

Chapter Nineteen

"Why should he suppose that the girl would pay any more attention to what I say than she does to him?" Connie's resentment burst out in spite of herself.

"The probability is that his scheme for getting the message to her won't work," Roger assured her. "If she's a dope addict, she won't care how many warrants are out for her or how many people are going to kidnap her. If she isn't, she has a good reason for staying away from the police. But, you know—"

He broke off and sat for a moment deep in thought. Connie waited in silence. Then he said,

"We'll go on the supposition that she is alive. How did she escape from her kidnapers? Are we to suppose that they released her as soon as they got their hands on the money? Did they turn her loose so promptly that she was able to get away from that house before the execution-murder took place? That's pretty remarkable. In fact, I find it unbelievable. The kidnapers would want to give themselves time to get away. They'd want to be well on the way out of the country, I should think, before she would have time to be back in the hands of her family. They didn't indicate, in that ransom note, how or when she would be released. Yet according to the time table we've been given, the money was left in the car about midnight, it was picked up shortly after, and the murder took place so soon after that that the money in the kit bag wasn't even disturbed. And the girl wasn't in the house—she wasn't one of the victims."

Connie felt a little faint. "Don't you think," she hazarded, "that the police must be aware of this? They must have plenty of experience to tell them how these things usually happen."

Roger glanced at her in a preoccupied way. "The point is, where is the girl? Was she being held somewhere else—not at that house? And is she still under restraint somewhere? If so, somebody had better hurry up and find her. She could die of hunger and thirst, you know, if she's tied up where she can't call for help."

Connie overcome by the note of real concern in his voice, blinked back tears. For a moment she wished it was possible to reward his touch of genuine kindness by assuring him that Tottie was safe.

"Though I suppose," Roger's voice broke in on her thoughts, "what is most probable is that her dead body will be found somewhere. They may have killed her even before they sent the letters demanding money. It would be by far the easiest way to handle the possibility that she would get away or would be rescued."

He was chiefly speaking to himself, pursuing the development of his thought with complete absorption. If I didn't know that Tottie was safe in my apartment, thought Connie, he would make my blood run cold. She made a move to get up and leave.

"I don't believe you need me here any longer, Roger. I assume it will be a day or two before we can possibly expect to know if Christeson's plan is going to work."

He lifted his head and gave her a long, dark look. She ignored it and got to her feet and picked up her handbag from his desk. Automatically he stood up also. When she started to walk to the door he stepped quickly around the desk to stand beside her.

"Connie," he said urgently, "I'm coming around to see you as soon as I can shake loose here."

Her expression was a little haughty as she said coldly, "There's no use at all in doing that. I think we have said everything that is to be said last night."

He rejoined angrily, "Some of it shouldn't have been said. You ought to be able to see that now. We can both make allowance for short tempers."

"Roger," said Connie, in a distinct, cool voice, "you must understand that I meant what I said. It is not a question of hasty tempers. I see no point in hashing the matter over once more. You don't owe me any duty of explanation and apology—and, what is harder, I know, for you to grasp—I don't owe you any. We're just ordinary friends—at least, I hope we are friends. I don't want to see you this evening."

His anger flared out. "You do owe me an explanation!" He was almost shouting as he glared at her furiously. "If you're walking out on me because of somebody else, I want to know who it is!"

Connie answered grimly, "What good would that do?"

"Then you admit it. You admit you're involved with somebody else!" The note of triumph in his voice matched the spark in his eyes. "You're infatuated with somebody you picked up while I was in Chicago. Why didn't you admit that in the first place?"

Connie, surprised at her own coolness, said ironically, "If that is what you think, it's a good thing you found out before we got married, isn't it?"

For a moment, he was silent, frowning furiously at her. "I'm beginning to agree with you that marriage is out of the picture." His voice had a spiteful sound, as if he sought revenge.

"I'm glad you see that, then. I can't contemplate marriage with you now. The sooner you accept the fact that I mean what I say, the better it will be for both of us."

He seemed about to lash out at her again, but he closed his mouth abruptly and turned away to shuffle the papers on his desk, obviously careless of what he was doing. Connie waited for a moment, watching to see if he meant to speak again. When he did not turn back to her, she walked quickly to the door and went out without a further word, closing it quietly behind her. To her relief he did not try to follow her to the elevator and she was able to leave the building alone, nodding a goodbye to the guard in the lobby.

Preoccupied, she waited in the empty Sunday street for the bus. No cabs were in sight. Vaguely she was conscious that the afternoon had worn away. It must be long past five o'clock. The bus was almost empty and she sat wrapped in her own thoughts until the sight of the park reminded her that the next stop was hers. As she walked up the street to her apartment building she felt she had reached a firm decision and that she must not allow any objections and persuasions of Tottie's to deflect her from the course she must take. Even Tottie must realize now that the time had certainly come for her to get in touch with her father. How she was to do so was something they would have to decide upon together. In some way Tottie must let her father know that she was safe, that she had never been in the hands of the supposed kidnapers. And—by all means—she must do this without letting anyone know that she had spent the past week in the apartment of Constantia Elizabeth Norton, an associate in the law firm of Bryanston and Clay. A feeling of disaster, like a shower of cold water, overtook Connie as she considered this last requirement. How? The question hung in her mind as she went up in the elevator and walked down the hall to her own door and inserted the key.

The reflected light of the late afternoon sun flooded the living-room, leaving only the corners in half-shadow. The room was empty. Connie dropped her handbag on the table and called, "Tottie!", gazing at the open bedroom door as she did so.

Before she heard a sound, Tottie appeared in the doorway. She wore her jeans and the white shirt, which was unbuttoned, with the tails hanging outside. Her hair was hanging over her face. She has been asleep, thought Connie, meeting the gaze of the still drowsy blue eyes.

"It's a good thing I didn't bring anyone with me, sleepy head," said Connie, with a nervous little laugh.

Tottie looked at her for a moment without speaking and then said, with sleepy seriousness, "You'd have made more noise if you had brought someone with you."

Connie, watching her to judge her mood, said tentatively, "I think I had better tell you what has been happening, Tottie."

Tottie made no effort to come to her but instead walked over to the armchair and sat down in it with her feet drawn up under her. Her shirt hung open and showed the ampleness of her breasts, so voluptuous on the meager little body. Connie longed to go to her and kiss her, on her lips, her cheeks, her breasts, but a second glance at the brooding, half-awake face deterred her.

"Was he there?" Tottie demanded suddenly.

"Your father? Yes, he was there. Tottie, you must listen to me carefully. You remember the story on the radio this morning— about those men who were shot to death?"

Tottie gazed at her through several strands of hair. She nodded.

"There is no doubt that they were the men you were hiding from. I told you that your father had arranged to leave the ransom money in a place for them to pick up. Well, the police found that money in the house where they found the murdered people. It was in the bag in which it was delivered, in a closet in the room where the men's bodies were found."

After a few moments Tottie answered, "Then Daddy's got his money back."

The contemptuous tone of her voice startled Connie. "Yes, but, Tottie, there is something more serious. Nobody knows where you are—whether you are alive or dead."

"And you didn't tell them?" The cool disdain in Tottie's voice threw Connie even further into dismayed confusion.

"No, I did not," she replied, indignantly, and then added crossly, "Though, as a matter of fact, if I'd had any sense, I should have."

"So you could lead the police here to come and take me off to prison," Tottie declared, melodramatically.

Connie said, "Oh, Tottie!", impatiently, and going over to the end of the sofa nearest the chair, sat down and leaned towards her. "All you have to do is get in touch with your father. He will arrange for you to give yourself up under the warrant that is out for you, he'll post bail for you and a hearing will be set to determine whether you really can be held as a material witness in the post office bombing. You've told me over and over again that you had nothing to do with that. If you convince the judge of that fact, you're free."

"If I convince anybody!"

"You'll have the best legal assistance—and the weight of your father's influence. Tottie, I don't see any alternative."

Tottie did not answer and Connie went on, "Tottie, I am really frightened that you will be traced here. If that happens, you will have to answer the summons anyway—and I—Tottie, it will be the end of my career. I couldn't possibly claim that I did not know I was harboring a fugitive from justice."

Tottie's small voice said quietly, "I see," and Connie glanced up to meet her eyes fixed on her in sober reflection.

"You've known that all along," Connie burst out, anxiety and chagrin at having to plead her own cause making her angry. "Now we have no choice."

"What did my father say he was going to do now?"

"His idea is to have Fairchild—the detective who has been trying to trace you—get in touch with some people who know you, so that they can transmit a message to you. He believes that the reason you did not answer his appeal on the radio and television was that you're angry and stubborn and did not want to talk to him. Now this message is to tell you to get in touch with me."

"With you!" cried Tottie, tossing her hair aside to stare at Connie with wide, alarmed eyes.

"Yes. With me, as a female member of the law firm, so that I can reassure you about dealing with him and with the police. He thinks you will not feel so hostile towards me. Tottie, we can use this scheme to solve our problem. In a day or so, to give Fairchild a chance to get in touch with some of the people you've been known to have associated with, you could get in touch with me at my office and we could carry on from there."

She gazed hopefully at Tottie as she spoke, trying to judge from Tottie's expression whether she was making any headway. But Tottie's face showed only absorption in her own thoughts.

"Tottie, you know, everybody really thinks you are dead—that they are looking for your dead body. Except your father. Tottie, if I weren't here looking at you, I would be pretty worried myself." Connie's voice faltered.

Tottie gave her a bland glance. "That's what Daddy really wants to know—whether I'm going to be around to get my share of the Christeson millions."

"Tottie, do give him the benefit of the doubt. I think he must feel some real concern for you."

Tottie smiled at her and Connie was once more astonished at the abrupt change of mood that so readily appeared in her face. Tottie was not now the fearful, clinging child she had so often seen in the course of the last week. She was instead a woman with a more sophisticated experience than her own.

"Dear Stantia, you must believe the best of everyone, mustn't you? Even Roger."

"Well," said Connie, warned by her voice of trouble ahead, "Roger is worried about you also. He's upset because he thinks you may be tied up or imprisoned somewhere, helpless, and that you may not be able to call for help and that you may die before you can be found."

"Kind of him!" Tottie exclaimed in an angry voice. "Why were you discussing me with him?"

"I wasn't discussing you with him. I was alone with him for a few minutes after the others left. He was threatening to come here to see me and I told him it wasn't any use. I told him I didn't want to talk to him."

"Coming here? When?" Tottie fired the questions at her peremptorily.

"I suppose he could come at any time. But I don't think he will. I think he is thoroughly angry with me now. I think he is ready to write me off."

A certain regretfulness sounded in her voice, even in her own ears. For days now, it seemed to her, she had been telling herself that any blame for the rupture between herself and Roger was to be shared between them, that he had always demanded too much of her, that if their positions had been reversed, he would not have reproached himself for having broken with her, that there had never been a real, unequivocal commitment between them. Nevertheless, a sense of guilt flourished under her self-assurance. Roger had succeeded in making her feel that she was wholly to blame, that she had inflicted a deep and lasting wound. She told herself that this was not true, that he suffered now from a sense of injury to his self-esteem more than anything else. Roger was not used to being rejected. To soothe his humiliation it was necessary for him to make her suffer the blame. It would not take him long to recover.

Absorbed in this reverie she was surprised to discover that Tottie had got up from her chair. She stood in front of her, just out of reach, the tattered jeans, insecurely fastened at the waist, lying over her bare feet, the ragged shirt hanging loosely open. The vivid blue eyes were alight with an angry glow.

"So you're mourning over your darling Roger," she said, contemptuously. "You want to be cosily back tagging at his heels, happy when he throws you a bone."

Connie turned white with rage and chagrin. "That's not true! You must not say things like that to me."

Tottie said with casual insolence, "Mustn't I? Well, you're welcome to him."

She turned away and with a stiff-legged dignity that overcame her tatterdemalion appearance she walked over to the door of the bedroom and disappeared.

Connie, overcome with wretchedness, buried her face in her hands. She struggled to suppress the tears but a few overflowed and rolled down her cheeks. What a whimpering fool she was, she told herself. Of course, she was overwrought and it was no wonder that Tottie was on edge, her uncertainties ready to come to the surface in such a silly thing as jealousy of Roger. But though she strove to argue her way back to calmness, the underlying strain would not dissipate. She longed to follow Tottie into the bedroom, to kiss her, to fondle her, to gain the reassurance of the small, eager body pressing against her own. But there was no use going after Tottie until she could control her own quivering nerves.

A slight sound penetrated her self-absorption. She looked up, to see Tottie standing in the middle of the room. But it was a Tottie she scarcely recognized. In place of the ragged jeans and white whirt, Tottie wore the pantsuit she had bought early in the week. Tottie's hair was brushed back from her face and her feet were shod in the soft shoes Connie had given her.

"I'm leaving," said Tottie, in a tight voice.

"Leaving?"

Tottie gave her a hard look and with a swiftness that left Connie helpless, walked to the front door, opened it and ran out.

Connie leaped to her feet and ran after her. She was in time to see her disappear through the door that led to the stairway. Racing after her, she called "Tottie! Tottie!", but the only answer she got was the slight sound of Tottie's softly shod feet running down the stairs below her and the muted sound of the elevator moving in its well beyond the wall. Then she heard a door open and close and realized that Tottie, hearing the elevator stop on the floor she had reached, had left the stairs and gone to catch it.

When Connie reached the lobby, there was no sign of Tottie. The Sunday switchboard operator, a wizened, crippled man, looked up from the magazine he was reading to watch her run past the counter. Out on the sidewalk she looked wildly about, in time to see Tottie's small figure running fleetly down toward the end of the block. Connie burst into a run, calling frantically, "Tottie! Tottie!". But the small figure with the flying hair disappeared around the corner of the building. When Connie reached the corner she was nowhere in sight. In a sort of frenzy of despair, Connie dashed up that block and then up and down all the neighboring streets, till, aware of the curious, unfriendly glances of the few passersby on the empty Sunday streets, she gave up and went slowly back to her apartment building.

"Something the matter, miss?" asked the crippled man at the switchboard, as she came back into the lobby.

She answered him with a shake of her head and went mutely back up in the elevator. The door to her apartment stood wide open as she had left it. She felt numb with bewilderment and nervous fatigue. Why? she thought helplessly. Why had Tottie run away? And where had she gone? The thought of Tottie again on her own alone in the world began to harass her. Where could she look for her? Tottie had run away in a sort of abandon, as if she herself had no clear idea where she was going. And she did not even have any money with her, unless she had picked up a few of the coins that Connie had the habit of leaving about on the tables or the top of the chest of drawers in the bedroom or the counter in the kitchen.

She dropped into the armchair in the livingroom, trying to convince herself that Tottie would come back, that this was one of those sudden storms of wilfulness that Tottie displayed, that when the dark came Tottie would grow frightened and come back to her. The room became dusky as the light of the sky beyond the windows grew first pink and then violet. The sun had long since set but the lingering brightness of the midsummer evening hid the fact that night was coming. Connie sat on in the armchair, without the will to get up and turn on the lamp. She tried to discipline herself not to listen for the sound of the elevator, for a tap on the door, but her anxious ears betrayed her each time one of her fellow tenants went in or out.

In the end it was the telephone that broke her vigil. Its ring seemed to shatter the quiet of the room like the clang of an alarm bell. She jumped up to answer it, her heart beating wildly. The voice that replied to her Hello was that of the man at the switchboard downstairs. Mr. Wellington was there. Was he to come up?

Connie said Yes, and putting down the phone, went quickly about the apartment, turning on the lights she usually had on in the evening. When Roger touched the door chime she opened the door at once and stepped back to let him in. He was hatless and empty-handed.

He paused as he entered, but noting that she stepped back, made no effort to approach her. She walked back to the chair and sat down. He followed and sat down opposite her.

She broke the silence by asking, "Would you like a drink, Roger?"

He said Yes and she got up and went to the kitchen for a glass. When she returned and placed the drink on the small table beside him, he asked sharply, "Aren't you having one?"

"Not now." She was aware that he was scrutinizing her and that her face probably showed traces of the anguish of the last hour or so. But she did not look at him. She sat down again.

Roger took a long swallow of his drink and said, "Connie, when are you going to come out of this?"

"Come out of what?"

"You know what I'm talking about."

"If you mean what we were talking about this afternoon and last night, there is nothing for me to 'come out of'. I've told you there is no point to further discussion."

He was silent for a moment, staring at her. Then he said, "I'm giving you one more chance. If you don't take it, we're really finished."

She did not flinch from his stare. "I have told you that I don't intend to marry you. Since I don't, our relationship is changed. From now on, we're just—acquaintances, if you want it that way."

"You're not going to get off that easy," he shot back. "I'm going to find out who you are involved with."

"It's none of your business whether or not I'm involved with anyone, as you call it." she answered, aware that she had flushed deeply and that he was noting the fact with avid interest.

He took another long swallow of his drink, half emptying the glass, before he said, with an unpleasant smile, "I'm just curious. Just curious to see who you are two-timing me with."

Connie struggling to control her temper, said, "There is no reason why I should put up with this, Roger."

His anger flared out and he got to his feet. "I'm going to find out. And I'm going to start by searching this apartment. You've been keeping me away, haven't you? You haven't wanted me to come here, have you? Well, I'm going to have a look."

With a sense of angry helplessness, she watched as he stalked to the bedroom door and passed out of her sight. She heard him rummaging about, slamming doors and cursing. Finally she felt compelled to get up and go and watch him from the doorway. He stared into the bathroom and ransacked the closet. When he had satisfied himself, he pushed past her to go to the kitchen and stood gazing angrily about the small space. She was aware then that Tottie had carefully straightened up the apartment while she had been gone in the afternoon. Tottie must have made the bed and washed up all the cups and glasses and plates they had used. Yet there was an indefinable air about the place of occupancy by two people. This, Connie realized, was what was baffling Roger.

Finally he came to the closet in the livingroom which she used for coats and outdoor wraps. When he flung open the door, her eye immediately lighted on Tottie's black felt hat and poncho and she felt her breath stop for a moment. But Roger's eye passed over them only cursorily. He had never seen them before, of course, and the police description of the girl Mary Gilray had apparently not fixed itself in his mind. Or perhaps he was too angry really to take in what he saw. The hat and the poncho hung there crowded by coats and jackets of her own. He shut the closet door with an impatient shove and turned to glare at her without speaking.

Connie, white with rage, said through gritted teeth, "Will you get out of here?"

He did not answer her but walked by her to the front door. When he opened it he paused to turn and give her one more furious glance. Then he went out, slamming the door behind him.

Chapter Twenty

Connie, suddenly weak and shaking, found her way to the bedroom. For a moment or so she stood and stared about the empty room, seeking Tottie or even some unmistakeable reminder of her. But there was no sign that Tottie had ever been there. She went to the open closet, drawn by the sight of the clothes hamper behind which Tottie had hidden the first night Roger had been expected. Without conscious thought she raised the lid. Inside, on top of the soiled towels and sheets, lay the ragged jeans and the white shirt. With a half audible cry, she snatched them up and hugged them to her. She was suddenly, certainly, aware that Tottie was not coming back, that Tottie was really gone.

She made her way blindly to the bed and threw herself on it, clutching Tottie's cast-offs tightly to her. She burst into the sobs she had been holding back for what seemed to her now an interminable time. They were uncontrollable now and she lost track of time and place. Only the void where Tottie had been was real, only the remembered sight and feel of Tottie had meaning.

Sometime near daybreak she fell into a troubled, exhausted sleep. She awakened to the taste of catastrophe still in her mouth, as the brightening sky beyond the uncurtained window began to light the room. She sat up and looked dully around. She had slept in her clothes and now, conscious of them, felt uncomfortable and constrained. She got up and undressed, throwing her clothes down on a chair with the feeling that she was divesting herself of the remnants of yesterday's conflicts. The shower revived her somewhat and the coffee she drank helped to clear some of the heaviness from her head. The same semi-dreamlike state stayed with her as she left for work, on the bus and into the office. The books and papers piled on her desk gave her a sense of refuge and she worked doggedly for a while, glad to have something outside herself to focus her attention on.

But within an hour she found herself once more off on the endless recapitulation of Tottie, Tottie's arrival in her life, Tottie's sojourn with her, Tottie's departure. She was amazed, in a moment of sharper awareness, of the minute details that were stored away in her memory, the clarity with which she remembered a phrase, a nuance of voice, a turn of the head, a glint in the eye. She spent the morning, then the afternoon, with a sandwich eaten inattentively at her desk, in a running battle with herself, striving to concentrate on the professional problems before her, having constantly to bring her wandering thoughts back to the tasks ahead of her.

She returned to her apartment in the same haze of preoccupation in which she had left in the morning. When she let herself into the livingroom she stood for a moment warding off the desolating feeling of emptiness that assailed her. There was no Tottie to call to, no Tottie to appear in the bedroom doorway, no Tottie whose moods and whims were to be guessed at and humored.

She sat for a long time in the big armchair, while the evening faded, before troubling to go into the kitchen and find something to eat, something that required no preparation and which she ate without savor. Once or twice it occurred to her to pour herself a drink of whiskey. Perhaps it would dull the ache of loneliness, but as soon as she was confronted with the whiskey bottle the remembrance of Tottie's disapproval rose before her and she put the bottle back on the shelf. It somehow comforted her to pursue as closely as possible the little habits and ways of doing things that had become her own and Tottie's. While Tottie had been with her they had lived every moment in company, truly in communion. There had been no blank spaces, no reserved corners. She had without conscious effort blithely laid bare her own every impulse and Tottie had seemed to have no shadowed niches. Oh, Tottie, Tottie! she cried silently, with a furious ache in her heart that surpassed any physical pain she had ever felt. Oh, Tottie! she cried to herself, where are you?

When she could stand her own brooding no longer, she put some records on the music-player and tried to drown out the sound of her own thoughts. But she soon realized that she had unconsciously chosen things that she and Tottie had listened to together and the patterns of the music became interwoven in her mind with the changes that Tottie had wrought in her life. She was no longer the woman she had been before Tottie had appeared at her door. Part of her had amalgamated with Tottie and the process was irreversible, even if she never saw Tottie again.

Whenever she reached this point in her reverie—whether she

would ever see Tottie again—her mind veered away and finally
she realized that this was something she could not contemplate.
It was impossible that she should never see Tottie again. Tottie
must come back into her life somehow. This running away was
just one of the inexplicable bits of behavior that were so much
a part of Tottie. It was this thought that enabled her at last to
fall asleep that night.

The next day, Tuesday, when she awoke and her mind went
back to that thought, she was assailed by a cold feeling that this
was by no means necessarily so. She hurried to dress and go down
to her office, in an effort not to dwell on the idea. Realizing that
she had forgotten to turn on the radio and listen to the news,
she bought a paper. She sat down at her desk and spread it open
before her. Her eye at once lit on the story in the right hand corner
of the first page. H.B. Christeson's Daughter Charged in Bombing
Attack, said the headlines. She read down the statement quickly.
The girl who had been sought by the police as a material witness
in the bombing of a United States post office ten days ago, had
surrendered and proved to be Charlotte Mary Gilray Christeson,
the daughter of the multimillionaire, H.B. Christeson. She had
been released on forty thousand dollars bail, which her father
had posted, and a hearing had been set for the following Tuesday.
If sufficient evidence was brought in then to support the more
serious charge, she would be held as an accomplice in the crime.
The account went on to describe her associations with various
youth groups who had staged protests and sit-ins in several cities
and mentioned that she was known as a writer of protest songs
under the name of Mary Gilray. It ended by stating that her
present whereabouts were unknown and that her father's lawyers
declined to make any statements regarding her. H.B. Christeson
himself was unavailable for comment.

Connie read the statement through the first time in a rush,
tripping over herself to get the whole of its import. Then with
a sigh of relief she read it two or three times again, lingering on
the details, as questions and doubts crowded into her mind. Tottie
had indeed gone to her father for help. Tottie, either on her own
initiative or under persuasion, had surrendered to the police. But
why had she done it just this way? No matter how hairbrained
and outwardly irrational her behavior might be, there always
seemed to be some very logical basis for Tottie's actions, there
was always some underlying motive that made sense to Tottie
herself. She had been angry when she had run out of the apartment. She had obviously been in a jealous rage. But what else

had come up, what other impulse had governed her once she was out of the shelter of that refuge?

Tottie's quick mind must have seized on some other idea and with her usual impetuosity she had acted on it. Connie read through the newspaper story once more. There was no clue in it to what Tottie might be doing in the week that was to intervene before the hearing. This latest development must surely be known to Roger and the partners of Bryanston and Clay. They must be the lawyers referred to. Yet Roger had not called her in to tell her about it. Late Sunday night or early Monday morning the lawyers of Bryanston and Clay must have been informed of what had happened. This was Tuesday morning and she had been left to find out through the public news.

Connie waited, uneasily expectant, all the rest of the day for a summons either from Roger or from one of the partners. But when the end of the day came and she had heard nothing from anyone, she was forced to face the fact that, without a formal statement from anyone, she had been dropped from the Christeson case. She went home to a disturbed evening of conjecturing, over and over again, what Tottie had told her father, what Roger had learned, what Christeson proposed to do on the basis of Tottie's statements. And where was Tottie?

The following day, Wednesday, she remembered, during the morning, that she would be expected to appear at the women lawyers' lunch. Hastily she told her secretary that she needed to spend several hours in research in the local bar association library and escaped before anyone could stop her.

"I must be getting neurotic," she muttered to herself, as she left the office almost at a run. But it seemed to her that the full details of her private affairs must now be known to everyone in Bryanston and Clay. She shrank from the thought that each group within the office must be discussing her, must be commenting on the sudden cooling of her relationship with Roger, on the fact that she was no longer active in the Christeson case. None of these details, she reminded herself, were necessarily known to anyone except Roger and the partners advising Christeson. But she was unable to reassure herself. It was a relief to escape to different surroundings where she would have a better chance to concentrate her attention on professional problems.

As each day came around she listened eagerly to the radio news as she dressed and breakfasted. Each morning, on the way to the office, she bought and read the newspaper. Each evening she listened again to the radio. But there was no further reference to the post office bombing or to those under arrest for it. Nor any reference to the Christesons.

Friday morning she awoke from a brief, troubled sleep to a feeling of exhaustion. The daily struggle to regain her equilibrium, to return to the sober, even, predictable pace of her life prior to Tottie's advent, was depleting her nervous energy. She thought with a sort of despair of the day stretching before her. She drank several cups of coffee and made an extra effort to return the office receptionist's good morning with an air of cheerfulness. By now she was convinced that rumors of her breach with Roger had spread throughout the office and were a favored topic of discussion. She stuck to her own room, hopeful that no one would seek some plausible excuse to drop in and chat, in the hope of gleaning inside information.

What she feared came to pass before the morning was over. Her door opened after a sharp knock, as Dorothy Sloan came in without waiting for her response.

"Hi, Connie. You've been living the life of a hermit these days. Where were you Wednesday?"

Connie did not look at her as she said, "I've been over in the bar association library, researching that Connally case. I don't know any way to do a job like this without living the life of a hermit."

She was aware that the other woman was scrutinizing her and she was determined not to acknowledge the scrutiny. For a moment there was silence and then Dorothy came over and stood close to her, her back against the desk, and crossed her arms. Connie saw only her legs below the short skirt and the glossy, square-toed shoes on her feet.

Dorothy demanded, "How do you stand with this Christeson business?"

"How do I stand? What do you mean?"

"I mean, do you know what is going on?"

Connie did not answer. Dorothy said, "I'm sorry, Connie. I suspected that you were being sidetracked out of the case."

Connie, chagrined, said, "Would you like to let me know what is happening?"

"You know what happened last weekend?"

"I know what the news stories said," said Connie, defensively.

"Really? Is that all? Well, last Sunday night Christeson's daughter turned up at his house. He called Tony Greig right away and they had a midnight conference—Christeson and his daughter and Tony and Roger. Next morning, early, I had a call from Tony

Greig. He said I was to meet him here in the office at eight o'clock. I said why such a godawful hour—I'm never awake then. He said he would explain when I got here. Well, I managed to get out of bed and down here by eight-thirty. They were all three walking the floor—Tony and Ralph Blythe and Roger. It seemed that they had reported to the police that Charlotte Christeson—whom, of course, the police had been hunting under the name of Mary Gilray—had been found and that she was prepared to surrender under the warrant. She was due to appear before Judge Hollaran at nine o'clock. Well, we all got there. I went with Tony and Ralph, of course, and the Christeson girl showed up with her father and Roger. I certainly got a shock when I saw her. She looks like a child. She was charged as a material witness and released in $40,000 bail. Her hearing is set for next Tuesday."

She paused and eyed the silent Connie closely. "I was expecting you to be there, Connie. When you didn't show up, I smelled a rat. I asked Tony whether you were sick. He said No. He said Christeson wanted a woman there with his daughter and Roger said I was to be called. Tony wouldn't say anything further."

Connie asked anxiously, "How did she seem?"

Surprised at her question, Dorothy said, "Charlotte Christeson? She's certainly an odd ball. She is very small. I said she looks like a child at first glance, but when you look again, you can see she is a woman. I certainly wonder what goes on in her mind. She played up to Hollaran. He was quite easy with her. And of course everybody else's attention was fixed on her."

"Was she frightened?"

The anxiety in her voice and the tenseness of her manner caused Dorothy to pause and look at her curiously. "It's hard to say. You'd think that someone like that, who is not used to police and judges, would be. Most of the time she didn't seem to be paying attention to what was going on around her. More than once she had to be asked the same question twice. I thought she probably was scared. But then she'd say something that showed she had not only heard everything but was 'way ahead of everybody in considering what came next. I suppose she could be on drugs."

"She is not on drugs," Connie said flatly, before she could stop herself.

Dorothy looked at her long and hard. "Well, I don't see how you can be so positive about that. But if that is the case,—You know where she is now, don't you? In the Careybrook Sanitarium, which caters to alcoholics and drug addicts with pots of money.

I'm told she committed herself there. Now, Connie, that's the place where her mother committed suicide. You know about that, don't you?"

Connie nodded dumbly.

"Of course, she might be an alcoholic. Her mother was."

"She is not," said Connie, as firmly as before.

Dorothy, still looking at her, said, "You seem to be very well informed about her personal habits. No, I agree with you. I wouldn't say she was an alcoholic."

"What about the hearing next Tuesday? If she is in the sanatorium, is she to appear?"

"Yes, that's evidently understood. I'm supposed to be there. Connie, I mean it when I say that I don't like being substituted for you in this case. There is no reason for the switch—except—"

Connie interrupted her. "You said it was Roger's idea."

"Yes, that is what Tony Greig said. But if that is the reason, I like it even less. It means that Roger does not want to work with you any more." She hesitated for a while and then said, "Connie, something has happened between you and Roger."

Connie looked up into her face. She was surprised to find sympathy in the sharp green eyes fixed on her. "What makes you think so?"

"Well, my dear, it's one of those things. Everybody in the firm has noticed that you and Roger aren't lovebirds any more. At least, you don't linger at the end of the day until he's ready to leave. You aren't summoned to his office at least once a day. When such wellknown habits are dropped from one day to another, people talk. What's up between you? This isn't idle curiosity, Connie. It's genuine, wellmeant concern."

Connie found nothing to say.

Dorothy smiled ironically. "You know, Connie, most people assume that you're the loser in this situation—that Roger has everything and that by breaking with him you're saying goodbye to a lot—including professional advancement here in the firm. *I* say that he's thoroughly spoiled and that if you're not ready to be a doormat, you're going to have a difficult husband. Not that it's any of my business."

Connie said slowly, "I think too much has been assumed about Roger and me. I've just come to some conclusions—in good time."

"He's not going to take it very well. But, Connie, you can't go through life dying of mortal wounds every time you break with a man."

Connie nodded absentmindedly. Her thoughts had already reverted to Tottie. She asked, "What did she say about the kidnapers?"

Dorothy, astonished, said, "She? Oh, you mean the Christeson girl. You know what? She claims she was never kidnaped—that the presumed kidnapers never had her in their hands. They must have been bluffing right along. But they must also have known something about her, because they knew that her father didn't know where she was, nor anybody else, for that matter. They must have been pretty sure she wasn't going to show up in the parental home."

"Where does she say she was?" Connie asked anxiously.

"That is something else she is not really explaining. I don't know why you're so categorical when you say she isn't on drugs, but there really isn't any other explanation for the way she has been acting. I do wonder how much credence we can put in anything she says. I suppose it is possible that she doesn't have a very clear recollection where she was. She is very disconnected in the way she talks. Half the time she is wandering off about things that don't have anything to do with the matter at hand. And sometimes she won't answer questions, just won't talk. Christeson gets very exasperated with her. They certainly don't get along."

"So I understand," Connie murmured. Clever, clever Tottie. Aloud she asked, "How was she dressed?"

"She had on a miniskirt, a long-sleeved blouse, and her hair was caught back on her head with a ribbon—it is a real corn-silk color. She looked just like a ten-year-old, a small one, at that. But when you get a good look at her face you see it's not a child's face at all—all hollows and blue shadows. How old is she?"

"Twenty-five," said Connie, with a little inner quiver at the memory stirred by Dorothy's description.

Dorothy moved away from the desk and looked at her watch. "How about lunch, Connie? It's twelve-thirty."

At Dorothy's suggestion they went to a restaurant farther afield than was usual for most of the members of the firm. It was a little more expensive and it catered to more leisurely lunchers in a luxurious, dimly lit atmosphere. Connie realized that it was Dorothy's intent to distract her from her woes and she strove to respond cheerfully to Dorothy's running commentary on people and events, voiced in Dorothy's usual, softly barbed manner.

But in spite of her efforts, Connie's mind strayed at each momentary pause in the conversation to Tottie and the problem of

Tottie. Each time she missed the point of some remark of Dorothy's she tried to cover up the lapse but she was uneasily aware that Dorothy noticed her lack of attention. Toward the end of the lunch Dorothy said abruptly,

"Connie, you're more upset than I thought you were. If you are so unhappy about breaking up with Roger, what are the chances of patching it up?"

"None."

"That sounds pretty final."

"It *is* final," said Connie flatly.

Dorothy persisted. "But if that's so, why so unhappy?"

Under her compulsion to be truthful, Connie answered, "I'm not so upset about Roger. I'm sorry he isn't taking it better, but that's not my problem."

"What is your problem?" Dorothy demanded boldly.

Connie was silent and after a while Dorothy said, in a softly insinuating voice, "Don't tell me it's you who have thrown Roger over for somebody else!"

Half-angry, Connie said, "I haven't said so."

Dorothy smiled, a satirical gleam in her eyes. "So you've shown Roger the door. No wonder he is sore. It can't have happened to him before. And who is his successor?"

"Does there have to be one?"

Dorothy looked at her speculatively. "Under these circumstances, I'd say Yes. Who is it, Connie?"

After a moment's silence, Connie said, smiling mechanically, "Sorry, Dot. I can't enlighten you."

During the rest of lunch she parried Dorothy's probing questions, making a game out of it in self-defense. Back at the office, as they took leave of each other, she said quickly, "Let me know, won't you, Dot, about the outcome of the hearing, as soon as possible?"

The note of anxiety which she had not been able to keep out of her voice caught Dorothy's ear. "You're really very much concerned about that girl, aren't you? Right. I'll let you know as soon as I do."

Chapter Twenty-One

Connie returned to her own office eager for solitude. The greatest relief was to know where Tottie was. Only now did Connie admit to herself the fears that had lain just beneath the surface of her mind and that had given her such vivid, horrifying dreams — Tottie wandering about, unsheltered at night, prey to the sort of unscrupulous characters she had always dreaded. So Tottie was at least safe.

Connie sat and thought with intense concentration, ignoring the work on her desk. Chiefly she tried to see Tottie through Dorothy's eyes. Perhaps if she could do this, she could come to some understanding of her own frame of mind, be able to distinguish between the Tottie who had somehow fixed herself in the center of Connie's universe and the Tottie who must exist independently. Dorothy's main impression had been of an erratic girl, unreliable and unpredictable, perhaps from the effects of drug-taking.

Connie turned the idea over and over in her mind. No, it was not possible. If Tottie took drugs by injection, her arms and legs would show the scars of needle punctures. There came vividly before Connie's inner eye the vision of the white, tender skin on Tottie's small body, unmarked and unblemished except for the gashes in her injured hand and the fading bruises on her thigh and buttock. And if Tottie smoked drugs in cigarettes, there would have been ashes and butts to be disposed of and a telltale scent in the air. But Tottie did not smoke and the few times Connie had lighted a cigarette, she had wrinkled up her nose and had taken the cigarette out of Connie's lips and thrown it away. The first time this had happened Connie had been too surprised to protest. When she had finally remonstrated indignantly, Tottie had said, with bland decision, that she did not like it and that Connie must not smoke.

"I wonder," Connie thought now, with chagrin, "why everything she wants has to be a law of life with me."

Connie brought her mind back to Dorothy's statements. If Tottie used any of the hallucigenic drugs, the effects would have been obvious in the close quarters of their week together in the apartment. Tottie could not have controlled her own reactions

so completely that Connie would not have seen something was
amiss when she returned home in the evenings. No, Tottie's un-
predictability did not originate in drugs.

It was just Tottie. But that only made it harder to understand
what Tottie might intend to do. There was no use her trying to
understand Tottie on the basis of reasoning. However unscien-
tific the method might be, she could only come near to grasping
the essence of Tottie and Tottie's mental processes by the sort
of intuitive insight she had been exercising ever since Tottie had
run away from the apartment. There was something behind Tottie's actions. If she could only be sure of what motivated Tottie,
she could understand what it was.

Suddenly impatient and overwhelmed by a sense of being in-
tolerably confused, Connie got up from her chair, bent on leaving the office at once. Her desk clock said only five o'clock, but
she nevertheless hastily straightened the books and papers she
had been using and took her handbag from the desk drawer. Her
secretary did not conceal her surprise when Connie announced
that she was leaving for the day and would probably not come
into the office the following day, Saturday. The receptionist made
a facetious remark as she passed on her way to the elevator, but
she found she really did not care what speculations might cir-
culate through Bryanston and Clay about her. She walked home,
to dissipate some of the restlessness that assailed her.

Throughout the evening Connie mulled over again Dorothy's
remarks. Somehow the feeling persisted that there was some
scheme operating, something that Tottie had devised. But what
it was and whether it included herself, she could not decide.
Obviously Tottie had no intention of communicating with her,
for whatever reason, and a heartsore shyness took possession of
her as this idea gained strength in her mind. Tottie did not intend
to get in touch with her, and from an amorphous sense of prohibi-
tion she did not consider making an effort of her own to get in
touch with Tottie. Tottie had deliberately chosen to place herself
somewhere where she could not be easily reached. She had chosen
to commit herself to the sanatorium. In all probability she would
realize that news of this fact would reach Connie—might have
reached her, in fact, sooner than today. Or am I, thought Connie,
just seeking comfort for myself in supposing that she would think
of that? Has she given me a thought at all?

Saturday morning was hot and sunny. In an attempt to escape
her own solitude Connie went up on the roof of the apartment
building to the swimming pool and spent several hours there

lying on a deck chair. The sunny heat and the cries and splashing of the other bathers induced a drowsy mindlessness that helped the hours go by. The afternoon was well underweigh before she went downstairs to her apartment and showered and changed and fixed herself a desultory lunch.

It was three o'clock when the phone rang. Dorothy's voice said crisply, "Will you give me a drink, if I stop by, Connie?"

"Yes, of course. Are you still at the office?"

"No, I haven't been in the office. But I've got something to tell you. I'll be there in twenty minutes."

When she arrived and had sat down on the sofa, kicking off her shoes and taking a long drink from the tall glass Connie had handed her, she said, "Your nose is peeling. What did you do? Roast in the sun all morning?"

Connie gave a forced little laugh. "You know just how to flatter, don't you, Dot? Yes, I've been in the sun all morning, at the swimming pool."

"And you don't give a damn. No Roger to complain. Anyhow, your friends can now call you up and invite themselves in. Do you realize how exclusive you've been lately—everybody afraid to disturb you when you might be with the great man? God! Its worse than being married."

Connie in spite of herself was amused. "I do have a sense of freedom."

"But you still listen for the phone. I can tell. Or are you waiting to hear from Roger's successor?"

Connie forced herself to go on smiling. "His successor isn't available for the weekend."

Dorothy's eyes widened. "Oh, so there is one!"

"I didn't say so," Connie said shortly and then added, "But you didn't come here now to cross-examine me about that, did you?"

"No. I came to tell you about interviewing Charlotte Christeson. I was sent for this morning, to go out to the sanatorium. I was told to find out from her, if possible, what she was doing at the scene of the post office bombing and where she was afterwards. The idea was that she might open up and talk to a woman."

Connie was slow to respond. "Did she?"

"She was loquacious enough—part of the time." Dorothy broke off to ask, "Are you going to have a drink, Connie?"

Connie jumped up. "I believe I will." She went to the cabinet and poured herself a scotch.

"But," said Dorothy, watching her, "I don't know any more about what she was doing than I did before I talked to her."

"Didn't she offer any sort of explanation?"

"No. She certainly is exasperating. When I was taken to her room—everything is pretty luxurious out there and she has a room to herself—it must be costing a fortune—she was wearing a yellow pantsuit with nothing on under it, as far as I could tell. She was barefooted and sitting on the bed with her knees drawn up and looking at me sideways like a kid who isn't sure she is going to answer or not. Halfway through the interview I could have smacked her. But she isn't really a kid and you can't tell just what is going on in her mind."

"So?" said Connie.

"So, after I had beat about the bush for a while, I lost patience and reminded her that in all probability she would be brought before the grand jury and charged with conspiracy or something of the sort and either sent to jail or released under much larger bail."

"What did she say to that?"

"She said she hadn't done anything criminal. According to her story, she was there at the post office out of curiosity. She just wants to know what makes people tick—in this case, people who make and throw bombs. That's a fine story to have to present in a court hearing, to unsympathetic ears." Dorothy's disgust overcame her and she took a long swallow.

"It might be the truth."

Dorothy made a rude noise and declared, "You tell me how to make it sound convincing. Then I asked her what she did after the bomb went off. She said she was frightened—of being picked up by the police, apparently—and ran away. So then I asked her what she was doing for the next seven or eight days. She said she couldn't remember. I said, why couldn't she remember? Was she taking dope? If so, where did she get it? Was it from those men who were murdered—the men who were supposed to have kidnaped her."

"What did she say?"

Dorothy hesitated. "This I find hard to believe. She says she met them in the street just after the bombing, that they helped her to hide from the police. So then I asked her if she knew anything about the ransom notes. Was she with them while they were trying to extort money from her father? She just denies she knew anything about that. She says she did not stay with these men. She got frightened of them and ran away and after that she doesn't remember very clearly where she went or stayed. I suppose she could have holed up somewhere and got onto drugs and been oblivious to everything that was going on."

"But she is not proved to be on drugs, is she?"

"No. But where was she during that week? She wasn't dirty and neglected when she turned up at her father's house. In fact, I gather she was wearing that pantsuit I saw her in and looked perfectly normal."

"Did you talk to any of the doctors out there at the sanatorium?"

"Listen, girl. Have you ever talked to the staff at a place like that? Do you suppose that they are going to tell you anything definite? After all, they are paid pretty well to keep their mouths shut. I did talk to one woman—I think she is a psychiatrist—it took me quite a while to get in to see her. I asked her if Miss Christeson was having withdrawal symptoms. She said No, because Miss Christeson wasn't addicted to heroin. But I couldn't get her to say whether the girl is addicted to anything else."

"Are any of the doctors to be subpoenaed to appear at the hearing?"

"Not as of now. I suppose if the case isn't resolved at the hearing on Tuesday, we may have to call on them."

She finished off her drink and ostentatiously looked down into the glass. Connie laughed and took the glass to replenish it. She said as she turned away, "So I suppose you're going to have to rely on what Tot—Charlotte Christeson says about what happened to her during that missing week."

"We're going to have to rely on her unsupported word about all of it. Presumably the only witnesses who could be called to corroborate her statements are now dead. There is one thing. The police have been unable to link her definitely with any of the suspects who have been questioned about the bombing. The two boys they arrested at the scene say they know her, of course —as Mary Gilray. But they say she was just a hanger-on of their group. Some others have been questioned—young people who have been arrested on other charges, for taking part in protest demonstrations and riots. They say they knew her chiefly as the writer of protest songs. None of them consider her to be an activist. In fact, the consensus is that she is too erratic and unreliable to be accepted as an active member of any of these hardcore groups—that she would not be trusted with vital inside information. Well, I'll tell you one thing. From everything I've heard of her and after talking to her, I wouldn't want to place any confidence in Charlotte Christeson. Maybe it isn't drugs. Maybe she is just wacky."

Connie looked at her in silence for a moment. "Was that your impression, really?"

"That she is wacky?" Dorothy paused thoughtfully. "Well, now, to tell you the truth, Connie, that's the impression she makes offhand. And I think most people would accept it without question. But, you know, I've been thinking over our interview, and there is something that sort of niggles at me. She could be playing a game—I mean, she could be covering up her real motives and intentions by acting like a nitwit. You investigated her life before she got involved with these hippies and bomb buffs. What would you say? Is she really unstable?"

"That depends. I suppose some people would call it unstable to get fed up with the sort of life you've been brought up to and to seek something different. A lot of these young rebels say, you know, that they don't want to mirror their parents' lives."

Dorothy eyed her. "I don't think I want to argue the pros and cons of that one."

Connie gave a little shrug. "But, don't you see, Dot? This girl is in conflict with her father and rebellious against the environment in which she was brought up. She is obviously dissatisfied with the sort of life she is expected to lead as H.B. Christeson's daughter. A lot of people will say she is unstable because she wants out of that."

There was a puzzled frown on Dorothy's face. "But, Connie, just because you're bored with life doesn't mean you need to leave home and bum around with a lot of self-styled revolutionaries."

"It has been done before. How about St. Francis of Assissi? And Florence Nightingale? I don't think their families and friends were very sympathetic to the things they wanted to do and the kind of people they insisted on mingling with."

"I don't think you'll find many St. Francises and Florence Nightingales in this crowd," said Dorothy drily. "So you think our little chum may only be declaring her independence. Well, she had better learn to be a bit more practical. Papa can't see her out of every scrape."

Connie sighed. "I don't believe she will expect him to, after this."

Dorothy looked surprised. "How's that? How would you know that?"

Connie, alarmed at her own lapse, murmured, "Oh, it's just a surmise."

The scotch was having its effect and Dorothy's restraint relaxed. She suddenly demanded, "So you think it is all right if somebody decides to cast discretion to the winds and take up the life of a tramp. It's not any better than that—what these girls do when they leave decent homes and go and live with all kinds of boys, bumming around the country like beggars, getting hooked on drugs. When I was their age you kept up some sort of front. Your parents might guess you slept with the boys who lived in the fraternity houses at college, but you didn't parade the fact."

"Some of the younger crowd would say we were hypocrites."

"You're bound.and determined to see it from their point of view, aren't you, Connie? Are you ready to cop out—I think that is the current phrase—of your job and social status? If so, where are you going?"

"I'm pretty sure I'm leaving Bryanston and Clay before long."

Dorothy studied her face for a moment. "Well, it's certain you don't have much of a future there, under the circumstances. You've probably frightened Roger to death, talking like this. He is going to have more and more to say about how the firm's run. Of course, he might mellow—when his interest is caught by someone else."

Connie gazed at her thoughtfully. "Have you ever been in love, Dot?"

Dorothy seemed startled. "In love? I'm not even sure I believe it really happens. What do you mean?"

"I mean, really in love, so that you don't have any doubt about the fact. You know then. It's not something you can fool yourself about. It—overtakes you."

"You mean you are in love—according to this definition?" Dorothy demanded. When Connie did not answer, she said, "Obviously you think you are. Then you were telling me the truth when you said it was you who broke with Roger and not he with you. Connie, this is a lot more dangerous. You're much more vulnerable, if you let yourself go like that. You can't count on any man. You're just heading for a real heartbreak. And if you're involved with some fellow who thinks he wants to abdicate from society, let me tell you, you're asking for it and you're going to get it."

"Get what?" Connie asked, smiling a little in spite of herself.

"Why, it's Q.E.D. that you're just going to be breadwinner as well as housekeeper and bedmate. That's nothing new, supporting an idle husband. It's been done for hundreds of years. You're too clever for that."

Connie gave a soft little laugh. "Don't worry, Dot. It's not that sort of situation.

"What is it, then?"

Connie hesitated. "It is something that has altered the whole course of my life. And it's permanent—at least, for me it is permanent."

"For you it is permanent? So at least you don't deceive yourself about expecting reciprocity. Really, Connie, I don't know whether to congratulate you on your perspicacity or feel sorry that you're not more self-deceived. It's a devil of a business, being involved with somebody emotionally."

Connie was surprised when Dorothy did not press her for further details. But when she looked at her friend she saw that Dorothy was, under the mellowing influence of her drink, musing on some personal recollection. When she suggested that she fix something to eat, Dorothy accepted, and when they started to talk again, it was about something quite different.

Chapter Twenty-Two

The next morning Connie awoke in plenty of time to go to communion. Sitting in the stuffy elegance of St. Thomas's, she felt a greater sense of quietness than she had experienced all week. As she waited for the service to begin she thought of her conversation with Dorothy and realized that it and her own veiled declaration had marked a change in her own frame of mind. Whatever the outcome of the situation, she was ready now to accept the fact that the future course of her life was not amenable to any intellectual decision of her own. She tried not to anticipate the stress of the coming Tuesday. She was aware now of Tottie as two people, the uncertain, clinging girl whose inner impulses and private fears were so wellknown to her and the Tottie who was really Charlotte Christeson, a mature woman, with experience in a style of life that was foreign and strange to her. How her own Tottie might be feeling, what she might be thinking, what she probably meant to do—all this Connie confidently thought she could readily imagine. But what were the intentions and desires of Charlotte Christeson?

The rest of Sunday Connie got through in a half-dream. And Monday she was thankful for the demands of her job. She tried to ignore the approach of Tuesday morning, deliberately closing her mind to what Dorothy obviously believed the probable outcome of the hearing would be—that Tottie would be bound over to the grand jury under a serious charge. Connie remembered, in a moment of weakness, Tottie's vividly expressed horror of incarceration. Surely, she thought, Christeson would come through with increased bail, if that was required. But even so, what would be the toll in nervous strain for Tottie, awaiting a trial for several weeks or even months? How would Tottie react to that? In the back of Connie's mind was the thought that Tottie, out on bail, would not await trial. She would escape through flight. And then where would she go and how would she live—again a fugitive from the law?

Resolutely Connie put aside these worries whenever they came to the fore. Yet she was aware of them even when she tried to think of professional problems. Monday evening she weighed the possibility of going to a movie, anything to engage her attention at least in part. But she gave up the idea and spent the evening and most of the night half-fearful, half-wishful that Tottie would come and take refuge with her once more. As day dawned she was aware that she was in poor condition for the demands of the next few hours. A dull headache undermined her spirits. She found trouble in reading the law reports and briefs she was studying. At last, as ten o'clock approached she gave up the struggle and sat in a sort of miserable anticipation at her desk. Her secretary, bringing her a cup of coffee at the usual midmorning hour, glanced at her and exclaimed in concern, "Why, Miss Norton! What is the matter? Are you sick?"

"I don't think so," said Connie, trying to pull herself together. "I didn't sleep well. I need that coffee. Thank you."

The girl gave her another lingering glance and left the room. The hearing could go on for hours, depending on how much testimony was presented. Dorothy had not told her how many witnesses were to be heard besides Tottie herself. Surely the attorneys for the government would be calling some to sustain its case. It might be adjourned at midday and re-scheduled for the afternoon or at some other date or it might be concluded within a few minutes. The shorter it was the more likely Tottie would be bound over on a more serious charge.

The lunch-hour passed and still there was no sign of any of the lawyers who were working on the case. The hearing, Connie decided, must have been held over till the afternoon.

It was almost four o'clock when the door of her office burst open and Dorothy walked in, obviously highly stimulated by an active day in court.

"She did it!" Dorothy cried. "She did it! I didn't think it was possible."

She threw her handbag down on the desk and sat down in the chair opposite. Connie looked at her dumbly, beyond the point of being able to respond.

"She is a consummate actress, I swear she is!" Dorothy exclaimed. "And I think I'm the only one there who appreciates that fact."

Connie made a supreme effort and said in a voice husky with nervous strain, "Tell me what happened, Dot."

"What happened?" Dorothy smiled at her with sparkling eyes. "She's sprung! And all through her own efforts. Precious little her lawyers were able to do for her. In the first place, the moment she came into the courtroom and I saw how she was dressed, I was prepared for something. A woman doesn't—"

"Begin at the beginning, Dot," Connie begged. "Tell me from the beginning."

Dorothy paused to look at her. "God! Connie, you're terribly upset! All right, I'll be as quick as I can. You know Judge Hollaran. He is a stickler for court ettiquette and he'll hold everybody up just to make sure every meaningless form is gone through in the traditional way. But we finally got the preliminaries out of the way and Charlotte Chirsteson was called to the stand. She came in with her father and Ralph Blythe and Roger. I went with Tony Grieg. I started to tell you how she was dressed. As you know, she is very small and I didn't get a good look at her until she took the stand. The men were all in the way before that. Well."

Dorothy paused to light a cigarette. Connie said nothing.

"I never saw a bigger contrast between the girl I interviewed at the sanatorium and the woman who took the stand. Do you know, Connie, she is actually beautiful. She had her hair done up in a chignon at the back of her head and as smooth as a cap in front. The pale corn color makes a wonderful complement to her eyes. She had on a long-sleeved dress with a conservative miniskirt and a lowcut neck. You know, she has a big bosom for such a small woman and she doesn't hide it. The men were all goggle-eyed. That lovely white skin of hers adds to the enticement. You should have seen Roger. I'm sorry, Connie. But he couldn't take his eyes off her."

Connie, pierced by the description, said impatiently, "Well, all right, get on with it."

"Keep your wig on. The government witnesses were on first and I must say that Roger did a good job of demolishing the case they had put together. You know, she was charged with personal knowledge of the actions and motives of the persons actually accused of making and setting the bombs. Well, by the time Roger got through, it was pretty obvious that the government did not have any real evidence to support that charge. They put an FBI man on who talked about how they had traced the girl to several places where there were groups that included some of those questioned as suspects, as well as the boys arrested at the scene of the bombing. And of course there was the evidence that she was at the post office when the bomb exploded. Roger made it amply clear that mere presence at the scene was not evidence of complicity and neither was acquaintanceship with suspect persons. There is plenty of law to cite on those two points."

"How about the week she was missing after the bombing, when they were looking for her?" Connie asked, her voice sharp with apprehension. "What did they do with that?"

"That was the weakness of our case, of course. Especially since, as far as I knew, nobody on our side had been able to get a statement from her about what she was doing during that week or where she spent it. Roger was able to make it clear that the government hadn't found out either, FBI or no FBI. She just dropped out of sight, everybody's sight, so that even the people who admitted knowing her as Mary Gilray weren't able to give a hint of her whereabouts. So of course everybody was pretty interested when she took the witness stand herself. If she could not give some sort of satisfactory explanation for that week, it was more or less taken for granted that the court could act on the obvious assumption that she must have had something to hide, i.e., association with those charged in the felony, which would mean a charge of conspiracy, to be tried later. The government lawyers tried hard on that one. But that is where she took over the hearing."

"How?" Connie demanded, too wrought up to disguise her curiosity.

"I've told you the impression she made when she got on the stand. Well, when the government attorney started his cross examination he asked her what she was doing at the post office. She said, in that soft little voice of hers, that she had just followed those two boys there, that she had been at a party somewhere earlier where they had been. So then she was asked why she followed them. She said she didn't have anywhere to go and she thought they might let her stay with them for a while. They had let her spend the night in the pad they occupied. Simmons was the government man and you know how sarcastic he can be. He began to insinuate, pretty broadly, that she was nothing but a little tramp and that she knew perfectly well what the boys intended to do. She didn't talk back to him. She just sat there looking miserable and forlorn and insisted that they had not told her anything. She managed it somehow so that she got old Hollaran on her side—you know, coming to the aid of a poor little girl who obviously hadn't very much on the ball but was just so sweet otherwise. I started enjoying things about then. It became a sort of three-way game—Simmons, Hollaran, and the girl. She was just passive, letting them fight it out."

"But what about that week when she was missing?"

"Simmons took her all through that. Didn't she know the boys belonged to a hardcore group that manufactured bombs? Didn't she know that they were armed with bombs that night? Didn't she know perfectly well that they were going somewhere to plant those bombs? She said No to all of it and insisted that she just followed them—well, like a homeless kitten, only she didn't use that description. She projected that image in the minds of the rest of us. So then Simmons made a crack about, Did she often follow strange men like that, implying that she was expecting to sleep with them. She put on a funny look—of injured dignity, you might call it—it's amazing how expressive her face can be—and said that wasn't any of his business. And Hollaran backed her up! After that round, Simmons asked her what she did after the bomb went off. She said she was scared and ran away. Roger had already established the fact that nobody—or at least, nobody who had been found to testify as a witness—saw her at the scene of the bombing after the explosion. So that meant it was her word alone about what she did afterwards. You remember, for a while it was believed that she might have been blown up in the post office."

"Yes, but what did she say? What did Simmons ask her then?"

"He asked her pointblank where she was between the time she ran away from the post office and Sunday a week ago when she showed up at her father's house. She said she did not remember anything clearly. She was very frightened. She did not know anything about the search going on for her as Mary Gilray. Under Simmons' cross-examination it came out pretty clearly that she had holed up somewhere with a man or several men but that she did not intend to admit who these people were. Simmons made quite a point of the fact that she must be promiscuous and just lives with anybody who is convenient. She did say that her companions had nothing to do with the bombing. They were just chance-met acquaintances. When she did come to the surface— or perhaps met somebody who recognized her and told her what was going on, she decided to go to her father's." Dorothy paused for a moment. "You know, it all sounds a bit far out, but while she was telling about it, it seemed perfectly plausible. After all, you read about such things every day in the newspapers—people who get into trouble and haven't the least idea what has been going on around them. I think she did just what she said she did—took refuge wherever she could and paid no attention to the news or anything else outside her own little orbit."

"How about the others? Were they satisfied with her story?"

"Well, yes—officially, in any case. Hollaran accepted it. If some had reservations, they didn't press them. After all, what she said could not be contradicted by any real evidence. Yes, her story was accepted. Oh, of course, Simmons resisted. He tried to make a big thing out of the fact that her lapse of memory was very convenient and all that, but even he had nothing to offer that could disprove her statements. Somehow she managed to get across the idea that her stay in the sanatorium was evidence that she is subject to these—what shall we call them?—moments of vagueness about her surroundings and associates. And her manner made it clear that she thought that Simmons, in doubting her, was just persecuting her out of ill will. By that time he and Hollaran were at such cross-purposes that Hollaran brought the whole case to an end abruptly and dismissed the charge against her. The government lawyers were pretty disgusted but they admitted they did not have sufficient evidence to hold her further as even a material witness."

"What happened after that, Dot?"

"After she was discharged? Oh, there was the usual milling around—congratulations and snide remarks from the opposition and all that. The FBI man was pretty annoyed. He said he didn't believe the girl was guilty of anything except foolish behavior but he hated to lose the chance of using her as a sort of stalking horse to entrap some of the people she has been associating with. Roger, by the way, didn't have much to say when it was all over, even though everybody was congratulating him on how well he handled the case, considering that criminal practice is not our line. Usually he is more expansive when he has a successful outcome."

"Why do you think that was, Dot?"

Dorothy was thoughtful for a moment. "To tell you the truth, I think he was in two minds. I think he is very much intrigued by the Christeson girl but at the same time he is afraid of her unpredictable way of acting."

Connie gaped at her in astonishment. "You don't mean he is seriously interested by her, Dot?"

Dorothy considered her for a moment. "Not his cup of tea, you would say, is she? But, you know, Connie, men are funny about that sort of thing sometimes. I think he is attracted and repelled at the same time. I'm sorry, Connie, if I'm treading on your toes, but I think I should tell you what I observed."

Connie said hastily, "What Roger does now isn't of any importance to me, Dot. I've told you that."

"Well, I'd say he is ready to look elsewhere—to assuage his own feelings, if nothing else, and he's definitely intrigued by this girl, in spite of her eccentricities. Personally, I think any relationship between the two of them would be a disaster. But I suppose on the surface it would look like a good match."

Connie asked quietly, "How did she respond to him?"

"She acted as if she wouldn't give him the time of day. But then that was her attitude to everybody once she left the stand. She ignored me. I just wasn't there. She scarcely spoke to her father. She did give old Hollaran a smile before she left the courthouse."

"Where is she now?" Connie could not keep eagerness out of her voice.

"She went home with her father. It seems that Christeson and his wife are leaving for Europe in the morning and he said they are taking the girl with them. Apparently he thinks that if he gets her abroad he will be able to break up these associations of hers."

"She has agreed to go with them?"

Dorothy cast her a look of surprise. "Why, I suppose so. She must have heard what Christeson was saying and she did not contradict him. I imagine she would be rather glad to get away from all this. I do believe she was a little frightened, though she put up a good front. Her moods are very changeable. Once the hearing was over and she knew she had been discharged she seemed to go into a sort of reaction, as if she couldn't get away from everybody fast enough. But I'm just surmising. She did not speak to me at all. Well, Connie, how about coming and having a drink with me and a couple of the boys? It will buck you up. You look a little downhearted."

For a moment Connie did not answer. Of course Dorothy thought she was unhappy over Roger in spite of herself. And Dorothy, under her usually acerbic manner, was kindhearted. Connie hesitated to say Yes. Tottie had been free now for a couple of hours and there had been no word from her. Dorothy had said she seemed eager to get away from everybody. It did not look as if Tottie intended to get in touch with her. Finally Connie said Yes and agreed to meet Dorothy and the others in half an hour.

As she straightened her desk in a languid sort of way and prepared to leave the office, a feeling of hopelessness fastened itself on her. The week of keyed-up suspense had exhausted her power to call up unsullied the memory of the Tottie who at the beginning seemed to fill her whole world. Her Tottie seemed to have receded into that most secret region in herself where she had first been truly aware that she loved Tottie. As she tidied the papers on her desk she thought that this evening's conviviality might well be a kind of farewell. In spite of distractions she had succeeded in finishing the job on which she had been working. Contemplating this fact she realized that, almost unbeknownst to herself, she had firmly decided that she was leaving Bryanston and Clay. That was the one clear fact in her mind. There was no going back to what she had been and how she had felt before she had met Tottie. Without Tottie she would not stay in the old surroundings where her old life had been lived.

She went with Dorothy and the others to a bar for drinks. The session there lasted a long time, or so, to her, nursing one drink, it seemed. Afterwards they went to a popular restaurant for dinner, where there was a band and a floor show. Throughout the noisy talk and joking she sat nearly silent, glad to be overlooked even by Dorothy, whose concern for her had vanished in the alcoholic euphoria. Finally the evening became intolerable to her and when the others started to argue about where they should go next, she was able to leave, depositing her share of the dinner check on the table and walking rapidly to the door through the crowded restaurant.

She found a cab and went back to her apartment building. It was already past eleven o'clock by the big clock over the door of a bank. She was aware that she had had more scotch to drink than she was used to and she felt thoroughly uncomfortable. The food she had eaten sat uneasily on her stomach and her nerves were jangled by the clash between her own emotions and the mindless hilarity of the group she had been with. It was with a sense of reaching a sanctuary that she arrived at her floor and stepped out of the elevator. The empty, carpeted, brightly lit corridor was a welcome change from the bar and restaurant. She inserted her key in the lock and entered the apartment, eager to close herself in from the outside world.

She stopped, tears in her eyes, unable to go on speaking. Tottie stood looking up at her, at first with a look of surprise on her face and then with thoughtful eyes. Connie, struggling to gain control of herself, wiped her eyes and walked over to the big armchair and sat down and covered her face with her hands. All the tension of the last ten days had broken in her and she was overwhelmed by a feeling of despair.

Gradually her fit of nerves subsided and she sat back in the chair. Only then was she aware that Tottie was crouched on the floor beside her. Now when she stirred Tottie placed a small hand tentatively on her knee. "Stantia." The small voice was troubled and unhappy. "Stantia, I was so frightened."

Connie, aware that her own resentment was waning rapidly, tried to be reserved. "I'm sure you were," she said in an artificially calm voice.

Tottie, noticing, said reproachfully, "Stantia, you're being very cruel!"

"Cruel!" Connie was goaded into attack. "Cruel! You're the one who has been cruel, Tottie. Why didn't you let me know where you were and what you were doing? Didn't you know that I would be half out of my mind about you? Even if you were angry with me, you must have realized what you were doing to me."

"I couldn't tell you. I didn't know, when I left here, what I was going to do. I didn't really plan it. It just developed. And it would not have been safe for me to tell you, even when I had thought it out and decided what to do. You would never be able to disguise what you knew or felt—not with Roger, not with my father. I saw that I had to stay away so that I would not be traced here. I knew I could not let them find out that I had been here all week with you. They must not know that you had known all about me all along and hadn't said anything to anyone. You would have been held responsible and I couldn't let that happen."

Connie, longing for comfort and yet unable to accept it, said as coolly as she could, "You were in a jealous rage when you left here. You hadn't all this in mind then. You wanted to get away from me and you wanted to punish me."

Tottie's eyes flashed briefly. "It was your fault, Stantia, that I was jealous. You shouldn't have been doing what you did. I couldn't stand it. I couldn't bear that you should be thinking about anybody but me. I hated the idea that you wanted to be with a man."

Connie looked down at her, covering the yearning in her own heart with a satirical grimace. "All that had taken place before

I met you. I couldn't undo it. But that's beside the point now. What I am saying is that you have shown some calculation in this. You were collected enough to take my key."

Again there was a brief flash of anger in Tottie's eyes and she said shortly, "Of course. I intended to come back. You should have known that. Stantia, I expect you to understand me, to understand what I will do."

"I'm not that much of a clairvoyant, Tottie," said Connie drily. Tottie said nothing but leaned her arm on Connie's knee and rested her head against it. The trusting gesture softened Connie's air of reproach as she added, "Tottie, nobody means anything to me now except you. You knew that when you left here. And I thought I had lost you forever."

Tottie did not raise her head but pressed gently against Connie's knee. "I hated to go back to Daddy," she said pensively. "But it was the only thing I could do. You said it was and I began to see that this was so. I couldn't let them find me here and accuse you of hiding me from the police."

"Yes, but when did all this reason suddenly dawn on you?" Connie demanded. "It was certainly not the cause of your running away. You were not exercising reason when you did that."

Tottie lifted her head to look coaxingly at Connie. She raised her hand and patted Connie's cheek. "Don't be cross with me, Stantia. No, I was too mad to think about anything except how furious I was with you then. But then when I got out on the street and began to think about what I was going to do, I got scared. I was scared, Stantia, out there on the street again by myself. Stantia, you're very unfeeling." She frowned at Connie as she said this.

Connie said crisply, "Stop beating about the bush. So when you discovered you were on your own again, you began to think about what your situation really was."

"Yes. And it came to me in a flash that that was the moment for me to go and see Daddy and stop all that business about the warrant. If I didn't say where I had been, nobody could trace anything to you."

"That was kind of you, Tottie," said Connie, ironically. "But it didn't occur to you that you could have come back for a moment and let me know what you intended to do."

Tottie sat up and began to undo the bun in which her hair was fastened. "I've told you why I couldn't tell you that," she said serenely. "I saw that at once."

"So you left me to agonize over you for ten days—without a

second thought!" Connie exclaimed bitterly.

"No, that's not true. I thought about you all the time. There just wasn't any other way." Her serenity suddenly broke as she went on, "But when I saw Daddy and he told me that I would have to surrender under the warrant and that I might have to go to prison, after all—Oh, Stantia, I was terrified! I thought the policemen would come and get me and put me in jail and I couldn't bear the thought. I almost came back here then. Then Daddy said he had put up the bail and I would be free at least until the hearing. That's when I decided I would go where nobody could get hold of me. I went to the sanatorium. I thought I'd be safe there."

She stopped speaking and put her head down in Connie's lap. Connie put an arm around her shoulders. "Oh, Tottie, I've been suffering tortures over you. I remembered what you told me about your feelings at being shut up somewhere. And I worried about where you'd be at night, about how frightened you would be if you were alone, and about the sort of people you might meet up with. There was no way in which I could find out anything about you. Thank God, Dorothy was able to tell me about seeing you in the sanatorium. At least for the time being you would be all right."

Tottie lifted her head again. "Dorothy? Is she the woman they sent to see me?"

"Yes. Dorothy is a good friend. She didn't know, of course, that I knew all about you—that you had spent a week here with me. She was upset because I had been taken off your case."

"I was very surprised when she came. I thought they might send you to me. They told me a woman lawyer from Daddy's firm was coming to see me. I wanted so much to see you and at the same time I dreaded to, because I didn't know what I could tell you. I was afraid if I told you anything you'd be sure to give something away, that somebody would be able to trip you up. I didn't want to tell you lies."

"Tell me lies? I'm not such an innocent, Tottie. I would have known whether you were lying to me."

"See?" said Tottie triumphantly, at her indignation. "You'd get all angry and upset and give things away. Anyway, it was better for that other woman to come. I didn't have to tell her anything. But I did wonder why they sent her and not you."

Connie said reluctantly, "They took me off your case right away. Roger doesn't want to work with me any more."

Her saying Roger's name produced a sudden deep silence between them. Without a word Tottie got to her feet and walked across the livingroom to disappear into the bedroom. Connie, surprised, sat still, in a mixture of fatigue and relief from nervous tension. She was startled when Tottie's voice reached her from the bedroom, "Stantia."

She started to respond and stopped, overcome by an almost painful pleasure. For ten days she had inhabited an empty apartment, an apartment that had not hitherto seemed so silent and deserted. Tottie's small voice, sounding sweetly across the space between them, filled her heart with an inexpressible joy.

She lingered without reply for so long that Tottie called again, "Stantia?" Connie stepped quickly across the big room to the bedroom door. Tottie stood in the middle of the floor, dangling the gold necklace in her hand. Her hair was streaming over her shoulders. She said, in a plaintively demanding voice, "You have to undo me, Stantia." Connie was astonished to see that her face was puckered as if she were about to cry.

"Why, Tottie, what is the matter now?" she cried, taking her in her arms.

Tottie buried her face in Connie's shoulder as she clung to her. "Oh, Stantia, please don't let me go. I was so unhappy when I was away from you."

"Let you go! Why, Tottie, you're the one who ran away!"

Tottie lifted her head to give her an angry glance. "That was because you made me do it."

Connie, defeated, said docilely, "Well, Tottie, after this you're going to have to let me know what's going on in your mind."

Tottie, dismissing the subject, turned her back. "Undo me, Stantia." She waited while Connie obediently drew down the zipper in the back of her dress. When the dress fell to the floor she stepped out of it and waited again while Connie picked it up and threw it on the bed. Pulling off the pantyhose she wore under it, she wriggled her naked body in the enjoyment of freedom from the constraining clothes, shaking the long hair off her face.

"That's a lot better," she said, smiling up at Connie like a happy child.

Connie, her heart overflowing at the sight of the so well-remembered small body, took refuge in practicality. "Tottie, didn't you bring any other clothes with you?"

Tottie pursed up her lips. "No. It was easier to walk out of the house without carrying anything."

"But what are you going to wear? You can't go around in a dinner dress and your jeans are worn out."

"Do you still have them?"

In spite of herself, Connie's eyes filled with tears. She tried to joke and failed. "Oh, yes. I couldn't part with them. They were all I had left of you."

Tottie, watching her face, put her arms around Connie's neck. "Dear, funny Stantia. You'll have to buy me some more clothes, the way you did before."

Connie, clasping her close, said simply, "Tottie."

After a while they separated and Connie fetched the bathrobe and put it around her. Together they went back to the livingroom and sat side by side on the sofa. Connie was aware of problems to be solved, of actions to be considered, but she put them aside in her mind. Tottie was silent, absorbed in thoughts of her own. Sitting there alone with her, Connie felt as if their combined presences filled the universe. She was startled when Tottie said suddenly,

"Daddy approves of Roger."

When Connie failed to answer, Tottie said, "He thinks Roger is a remarkable young man. He thinks he's going to be a famous lawyer."

Connie, forced to speak, said carefully, "Everybody thinks Roger will have a brilliant career." She kept her eyes on the floor, aware that Tottie was watching her closely.

Tottie said, "But Daddy thinks more than that. He thinks Roger is just the right influence for me. He thinks Roger is forceful enough so that he could keep me out of mischief. That's all Daddy thinks I do—get into mischief. He's tired of having to deal with me himself, so he's thinking about getting Roger to do it."

Connie, at sea, said, "Roger?"

Tottie nodded. "He wants me to marry Roger. He'd like Roger for a son-in-law, and as my husband, he could keep an eye on me."

Connie raised her head cautiously to look at her. Tottie was watching her with bright, satirical eyes. "Don't look so browbeaten, Connie. I couldn't stand him. How did you ever put up with him? He's so bossy."

Connie demanded, with sudden asperity, "How about Roger? He's quite attracted to you, isn't he?"

Tottie's face grew more serious. "Where did you hear that?"

"Dorothy saw it, at the hearing. She knows Roger quite well. She was afraid I was still grieving over him."

There was a flash in Tottie's eyes. "Grieving over him? He can't mean anything to you now. You've told me so."

"Of course. But I couldn't tell Dorothy about you. She is sure

I've found someone else, and she is very curious about who could supplant Roger."

Tottie made a sound of disgust. "Roger, Roger. Daddy had him come to dinner with us tonight. That's why I had trouble getting away. I had to wait till he and Daddy were absorbed in talking politics. He can even put Daddy straight over a thing or two. Daddy is very impressed."

"How did you get away?"

"I just walked out of the house. The guard at the gate was upset. Daddy still has guards there. And I expect the guard went and told Daddy right away that I had left. But they haven't the least idea where I am. They won't know where to look for me. They'll have to leave on that plane for Europe tomorrow without me."

"But, Tottie, will they? After all this?"

Tottie said contemptuously, "Of course. Especially after all this. I was being given a last chance. Daddy will have a fit of temper—he is probably having it right now. And then he'll announce he is washing his hands of me. After a few days it won't matter. I'm not a minor. Nobody can tell me what to do."

"What *are* you going to do, Tottie?"

"Me? Why, I'm here. I'm going to stay here—unless you go somewhere else, because then I am going with you."

Connie said soberly, "I've already made up my mind to leave Bryanston and Clay. There is no future for me there. I'll have to look for another job."

Hearing the note of bitterness in her voice, Tottie said nothing for a moment. Then she put her arm around Connie's shoulders. "You don't have to worry about that, Stantia," she said gently. "I've got enough for both of us."

Connie said stiffly, "I can always earn a living."

Tottie gave a little shrug. "What does it matter? As long as we're not separated. You can do as you like. But we have to be together."

Connie said uneasily, "It may not be very easy for us, Tottie."

Tottie looked at her closely, gauging the depth of her anxiety. "Does anything really matter, Stantia, as long as we've got each other? Do you really care what anybody else thinks?"

"Not really," Connie said slowly. She looked up with sudden happiness in her face, and said cheerfully, "It's just that I'm not quite so irresponsible as you are, Tottie."

"Irresponsible!" Tottie laughed and pulled Connie's head down close to her. She said softly into the ringlets behind Connie's ear.

"İt's just you and I, Stantia. We don't have to worry about anybody else. Kiss me, kiss me, Stantia."

THE END

A few of the publications of
THE NAIAD PRESS, INC.
P.O. Box 10543 • Tallahassee, Florida 32302
Mail orders welcome. Please include 15% postage.

We Too Are Drifting by Gale Wilhelm. A novel. 128 pp.
ISBN 0-930044-61-4 — $6.95

A Hot-Eyed Moderate by Jane Rule. Essays. 252 pp.
ISBN 0-930044-57-6 — $7.95
ISBN 0-930044-59-2 — $13.95

Inland Passage and Other Stories by Jane Rule. 288 pp.
ISBN 0-930044-56-8 — $7.95
ISBN 0-930044-58-4 — $13.95

Amateur City by Katherine V. Forrest. A mystery novel. 224 pp.
ISBN 0-930044-55-X — $7.95

The Sophie Horowitz Story by Sarah Schulman. A novel. 176 pp.
ISBN 0-930044-54-1 — $7.95

The Young in One Another's Arms by Jane Rule. A novel. 224 pp.
ISBN 0-930044-53-3 — $7.95

The Burnton Widows by Vicki P. McConnell. A mystery novel.
272 pp. ISBN 0-930044-52-5 — $7.95

Old Dyke Tales by Lee Lynch. Short Stories. 224 pp.
ISBN 0-930044-51-7 — $7.95

Daughters of a Coral Dawn by Katherine V. Forrest. Science
fiction. 240 pp. ISBN 0-930044-50-9 — $7.95

The Price of Salt by Claire Morgan. A novel. 288 pp.
ISBN 0-930044-49-5 — $7.95

Against the Season by Jane Rule. A novel. 224 pp.
ISBN 0-930044-48-7 — $7.95

Lovers in the Present Afternoon by Kathleen Fleming. A novel.
288 pp. ISBN 0-930044-46-0 — $8.50

Toothpick House by Lee Lynch. A novel. 264 pp.
ISBN 0-930044-45-2 — $7.95

Madame Aurora by Sarah Aldridge. A novel. 256 pp.
ISBN 0-930044-44-4 — $7.95

Curious Wine by Katherine V. Forrest. A novel. 176 pp.
ISBN 0-930044-43-6 — $7.50

Black Lesbian in White America. Short stories, essays,
autobiography. 144 pp. ISBN 0-930044-41-X — $7.50

Contract with the World by Jane Rule. A novel. 340 pp.
ISBN 0-930044-28-2 — $7.95

Yantras of Womanlove by Tee A. Corinne. Photographs.
64 pp. ISBN 0-930044-30-4 — $6.95

Mrs. Porter's Letter by Vicki P. McConnell. A mystery novel. 224 pp. ISBN 0-930044-29-0   **$6.95**

To the Cleveland Station by Carol Anne Douglas. A novel. 192 pp. ISBN 0-930044-27-4   **$6.95**

The Nesting Place by Sarah Aldridge. A novel. 224 pp. ISBN 0-930044-26-6   **$6.95**

This Is Not for You by Jane Rule. A novel. 284 pp. ISBN 0-930044-25-8   **$7.95**

Faultline by Sheila Ortiz Taylor. A novel. 140 pp. ISBN 0-930044-24-X   **$6.95**

The Lesbian in Literature by Barbara Grier. 3d ed. Foreword by Maida Tilchen. A comprehensive bibliography. 240 pp. ISBN 0-930044-23-1   **$7.95**

Anna's Country by Elizabeth Lang. A novel. 208 pp. ISBN 0-930044-19-3   **$6.95**

Prism by Valerie Taylor. A novel. 158 pp. ISBN 0-930044-18-5   **$6.95**

Black Lesbians: An Annotated Bibliography compiled by JR Roberts. Foreword by Barbara Smith. 112 pp. ISBN 0-930044-21-5   **$5.95**

The Marquise and the Novice by Victoria Ramstetter. A novel. 108 pp. ISBN 0-930044-16-9   **$4.95**

Labiaflowers by Tee A. Corinne. 40 pp. ISBN 0-930044-20-7   **$3.95**

Outlander by Jane Rule. Short stories, essays. 207 pp. ISBN 0-930044-17-7   **$6.95**

Sapphistry: The Book of Lesbian Sexuality by Pat Califia. 2nd edition, revised. 195 pp. ISBN 0-930044-47-9   **$7.95**

The Black and White of It by Ann Allen Shockley. Short stories. 112 pp. ISBN 0-930044-15-0   **$5.95**

All True Lovers by Sarah Aldridge. A novel. 292 pp. ISBN 0-930044-10-X   **$6.95**

A Woman Appeared to Me by Renee Vivien. Translated by Jeannette H. Foster. A novel. xxxi, 65 pp. ISBN 0-930044-06-1   **$5.00**

Cytherea's Breath by Sarah Aldridge. A novel. 240 pp. ISBN 0-930044-02-9   **$6.95**

Tottie by Sarah Aldridge. A novel. 181 pp. ISBN 0-930044-01-0   **$6.95**

The Latecomer by Sarah Aldridge. A novel. 107 pp. ISBN 0-930044-00-2   **$5.00**

VOLUTE BOOKS

Journey to Fulfillment	by Valerie Taylor	$3.95
A World without Men	by Valerie Taylor	$3.95
Return to Lesbos	by Valerie Taylor	$3.95
Desert of the Heart	by Jane Rule	$3.95
Odd Girl Out	by Ann Bannon	$3.95
I Am a Woman	by Ann Bannon	$3.95
Women in the Shadows	by Ann Bannon	$3.95
Journey to a Woman	by Ann Bannon	$3.95
Beebo Brinker	by Ann Bannon	$3.95

These are just a few of the many Naiad Press titles. Please request a complete catalog!